Readers love *Dog Days*
by TA MOORE

"Wow. *Dog Days* turned out to be even more than I expected… Trust me when I say you won't regret reading this… not if you love twists, turns, and horror."
—Rainbow Book Reviews

"…an amazingly captivating shifter story that is by far one of the most unique I have read in a quite a while. And I want more."

—The Novel Approach

"…I highly recommend this to all the shifter lovers out there."

—Diverse Reader

"I loved this story for the beautiful way that it was executed…"

—MM Good Book Reviews

By TA MOORE

Every Other Weekend
Ghostwriter of Christmas Past
Liar, Liar
Wanted – Bad Boyfriend

DIGGING UP BONES
Bone to Pick
Skin and Bone

WOLF WINTER
Dog Days
Stone the Crows

Published by DREAMSPINNER PRESS
www.dreamspinnerpress.com

DOG DAYS
TA MOORE

Published by
DREAMSPINNER PRESS

5032 Capital Circle SW, Suite 2, PMB# 279,
Tallahassee, FL 32305-7886 USA
www.dreamspinnerpress.com

Dog Days
© 2016 TA Moore.

Cover Art
© 2016 Anne Cain.
annecaine.art@gmail.com
Cover content is for illustrative purposes only and any person depicted
on the cover is a model.

Mass Market Paperback ISBN: 978-1-64108-189-4
Trade Paperback ISBN: 978-1-63477-576-2
Digital ISBN: 978-1-63477-577-9
Library of Congress Control Number: 2016946140
Mass Market Paperback Published February 2019
v. 1.0

Printed in the United States of America

∞

This paper meets the requirements of
ANSI/NISO Z39.48-1992 (Permanence of Paper).

With thanks to the Five, who encouraged me to believe I could write, and to my mum and grandparents, who encouraged me to believe I could do anything.

"Environmentalists used to worry about the ramifications of reintroducing the gray wolf to Britain. What they didn't understand was that we've never left."

Chapter One

WINTER HAD fallen like a hammer. The cold tasted like needles, and the wind knotted snow in Jack's hair. The wind shoved at him like a hand, trying to push him back up the hill. No one could remember a harsher winter—bearing in mind his family had a long memory—and the calendar had only reached September. Strange weather. Wild weather.

His boots slid on the ice that glazed the beaten dirt of the old track, and when he cut over the moors the frost-brittle heather crackled like small bones. By the time Jack got to the old stones, his T-shirt was stiff with frozen sweat, and the cold had crept down to his balls. If anyone from Lochwinnoch saw him they'd think he'd run mad. Gods knew what they'd make of the scene on the loch.

The old man stood bollock-naked in the dark water, six foot from the rocky shore. The tattoos covering him from hips to shoulder blade, ink faded from black to blue with age, stood stark against chill-paled skin. The rest of the family crouched on rocks or sat cross-legged on the ground, waiting.

For him.

Jack's brother stalked out of the crowd, shoving their kin out of his way roughly. "You're late," Gregor said, breath misting around his lips. He jabbed a finger against Jack's chest. "You ignore a summons again, and I'll break your legs. Can't walk far then."

Jack grinned at him, humorless and toothy. "Touch me again, and I'll—"

"Boys. Enough." The voice sounded thin, the usual timbre stripped by the wind, but it still scruffed them both. Mouth set in a sneer, Gregor backed off. Jack nodded to the broad, scarred back.

"Da."

The old man turned around, ice crackling around his knees as he moved. He must have been standing out there for hours, letting the water freeze around him.

"Jack." The old man dragged his hand down his face, wiping the frost out of his beard, and jerked a thumb over his shoulder. "D'ya see?"

Not well. The snow was like a blanket, with only glimpses visible through the weave. If Jack squinted, he could just make out a string of lights crawling out of town. They were heading west, to the road.

"They're leaving."

"Aye." The old man sounded smug. He'd no real grudge against the humans that lived there, but the settlement had offended him on the day the humans built it. "Evacuatin'. They sent us a letter too."

Everyone laughed—a low growling roll of amusement.

"What does it mean?" Jack asked.

His da scratched his beard. With the cold snap, they'd all spent more time in fur than not, and the old man's nails were sharp enough to shred the gray and black bristles. "The great winter is here at last. Our prophets were right. Mad bastards, but right."

A ripple of excitement ran through the crowd. Eyes glittered black and eager as they whooped and clapped, smacking hands against their thighs. They'd all been waiting for this day for a long, long time—ever since Hadrian had turned on the monsters he'd found in his legions and banished them over the wall. Rome had turned its back on them, but in the old, high places up here they'd found gods who shared their fangs, and their hunger. Gods born of cold lands and bitter winters, who'd promised to one day give them the world to eat.

Now that day had come.

So why did Jack feel in his marrow that something bad was coming?

The old man waded out of the water, absently waving off a wee lad with a blanket, and walked over to the brothers. He was hairy as a boar, gray thick over his chest and shoulders, and so broad with muscle that he looked short until you found yourself looking up at him. Habit made Jack pull himself up straight, and out of the corner of his eye he saw Gregor do the same.

They were the same height, the same way they wore the same face and the same eyes and the same sandy-fair hair. The only thing they didn't share was the twelve-minute head start one of them had gotten on life, although their ma would never tell them which had come first. Even on her dying day, she'd eaten that secret.

Ignoring their automatic posturing, the big man dropped a hard hand on Jack's shoulder. "And it means something else, boy. I'm heartsore over it, but it means you ain't one of us anymore. You have to go."

For a second Jack didn't feel anything. Maybe the chill had gotten deeper than he thought. The pronouncement of his exile cramped dully in his gut, a feeling of loss as unavoidable as gravity.

Gregor laughed, a startled blurt of triumph. Their da backhanded him, slapping the sound back into his mouth and laying him out on the ground.

"Losing one of us is nothing to gloat over," he growled. "Not at the best of time, not now. And you, boy, you didn't win the toss by some grand margin. There wasn't even twelve minutes in it."

Propping himself up on his elbow, Gregor wiped his mouth sullenly on the back of his hand. Blood smeared bright as a crayon over his knuckles. His eyes were dark and bitter under the straight line of his eyebrows.

Both of them wanted to know. Jack asked first.

"So what was it, then?" he asked, the dullness giving way to anger. "If he wasn't older, or better, why exile me and not him, Da?"

Annoyance crimped the old man's mouth, lips bleeding white, and he looked away. "You know why. I take no pleasure in this, but if you will not change your ways, then you have to leave. It's how things are."

"What things?" Jack asked. He knew—he'd known when he got the summons—but he wanted to make the old man spit the fucking words out. "If there's not even twelve minutes in it, Da, then why does Gregor get to stay, and I have to go?"

The old man shook his head…. "It's the end of the world, boy. Too late for any of us to change now."

"What. Things," Jack growled, voice rasping in his throat. If it had been *fair*—if he'd been weak, or ailing, or if he'd lost a challenge—he could have accepted it. Strength was the rule that ordered all their lives. Except he was a good son, a good wolf, and this wasn't fair. He shouldered into the old man's space, smelling the dander and musk of him on the air. "If you're going to exile your own kid, have the balls to say why, Da."

Hooded, stony eyes met his. They held grief, and pity, but no regret. When the old man *still* didn't say anything, Jack's temper bubbled over into stupidity. He shoved the old man, punching the heels of his hands against heavy shoulders. His da stepped back, and everyone gasped. It had been thirty years since anyone had laid hands on the Numitor, and then it had been Jack's ma in a temper.

Buoyed on the hot rise of his anger, Jack thought about it for a second. Challenge the Numitor and win, and it wouldn't matter what the old man said anymore. It wouldn't matter what anyone thought—

Jack didn't even see the old man move. One minute they were glaring at each other; then the old man's hand closed around Jack's throat. His thumb, callused to leather from work, pressed against the fast throb of Jack's pulse.

"I don't answer to you, boy," his da said. "I've told you my ruling. That it's my fucking whim is all the words you need to know."

Jack cast his eyes over the crowd, seeing kin and friends he'd known for long enough it didn't seem like there was much difference. All of them avoided meeting his gaze. He twisted his mouth in a hard smile, because why pretend anymore? "So it's the length of a dick, is that it, Da?" he said, feeling the word squeeze past his da's thumb. "If I'd just fucked some girl from town every now and again, you'd have let me stay?"

The old man let go of him. Jack stumbled back, swallowing hard and resisting the urge to rub his throat. He wanted to cower, to beg, but he kept his chin up and met his da's glare defiantly.

"It ain't in you to change," his da said. "And it ain't in you to serve. All that's left is leaving, boy. It can be as hard or as easy as you like, but you *will* go. Or I'll send you for a priest."

That threat made Jack flinch, breaking eye contact in a mute admission of defeat. He wasn't a coward—he had taken beatings before—but the thought of a priest's fate scared him.

Mutilated. Castrated. Hobbled. No, he'd rather take exile than that.

Jack bent his stiff neck, swallowing pride that scraped like rocks, and submitted. "I'll go."

The old man turned his back and walked away, snatching the blanket off the hovering lad and throwing it over his shoulder. Left alone, Jack looked down at his brother and, on a whim, offered him his hand. When she'd been dying, their mam had begged them to stop fighting, damned them for fighting like dogs even when they were inside her. Well, now they had nothing left to fight over. Gregor had won.

Rage twisted Gregor's face into something ugly, and he slapped Jack's hand away, knuckles bashing. He scrambled to his feet, spitting a wad of clotty blood into the ground. "I didn't need him to *give* me this. I could have taken it. I *would* have taken it, and my face and my twelve fucking minutes back."

Jack relaxed back into the familiar enmity, a sneer curling his lip. At least their da had given him one last gift. "Except you didn't, did you," he said. Leaning forward, he murmured in his brother's ear, "And now that's what everyone will remember. That you didn't take it, you just... got it."

He left his brother with that, holding on to the smirk until the dark blocked the pack from view. Then he let it hit him, shoving the air out of his lungs in a desperate gasp. He staggered and dropped to his knees on the hard ground, scrubbing a hand over his face. Exiled. Alone. Just thinking about it made his chest crack with anger and a hot, sticky fear. In his whole life, he'd never been alone. He didn't even know how you went about it.

The bitter cold masked the smell, but the frozen ground was no friend to stealth. Jack heard the crunching shuffle of someone approaching in time to pull himself together. He staggered to his feet, growling at the wind that shouldered him, and turned to face the intruder.

He hoped to see his da, come to change his mind. He *expected* it to be Gregor, back for one last fight. Instead a prophet limped into view, scarred and shabby in heavy layers of winter charity.

"What do you want?" Jack demanded. He retreated a step, then made himself hold his ground. "Why did you follow me?"

The prophet grinned, showing the gaps where his incisors had been wrenched out of the gums. "Things change," he said, spitting Jack's words back at him. "Your da's wrong. The end of the world changes everything. If you want it to. Do you want it to, Jack? And are you willing to pay the price for it?"

In the end, no. He wasn't.

Chapter Two

THIS TIME of year, the streets of Durham were usually full of people. Tourists heading up to the Castle to get a glimpse of where they'd filmed *Harry Potter*, students looking for secondhand text books in the Oxfam shop, and residents just trying to live in the middle of it all. This year, the streets were empty, and the shops were boarded up. The only people left were council workers, slogging through flood water in waders as they tested foundations for subsidence, and the few poor souls who'd not found anywhere better to go.

Danny stood in the doorway of St. Chad's, shivering and rubbing cold-raw hands together, and watched the old Land Rover crawl its way out of the pea-soup fog that had come in when the storm slackened. It jolted and clattered over the battered cobbled road, wheels hitting the frost-cracked ruts and gaps. The driver was a local farmer whose son had talked him into helping out with transport after they'd closed off the motorways.

"Al," Danny said as the jeep pulled in next to him. He ducked his head to peer through the window. The air inside, blasting out of the vents, was hot enough to make his glasses mist as it hit them. He whipped them off, giving the lenses a quick polish on his sleeve. "We appreciate this. These are the last of the students. Thank God they reopened the train line this morning."

"That's one bit of good news, then," Al said, pulling his hat off and wiping a gloved hand over his sweaty scalp. He pointed to the windshield on the passenger side, a spiderweb of cracks shattering out from a golf-ball-sized hole. "Hail last night did that. Took out most of the windows in the farm too. Mad fucking weather."

"Can't keep it up *much* longer," Danny said. It was the party line, rote response to any commentary on the weather. So far the weather had kept it up for two months, and the words were starting to sound a bit empty. "You okay up there?"

"For now," Al said grimly. "I've been thinking I might lock the place up and head down to my sister's in Birmingham. It's not been hit as bad."

Danny grimaced his uncertainty about that, not after some of the news reports, but it wasn't his job to keep Al on the farm. It was ground; it would be there when he came back. He slapped the hood of the car instead. "Keep her running," he said. "I'll get your passengers."

He headed back into the building, feet crunching in the half-frozen puddles that filled the foyer. There were twelve students left, sitting on suitcases and the plastic-sheet-covered chairs. He hustled them outside and into the cab.

Larry stalled at the curb, shoving his hand through his shaggy hair. "Maybe I should wait a couple more days, Professor Fennick," he said. "If the weather lets us, they've said they might open the roads up to Scotland back up. I could head home."

"If the roads open up, your mum will be coming down to her sister's," Danny reminded him. "That's what she told you when she called, right?"

Twisting his mouth, Larry admitted, "Yeah," but didn't move.

"I'm heading for Cornwall," Rhiannon said, tossing her backpack in and shoving past him. "I heard there were surfers catching thirty foot waves off the beaches there. I'm gonna make the most of it."

"We'd rather like you to come back when the university reopens," Danny said dryly. He shoved Larry into the Land Rover, and the rest of the students scrambled in after him. By the time mousy little Neil squeezed in, clutching his laptop like a talisman against missing months on his thesis, the Land Rover looked like a clown car. Somewhere over Durham a clap of thunder grumbled disconsolately through the clouds.

"What about you, Professor?" Alison asked, rolling the front passenger window down enough to stick her nose out. "Aren't you leaving?"

"Once I get you guys safely away, I'm locking up and heading home," he said. "Don't worry about me. Travel safe."

He stepped back, shoving his hands in his pockets and shuffling his feet restlessly on the pavement. Al honked the horn—just in case—and pulled away from the curb slowly. The Land Rover lumbered away in the direction of the train station, damage-pocked rear end disappearing into the fog like a retreating dinosaur. Danny waited until he couldn't hear the engine, then went back inside to grab his bag and lock up. He hesitated, ducking his head to settle the heavy satchel over his shoulders. The tiled floor in the entrance was muddy and cracked, the cardboard tacked up over the broken windows sodden and leaking damp down the wall. It felt like he should do more than just lock the doors, but with no one here anything he did would just be a Band-Aid. Besides, one thing no one had ever called him was handy.

He huffed out a breath, tasting fresh rain in the air, and let himself out, locking up behind him.

The wind had picked up while he was inside. The tattered festival banners strung from lampposts rattled and flapped, the ones that hadn't already ripped belling out like sails. Danny ducked his head and walked into the wind, clutching his satchel close across his body. He felt like a mime, at least he did until the rain came on like a tap. Then he just felt like a drowned rat. His hair plastered itself down over his face in sodden, matted tangles—the length of it reminding him he'd been meaning to get to the hairdressers—and he spluttered on the pelting water hitting his face.

Tucking his chin down, he broke into a loping jog past the shuttered-up Waterstones and into the Market Place. The wind caught him from a different direction, making him stagger, and he caught the taste of ozone on his tongue a second before the lightning struck.

It hit Neptune's upraised trident, shattering the stone into blackened shards. Danny cursed breathlessly and threw his arms up over his face, yelping as the shrapnel hit him. His forearms took the brunt of the biggest bits, but what was left scattered wasp-sting pinpricks of pain over his forehead and jaw. He was still blinking away the glare spots burned through his field of vision when the next bolt struck, agitating up enough static electricity to make his hair bristle even through the rain. Then again, and again.

Forks of lightning staggered across the square like a drunkard's walk. It left charred patterns on the stone-paving slabs and shattered windows. Small fires spat and caught in the grass and behind glass, guttering stubbornly against the battering wind and rain.

In the middle of it Danny stood frozen, gaping openmouthed like an idiot. He knew he should run, but some atavistic instinct froze him in place. As if the lightning was a predator, and he just had to avoid catching its attention.

Besides, in a totally terrifying way, it was beautiful.

The growl broke the paralysis holding him in place, the guttural, hollow noise making him flinch and look around. A wolf stared back at him, hunched and sodden in the rain. It was quite clearly a wolf, from the green-eyed broad head to the muscle-coiled haunches. Only an idiot would have thought it was anything else.

It was looking at Danny.

He sucked in a startled breath, but all he could smell was stale water and ozone. "Oh hell." Danny turned to run, feet sliding on the wet stone, but the heavy weight of muscle, flesh, and fur hit him first. The impact threw him off his feet, breath hiccupping out of his chest, and sent him crashing into the window of the abandoned Cafe Nero. It had been boarded up, but the sodden plywood cracked easily on impact, and Danny and the wolf fell through into the store.

Chairs and tables went flying as the two of them landed on the floor. Danny grabbed the wolf's ruff, digging his fingers in and locking his elbows to keep the white, white teeth from his throat. Slobber drooled on him, and the wolf snarled into his face, flews wrinkled back tight from long fangs. It wasn't like the rangy, tired wolves you saw at the zoo. This was an old Scottish werewolf, big as a pony and muscled like an ox. The weight of it on Danny's chest made his ribs creak, his lungs compressed.

He growled back. "What the fuck is wrong with you?"

Green eyes in a dark mask of fur blinked at him, and then a naked man was straddling his waist, hands braced against his chest. He was all sculpted lines of heavy muscle, tattoos of rank curling down his ribs and low across his stomach. His hair was short, tawny blond, and Danny's hands were still buried in it. Flushing, he moved them quickly.

"Me?" the wolf asked, voice burred with a Highland accent. Straight brows arched over those rare green eyes. "I wasn't the one dancing with the lightning. Do you fancy yourself a priest now? Were you looking for augury in your cooked brain meats?"

"Go to hell, Jack," Danny snapped. "And get *off* me."

Chapter Three

JACK DIDN'T move. Asshole.

Instead he ducked his head, burying his face in the crook of Danny's neck, and sniffed noisily. Danny set his jaw and tolerated it for a minute, then shoved his face away. The scruff of stubble along Jack's jaw was rough against his palm. "You done?"

"That hasn't changed. You've still got a mouth on you." Jack rolled off Danny and got easily to his feet. Rainwater dripped down his body, wrung out of the coat of fur he'd just shrugged off. He stretched, long, lean muscles sliding under tanned skin, and scratched his chest, unabashed by the fact he was naked and wet.

Of course not, Danny thought with dry-mouthed irritation as he straightened his glasses over his ears. Wolves had no nudity taboo. Neither had Danny once; somehow, though, none of that scarred and inked skin felt safe to look at. He dragged his eyes away from the water dripping off ridged stomach muscles, glanced at the cock hanging loose between lean thighs, and then settled on Jack's collarbone.

The sharply unamused voice of his PhD supervisor echoed in his memory: "My eyes are up here, Mr. Fennick."

It had taken him a *long* time to get used to the idea of looking people in the eye. It took no time at all to fall back on the old social cues. He kept his eyes on Jack's throat as he scrambled to his feet, exaggerating his always terrible posture to steal a couple of inches from his height. That still left him too tall, but it was the effort that mattered.

"What are you doing here, Jack?" he asked. "This isn't your side of the wall."

Jack rubbed his jaw, dragging his thumb along the line of his chin. "It ain't?" he said, mocking surprise in his voice. "I'll have to send word to Da that he ceded his claim. Age is a sad thing, to take you from Wolf King of the British Isles to the laird of a soggy marsh." He shook his sandy head ruefully.

And people accused cats of playing with their food. Wolves were worse. Danny grimaced and looked up as far as Jack's sharp, toothy grin. He hesitated there. It wasn't—necessarily—friendly on a wolf, and there were a *lot* of teeth.

"I wasn't disputing… that's not what I *meant*, Jack," he said. "But wolves go north to pay their respects. The Numitor doesn't come down over the wall and out of the wild. Neither do you."

There was a pause; then Jack thoughtfully said, "Things change."

Danny snorted. "Wolves don't."

He could have said "you don't," and it would have been as true. Except the last time they'd had that argument, it had been on a crag in the Highlands, the loch below and the sky above the same freakishly perfect blue. It hadn't ended well there—with fucking, fighting, and fuck-yous—and it seemed like a letdown to run it through again in a musty coffee shop.

From Jack's glare, and his silence, he remembered and he agreed.

Outside the lightning had exhausted itself battering the ground and spluttered out, sparks of electricity dancing in the puddles. That left the rain, sleeting down sideways as if it had somewhere to be. Just like Danny did.

He took a deep breath, absently shifting his satchel across his body like a talisman, and pointedly changed the subject back. "I wasn't expecting to see you," he said. "That's all."

Jack prowled closer, sniffing him as he circled. On the back of Danny's neck, his hair prickled with something between discomfort and a heavy, hot awareness. He wasn't a wolf, but he wasn't human either—and this was what he'd grown up expecting to want. Or else his cock was an idiot with a thing for very bad lads and an inability to learn. He shifted his weight, ignoring the ache of weight in his balls and the heady soup of pheromones Jack was leaking like snot. Maybe it could be a bit of both.

"I wasn't expecting to see you either," Jack said. This time the circuit was closer, shoulder bumping against Danny's. "Last your ma heard, you were in Leeds."

Danny glanced to the side, watching Jack out of the corner of his eye. How long had Jack spent in wolf form? The longer you spent in fur, the more you brought back with you. It sounded a fair trade, but the stories were only of monsters. "Last time I spoke to her,

I was. When I moved up here, I didn't see how it would make a difference to her. She'd not cross the wall, not to see me."

Jack grabbed his ear with hard fingers and pinched, startling a yelp out of him.

"Don't see *you* crossing the wall to see her," Jack pointed out. He twisted and let go. Danny clenched his jaw and rubbed his ear resentfully, feeling the heat of it against his head. His hand stopped midrub when Jack stopped behind him and asked, "Since when are there wolves in Durham?"

Ah. Danny shifted and cleared his throat uncomfortably, dropping his hand to grip the strap of his bag. Explaining *that* was part of the reason he hadn't gone home to see his family. There were no wolves in Durham, not permanently. The north of England was a place to pass through for their kind, heading up to see the Numitor or fleeing south in disgrace.

It wasn't a problem for Danny, but Jack....

Jack had grown up in the oldest pack in Britain, all centuries-old grudges and rules codexed by *howl*. His kin were so purebred that they thought interbreeding with real wolves would be better for the bloodline than dilution by humanity—and mutts like Danny were their proof. Thing was, they might not like dogs, but they liked their rules even more.

"There are a couple of us," Danny hedged.

He got scruffed unexpectedly, the hard squeeze of Jack's hand on the back of his neck making him jolt, and then released. Jack wandered back into view, sniffing his fingers. "I smell paper and mint and lye," he said. "I smell humans and curry sauce and sweat. I don't smell *us*."

Danny looked all the way up, meeting pale, wild-green eyes in stubborn defiance. "I'm not a wolf."

It was another old argument, and Jack batted it away the way he always had.

"You're still *pack*."

"Not anymore."

Jack narrowed his eyes, anger tightening his skin over the sharp bones of his face. "Did they drive you out?"

"No," Danny snapped. He'd not liked the Leeds's pack much, but then he'd not liked his own pack any more than that. "I don't *want* a pack, Jack. I don't need one."

Jack eyed him like he was a lunatic. Danny shrugged and shifted his weight onto the balls of his feet. He spread his arms. "Look at me. I'm fed, I'm wormed, I've got a job and a place to sleep. I'm *fine*. I'm not a wolf. I don't need anything the pack has to offer."

He was shouting by the end, the angry crack of his voice startling them both. There weren't a lot of people who shouted at Jack, and none of them had ever been Danny. He'd snarked and questioned and sometimes ignored, but never directly challenged. Danny closed his mouth so hard his teeth clicked and raked his hands through his hair. Cold water dribbled down the back of his neck.

"Jack...."

He was going to apologize. Before he could get the words out, Jack grabbed him and shoved him against the counter. The impact made him gasp. His body bent back along the curve of plastic, pinned over the fusted remnants of lemon cake and scones.

"It's not about what *you* need," he snapped, twisting his fists in the soft fabric of Danny's jacket. Heavy muscles clenched over his shoulders as he pinned

Danny down. "The pack keeps us all safe, keeps us secret."

"I'm twenty-eight—I don't need rescued. I don't need *adopted*." He braced his hands against Jack's chest and shoved. It won him a few inches of space. Jack took it back and a few inches more. A hard cock pressed against Danny's thigh, the usual confusing mix of lust and submission hitting him like a bat to the gut.

"You don't get to decide that."

"Fuck you."

This time the smile was close-lipped, relaxed and interested, and his hips shifted, thrusting his cock against Danny's thigh. "If you want."

Danny's chest hitched, lust yanking down from his balls, and his cock thickened eagerly. It was a bad idea, but for a heady second he didn't care. He hadn't been celibate, but like he'd discovered with Jenny—it just wasn't the *same* with humans. They didn't smell right, they didn't *want* right. Jack did. Always had.

Except he'd nearly chewed his foot off to get away from the pack, from his mum and his siblings and all the cousins and uncles and fifty-three times removed, second cousins by marriage. From Jack. The pack might feel right, but it was also confining, clannish, and frequently cruel.

"I don't," Danny said, voice thready and unconvincing. He cleared his throat and tried again. "I don't. Get off me, Jack."

"Sure?"

Danny shoved him again, bracing his forearm against the wolf's broad chest.

"Sure."

Jack leaned in, sandy hair rubbing against Danny's jaw, and licked him, a wet swipe from collarbone to jaw. The noise that escaped Danny was trying to be a gasp, but wanted to be a groan.

"Maybe another time," Jack said. "But you're still coming with me, Danny. You can't stay here on your own."

He let go—as unabashed about naked and hard as he had been with being naked and soft—and stepped back. Sharp green eyes stayed focused on Danny, narrowed enough to squint the fine wrinkles at the corners, and he waited.

Danny shrugged his jacket straight on his shoulders and yanked uncomfortably at his trousers—in no way as unruffled.

"I'm not on my own," he said. "Look, Jack, you weren't sent looking for me, so just forget you found me. Forget I asked why you came down over the wall. It isn't my business anymore. Just do me a favor and *forget me*."

Jack cocked his head to the side and frowned, brows knitting together over his aggressively straight nose. "Don't be an idiot, Danny," he said. He waved one hand at the storm battering the city behind him, the extension of his arm exposing the crown-and-mistletoe tattoo scored into the tender hollow of his armpit. "The prophets have Da's ear now, Danny, and they think this is the end of the world. I might be the first wolf to come down over the wall, but I won't be the last. Do you really want to be denning with humans when Da cuts us loose?"

The memory of a hunt cracked through Danny's brain, the smell of blood layered over piss, concrete, and booze. Stained fur and fangs, going rancid quickly as it clotted and curdled. Their quarry had been a branded exile, sentenced to be a prophet and running from the gelding, but that hadn't been the only prey they found that night. No one had ever told Danny what the exile had done wrong to be sent for maiming, but it had been a comfort to know it was something bad enough the Numitor would loosen his leash for a night.

Imagine the leash gone entirely?

"He's not going to do that," Danny protested. "The Numitor's spent his reign keeping us secret, laying down the laws that keep us separate from humans. He'd not just undo them."

Jack's mouth tightened, and he looked away for the first time, rubbing the back of his hand over his jaw. "It might not be up to him."

"He's the *Numitor*. Who the hell is going to over-rule him? Selene, yelling orders down as she swings by on the moon?"

Amusement tweaked Jack's mouth for a second, then faded away. He looked grim and oddly guilty. "You don't want to be here to find out, Danny. You need to come with me."

It wasn't ten years ago. Danny wasn't a shit-scared eighteen-year-old half hoping someone would talk him out of his dreams. Jack wasn't the prettiest damn thing he'd ever seen anymore. Okay, that last was a lie, but the rest wasn't.

"No," he said and then took a deep breath. "I don't need to do anything. *You* do, so why don't you get back to chasing whatever you came down the wall after—before the weather washes away the trail."

He shoved past Jack and hopped out through the broken window. The rain hit him like a wet sheet, cold and hard enough to feel like a slap. He hissed and hunched his shoulders, quickly soaked down to the skin as the rain penetrated through the layers of tweed and bulk-bought Marks and Spencer's shirts. Lightning scars forked in splintered lines across the square, and Neptune had sacrificed his trident arm to the storm.

A prophet would call *that* a bad omen. It made Danny hesitate, doubt crawling out of some superstitious pit in the back of his brain.

"Danny, you've been gone too long," Jack said. "You don't understand what's going on."

Turning around, Danny squinted at Jack through the rain, lifting one hand to shield his glasses from the downpour. "Good," he said. "I'm not a part of that world anymore. I'm not a wolf."

He turned and stalked away, but not fast enough to escape Jack's parting words through the rain: "You're not human either, Danny, no matter how hard you pretend."

Chapter Four

SOMEONE HAD put the window of the co-op in a couple of days ago. The shelves were stripped bare. All the looters left behind were the dregs: newspapers turning to pulp on the shelves and a split bag of mixed veg ground into the muddy tiles. From somewhere inside the store the alarm droned on, the shrill sound rattling off the empty walls.

Danny had been coming home to the noise since Monday. He knew exactly how long it took to get used to it. One piss, a mug of coffee, and twenty minutes on hold to the police before he gave up. Jack wasn't so easily ignored.

The end of the world. He knew all the prophets' claims, repeated like catechisms every new moon. The wolf winter. The long hunt. Myths broken into pieces and stitched back together again over the centuries. It had never been for him—not for the mutts—but he'd still listened. When he'd gotten books from the library, he hunted *their* stories like rabbits through legend and history.

It had fascinated him. The old stories were why he'd studied theology at university, why he was here at Durham. They weren't real, though, not in a tangible sense. Reality was national insurance, a freezer that creaked in the night, and occasional guilty sex with an ex-girlfriend. The wolf winters were metaphors, symbolism, and the anger of exiles. He'd never believed in them; only the prophets did.

Danny crossed the road, wading through the dingy brown runoff bubbling out of the drains. There was a jaunty red-and-white Mini Cooper blocking the gate into his flat. It was sitting chassis-deep in the puddle—well, more a lake at this point—with the hood left popped to let the steam out.

Stupid. Most people had given up trying to drive around in anything other than a four-by-four after the story in the newspaper the other week. A Smart car had actually been blown off the road, tossed into the wall of the HSBC bank like an old bottle. There was always someone who thought the "stay off the roads" advisories didn't mean *them* or where *they* needed to go.

Absently hitching his satchel up out of the way, Danny squeezed between the bumper and the gatepost. He stopped halfway through, knees pressed against the side of the car. It was still warm, and it smelled like…. Bending over under the hood, he sniffed the air over the engine. He mostly got wet metal, oil, and emptiness, the narrative scents washed away in the rain, but there was—

BANG!

Danny jumped backward, cracking his hip and shoulder against the gate. All the banked tension of the day—herding the students, the terrifying spectacle with

the lightning, the meeting with Jack—flooded his sys-
tem with adrenaline and made his heart stutter faster in
his chest. Not that there was anywhere to go. If another
car had hit the Mini, he'd be crushed.

Instead of an image from a "Drive Safely" cam-
paign, he got a ginger wanker laughing at him over the
roof of the car.

"You should see your face," Brock hooted, slapping his hand against the roof of the car again. "Bet you
near shit yourself."

It wasn't that hard for "flight" to turn into "fight."
Danny licked dry lips and looked away from Brock's
smirking face, clenching his teeth on his temper. It was
never exactly pleasant running into his replacement in
his ex's bed, particularly when that replacement was a
macho asshole, but he prided himself on being an easy-
going man. Today, after the adrenaline shot of Jack's
arrival, he'd been reminded that he wasn't exactly a
man, and his knuckles hurt from not being fists. He
flexed the ache out of his hands.

"Did you see who left the car?" he asked instead,
squeezing the rest of the way from behind the car.

Brock shrugged broad shoulders, battered camo
jacket hitching up over his hips. "Nah," he said. "Why,
you need to get your car out?"

"The engine's still warm. If they were around, I
thought I could help."

That got him a snort. "You? Since when do you
know anything about cars?"

Since he'd grown up in an isolated farm in Scotland, with the only thing between him and a world with
no books the battered old Range Rover a local farmer
used to let him borrow. Wolves didn't read for pleasure,
and they didn't much trust those who did. The Range

Rover had been a decade old and change, had holes in the floor, and ran on fumes, swearing, and hitting the engine sporadically with a wrench. Danny had ripped his knuckles on spark plugs, scalded his arms on the radiator, and turned up at the library covered in enough oil to make the librarian tch at him—but it had been worth it to have something other than *Farmer's Life* and circulars to read.

Instead of saying any of that, Danny shrugged and pushed his glasses up his nose. "I could have called someone."

Brock snorted and thumped Danny's shoulder with a closed fist. "That's the problem with you, Danny Boy. You gotta have the balls to fix your *own* problems."

The fact was, the less people knew about him, the easier it was to fit in. If you were what people expected—the geek with a satchel, desk job, and no car-repair skills—they didn't go looking for anything out of place. Sad but true.

Shoving Danny out of the way with shoulder and hip, Brock leaned over the engine. He leaned one arm against the raised hood and poked the engine with the other. Danny looked. It wasn't a bad view. The guy might *be* an ass, but it didn't stop him having a nice one too. Wiping his greasy hands on his jeans, Brock pushed himself upright. "Probably just flooded. I'll get some of the guys later, and we can push it out of the water, give it a chance to dry out. No need to get your hands dirty, Danny boy."

"That's a relief."

Danny left Brock to finish up at the car, the clunk of the closing hood echoing behind him, and headed inside. The security door was meant to be kept closed at all times, but Brock had propped it open with the fire bucket. Fresh butts were shoved into the sand.

He met Jenny at the lift inside, wearing a cardigan over a sweater and her jogging bottoms tucked into her Uggs. She stopped when she saw him, tugging self-consciously at her braid.

"Dan."

"Jenn."

It was an old joke. It still used to raise a smile. Today Jenny just looked unhappy, shoving her hands into the pockets of her cardigan and biting glossy balm off her lips.

"Did you...," she started, trailing off as she glanced past his shoulder. "Oh. So you did."

They'd been friends, the two outsiders in a PhD program full of Durham graduates, and then flatmates. When she kissed him one night two years ago, it had seemed to make sense. It had been very normal—pizza, late nights, and *EastEnders* omnibuses every weekend. It had been fun. It had been *human*.

He heard the echo of Jack's words in his head again: "You're not human." Jack said it like it was something Danny didn't know. Except he'd had a hard lesson in how he wasn't quite human *enough* a while ago. It just wasn't how he'd been brought up. When she'd cheated on him after a year, it had been kind of a relief.

"Someone abandoned their car," he said, wiping his sleeve over his face. Both were wet, so it didn't make much difference. He swiped his hand over his head, slicking his hair down. Water ran down the back of his neck in a chilly trickle. "We were just having a look."

Jenny nodded and looked down at her feet, her tongue curling over her upper lip.

"Brock—I've asked him to stay over," she said. Blue eyes flicked up, a strained smile curving her lips. "With the weather and… everything… it's just nice to have someone here. I was going to tell you. I don't want it to be weird."

"It's not," Danny said after an uncertain hesitation. "It's fine, Jenn."

She wrinkled her nose at him, looking sad. Danny shuffled his feet and awkwardly excused himself, ducking into the lift as Jenny went outside. The door slid shut, and he slouched back against the wall, thumbing the third-floor button to make it light up. Maybe he shouldn't have just moved up a floor when they broke up. Maybe that hadn't been the *human* thing to do.

The lift engine hummed, and the cab jolted upward. Closing his eyes, Danny sighed and absently rubbed his throat where Jack had licked him. He could still smell the wolf on his skin, heather and high places and… blood.

He straightened up suddenly, making the lift rock, as his brain linked the two scents. Blood. That had been the elusive scent on the car. Someone had bled there.

"Shit," he muttered.

WHEN DANNY and Jenny had moved in, the estate agent had told them that before the building was converted into flats it had been a chapel. Methodist, she'd said, as if Danny couldn't tell from the severity of it. Inside it was a box, neatly boxed off into smaller boxes. The flat Danny used to share with Jenny had bare stone walls. The one he lived in now was flat white plaster throughout. Like a monk's cell.

Sometimes it made him feel guilty that he missed the bare, old stone more than he missed the sex.

Habit made him turn into the narrow galley kitchen and turn the kettle on. He leaned on the counter, the plastic edge digging into the heel of his hands. While the kettle bubbled and rattled, he thought about the smell of blood on metal.

It had been a trace. A remnant of a smell.

Shoving himself off the counter, Danny rattled distractedly through the drawers and cupboards. It had been four months, and he'd been the one to decide where everything went. Things should be easier to find. It still took him two tries to find the cups, and he had to dip into the dishwasher for a spoon. He ran it under the tap, scrubbing the bowl with his thumb, and dried it on a sheet of kitchen roll.

The driver had probably just cut himself trying to fix the car. Dumping coffee into a cup, adding enough milk and sugar to gag a builder, Danny snorted to himself. He'd *just* been standing by the car, thinking about how many times he'd barked his knuckles or opened the pad of his thumb on a ragged bit of metal.

It was nothing. The kettle clicked off, and Danny added water to the murky paste in the cup. Picking it up, he cradled it in both hands as he drank. The heat of it baked through his cold, chapped hands, almost painful as it reached his bones. Even if it was *something*, it wasn't his problem.

He gulped down another mouthful of coffee, still hot enough to scald his tongue smooth. It warmed him up enough he couldn't ignore the clammy weight of tweed and wool anymore. Stripping off—mostly one-handed, although he set the cup down long enough to pull his shirt over his head—he shoved the bundle of wet cloth into the machine. He left it to molder and stalked into the living room in his boxers, then folded his long, bare body down on the dog-hair-covered couch.

It felt too long—challengingly *tall* at six foot four for all he was all bone and no muscle—and his skin too bare. There were a few scars, but only wolves got rank tattoos. Working at the university, the lack had been an advantage. Oh, there were a few professors who had discreet tattoos, mostly *not* in the theology department, though. Seeing Jack had reminded him why he was lacking what he was lacking.

He didn't *care*, not really, but he remembered. It had been why he'd had to leave.

The rain was hammering down again, sleeting down the windows as the wind blew it sideways. It sounded like the end of the world out there. The phrase slid into Danny's head when he wasn't paying attention and squatted there.

He swore ripely—it would have made his students whoop—and grabbed the remote. The TV clicked on, and he flicked down static-jumpy channels to BBC One. A woman with the vaguely familiar face of the junior that usually gets the special-interest stories was standing on Quayside. She was clutching a mike with one hand and had her free arm hooked around the railing. The Tyne had overflowed its banks, soaking into the hastily constructed bulwarks of sand and rice bags. It came up to the reporter's knees.

She spat hair out of her mouth and squinted at the camera. "Bad as it looks here," she said, freeing her arm long enough to gesture and then grabbing the railing again as the wind tried to turn her coat into a sail, "There has been worse, and stranger, weather across the UK. According to reports from the BBC in London, a *tornado* touched down in the center of the city today."

The image cut away from her face, replacing her drenched pallor with a shaky, water-spotted video someone had shot on their phone. In the middle of the road, a twisting streamer of weather as tall as the nearby buildings twirled erratically as a top, old bags of crisps, lost shoes, and other bits of rubbish tossed about inside it. A bottle broke free of the tornado and shot across the road like a rocket. It must have passed close enough to whoever was holding the phone that they felt it, because they swore sharply. The image blurred and wobbled as they turned, revealing the bottle drive through a wooden door and a boy bleeding on the ground with a bloody gash on his head.

"Holy shit!" the kid holding the camera said.

Then the screen went black for a second, before shifting back to the shivering blonde soaking her legs in Newcastle. She wiped her face on the puffy sleeve of her down jacket.

"In Scotland the weather is said to be even—"

Danny turned her off. It wasn't the end of the world. That was superstitious rubbish. There was magic in the world—it would be stupid to pretend otherwise when he'd just touched it today—but that wasn't the same as prophecies and apocalypses. He could see why the prophets might not agree, though. And if the prophets believed it, then so would the Numitor. Wolves lived a long time. The Numitor hadn't come over from Rome with Hadrian, but he remembered the witch trials. He'd believe in the end of the world, especially if it was what he *wanted* to believe.

That would be…. Words failed Danny. Bad was too small a word. Bad was spilling coffee on your tie before a meeting. Bad was forgetting goat cheese at the back of the fridge. Disaster was too big. Not *wrong*, but it left too much for his imagination. Jack was civilized, as wolves went. The old man-eaters in the Numitor's pack weren't.

Nervous energy drove him to his feet, his muscles twitching with the adrenaline-kicked-in expectation of flight-or-fight. That was a joke in itself—he'd no chance if he fought, and once the Numitor loosed the choke chain… there'd be nowhere to run *to*.

He clenched his hands, squeezing his fingers into his palms until his knuckles creaked, and rolled his neck. The itchy restlessness refused to shift, his brain full of how it could all go wrong. Or not, he reminded himself. He rubbed his fists against the sides of his thighs, digging his knuckles into the tight strap of muscle.

The weather could break before the Numitor decided to cut the pack loose of Hadrian's Ban. Or maybe the wolves would bleed the country like a deer at bay, crippling and gutting it to eat later. Maybe the wolves would cross the wall, and Hadrian's curse would turn out to be real too, although Danny thought the world ending was more likely. Either way, any of the ways, there was nothing to be done about it.

Not that it stopped the restless feeling in his legs, the need to be moving toward something. With a choice between running to Scotland to face down the Numitor—a long run, a short confrontation—or going to track down a smear of blood, Danny picked the blood.

He padded over and cracked the window, swearing as the wind shoved at it. Cold rain slashed through the gap, making his balls shrivel as it hit him. It was gray outside, a murk of fog, rain, and dimming, weak sunlight.

Just under the window was the tar-paper roof of the garden shed, a rickety, wooden half shed full of rusted spades and the spider-filled BBQ. Danny let the window swing open—repeating his curse as the full blast of the weather hit his bare skin—and climbed out. His gasp at the cold filled his mouth with water, the windowsill wet and slimy with wet bird shit under his feet.

He jumped, pulling his fur on as he fell. The dog landed on the shed with a thud, staggering as it got all four feet under it. It shook itself, sneezed out the water the man had inhaled, and hopped down into the garden.

The rain battered it, sodden ears drooping, and washed out the world around in smears of odor and stench. Under the stunted willow the watered-down spoor of a fox was seeping away into the grass, and the air smelled of wet concrete and clean water.

Instinct sent it snorting around the small patch of greenery, sticking its head under the rosebush, and pissing on the fence to make a point to the fox.

Thinking was harder as a dog, or at least it was harder to remember what things in its head were important. The possibility of a bloody tide of fur and fang from Scotland ceded its position in the forefront of the dog's brain to the certainty that acrid spaniel had been walked past again.

The dog and the man *were* still the same, though, so after a minute of huffing and gruffing at the fence, it remembered why it was here. Blood on metal and a mystery it trusted would make sense when it put its skin back on.

THE CAR had moved. Brock had bumped it up onto the pavement, dinging the side panel against the wall, and closed the hood. The dog sniffed around the car, getting down on its elbows to crawl under the car. It smelled of oil and road, a bit of Brock.

With his skin on, Danny didn't care much about Brock. The dog was less sanguine. This was *its* territory, and it didn't like having someone else marking it as theirs. It put its hackles on end.

After crawling out from under the car, the dog jumped up onto the hood of the car, nails scraping against the paintwork. The ghost scent of blood it had picked up earlier was gone. It had been there, though. The dog knew what it knew, and it didn't doubt it.

It shook its head, ears flapping, and dropped its nose to the pavement. Brock's stink and Brock's cheap rubber and pleather sneakers, the sharp yellow reek of a cat on a weed, and a wispy thread of jasmine orange and a sour, flat gray smear of fear. That wasn't part of the territory's usual scent map. It was barely there, the wind tattering it and blowing it away.

The hook of the chase caught in the dog's instincts, and it loped after the trace. Twice the wind nearly ripped the scent from under its nose, sending it on a detour, but it managed to catch the tail end of it again each time. The fear smelled louder, burnt-out and acrid, but the chemical potency of the jasmine weathered better.

It stopped abruptly, a puddle of smell in a doorway the last trace. The dog whined confusion in its throat and cast around, tongue lolling out of its mouth as it panted hot plumes of breath into the air. It made no sense for a smell to just stop, like it was cut off by a knife.

"Oy!" a woman yelled. "Get out of there."

A stone clattered, skipping along the pavement and bouncing off the dog's haunch. It yelped and spun, wrinkling its lips back from sharp white teeth. The woman in the road, hunched under a blue and pink umbrella in a onesie and wellies, quailed and took a step back.

Her fear was jagged and bright even through the sheeting water, but one step was all she was willing to surrender. "Go on," she said, cocking her hand back like she had another weapon. "Shoo, you mangy thing."

Under its shaggy gray coat, the dog's lean muscles clenched. It took a stiff-legged step forward and then stopped, legs trembling with leashed aggression. The woman wasn't a threat, and humans weren't prey. Licking its teeth, the dog slowly backed away until it put enough distance between itself and the woman to turn around. It spun and ran down the street at full pelt. With no need to follow a dead scent, its nose swam with the brewing, fresh scents on the street.

Charred steak, fresh boiled eggs, vibrant orange and green of a baby's diaper, and the pungent, sweet meatiness of fresh rot. After the blood congealed and before the skin split, the flesh still tough enough to chew.

Its belly grumbled. The dog hesitated, torn between what it had set out to do and its stomach. In the end hunger won. It followed the stink down the street to a tall slatted fence that smelled of paint, intoxication, and piss. A ragged flag of soaked red hung from a post, plastered to the wood and any flap it used to have gone.

One of the slats was cracked in half, leaving a splinter-lined gap. The dog sucked its sides in and squeezed through, losing a hunk of gray fur and a bit of skin on the wood. Despite the stink outside, the garden had been well tended once. Now the lawn was a mire of mud, and the shrubs had been beaten down by the rain into the moldy leaf mulch.

Too much smell for a rat; it was something bigger. Cat? Dog? It knew—vaguely—that eating a dog would make it gag when it was skin side again, but it didn't care. It slunk through the garden, keeping a wary eye on the house. The curtains stayed pulled, the flickering lights of the TV spilling out the gap where the fabric didn't quite meet. The dog could hear the muted mumble of voices and music, soundtrack laughter vibrating through the glass.

The dog skulked around the edge of the garden, paws sinking in the cold mud, and down the narrow alley to the side of the house. Three plastic bins were lined up along the wall, leaving barely enough space for someone to get by. The narrow space reeked of death, strong enough that the dog thought it could smell it even skin side. It stood on its back legs and pawed at the top, using paws and nose to wedge the flimsy plastic lid open. The smell hit it first, ripe enough to make its mouth water, and then the lid fell open. It hit the bin behind with a hollow thud, and the dog jumped back from the mess of... flesh... shoved in on top of the rubbish.

Viscera tied in ribbons and slabs of meat stuck to the sides of the bin, the edges curling and dry. In the middle of it all, a nest of brown curls and a pale blue eye staring up at the sky.

The dog sneezed, snorting the smell out of its nose like it was evidence, and shed its fur. It needed a human brain to think around these corners. Danny knelt naked on the cold stone pavers, goose pimples crawling over his pale skin.

"Fuck me," he muttered. Standing up, he covered his mouth with his hand, pinching his nose shut. His nose wasn't as sensitive in this form, but he didn't like the smell either. He stepped forward and peered into the bin. Even without his glasses, he could still see it was a dead woman. Moistened by the rain, one of the bits of flesh peeled off the plastic and flopped into the pile of meat.

When he leaned in, careful not to touch anything, he could swear he could smell a hint of jasmine layered under the rot. Maybe that was just expectation. His stomach roiled unhappily, a burble of acid crawling up to burn the back of his throat. The sourness of it cut through the smell in an odd kindness. He'd seen bodies before. Old wolves died in the Highlands and rotted among the stones, and—no matter how rigorous the Numitor's justice—accidents happened when wolves and humans came together. That was just death. This was slaughter. It was the frenzy of the fox in a henhouse, with too many necks and only one mouth.

It was murder, and the only wolf he *knew* was in town was Jack.

The idea—not even quite a suspicion yet—slid queasily into Danny's mind. Before he had time to reject it, and he was sure he *would* reject it, the background mumble of soap voices suddenly went quiet.

"I'm telling you," a man said. "I heard something out there."

"It's nothing," a lighter voice, but still male, said. "Come in, before you catch your death."

Shit. Shit. Shit. Danny held his breath and didn't move, shivering naked in the rain as he tried to will the suspicious man back inside. It was cold, it was wet, and what did Mr. Warm-and-Dry care if a fox was sniffing around an empty henhouse—he should really just go back inside.

As always, the Wild stayed under his skin and out of his control.

"Just give me the torch and that poker," the man said. "We don't want to get rats on top of everything else."

Some benighted instinct made Danny grab for the bin lid. He flinched back before his fingers touched the slimy plastic. Last thing he needed was to leave his fingerprints on the scene of *this*. He pulled his fur on, dropping to all fours just as the man came around the corner and played the beam down the alley. His eyes widened when he saw the big, bony animal lurking in this ginnel.

Maybe he wasn't a wolf, but for a dog he was *wolfish*.

The dog bolted out into the garden, the homeowner quickly hopping out of the way, and across the grass. He jumped the fence instead of squeezing through, hooking his paws over the slats and hoisting himself up and over, as the man asked, "D'ya see the *size* of that?" behind him.

By the time the screaming swears started, the dog was halfway down the street. It tucked its tail, obscurely ashamed, and kept running. It didn't stop until it reached the den, fur dank with sweat and tongue flopping out of its mouth as it panted in great, rasping whoops.

The car was still there. It smelled like cigarette smoke, butts littering the pavement next to the passenger door. Usually the dog would get back into the garden and unearth the ragged pair of jeans Danny left behind the shed, pretending he'd been taking the bins out if any looked askance on his way in. Since Brock had left the front door propped open, the dog just let itself in and pressed the button to call the lift with its nose. The button lit up, and the dog sat down to wait, its tail pattering against the rug in a lazy wag. It liked the lift, and the run had worn the nerve-twitching adrenaline of its discovery out of it.

When the lift arrived, it stood up, shook itself politely, and then stepped carefully across the gap. It waited until the doors slid shut to pull on its skin again, leaving Danny naked and nauseated and reflected in brushed steel.

The dog could see better. The world was blurred again around Danny, but from what he could make out, he looked pale and strained, dark marks ground into the skin under his eyes. The dog might have run off its distress, but Danny couldn't get the image of that mess of blood and bits out of his head. It made him retch, tasting coffee and the cheese sandwich he'd had for lunch, and he had to struggle not to empty his guts all over the floor. It would hardly improve the smell. He leaned back against the cold metal wall, feeling the bump and thrum of the lift's workings through the surface. Maybe his mother had been right, and going to university had made him soft. He doubted a dead body would make that hard old bitch sick.

Luckily, no one between the ground and Danny's floor wanted the lift. It wasn't *that* late, but it was dark and miserable. People were sticking close to home and in the warmth. He made the naked dash across the landing and let himself in. The door wasn't locked. It wasn't as if he had much worth stealing, and if someone did break in, he could track them down more easily than the police.

The flat was cold, the open window letting rain and wind in. The carpet under it was sodden, squishing underfoot as Danny went over to latch the window. He had to wrestle it over, putting his shoulder to the frame as the wind fought him. Finally a sudden, gusting change in direction took the pressure off it, his weight slamming it over.

He should have gotten something to eat, but the thought of eating made his stomach twist again. He could have tried to get in touch with the Numitor, going through the creaky old contact tree of shop phones and pups sent belting up the crags with messages, but he wasn't sure what that would do. An hour ago, the last thing he'd wanted was for the wolves to break Hadrian's Ban and head south.

He grabbed the curtains and dragged them shut, closing out the storm.

He didn't even *know* that Jack was involved. Humans might not have teeth and claws, but they made do. Danny thought of that untouched face, waxy as a doll as it looked up out of the ruin of its body. That wasn't the casual cruelty of wolves; that felt like a human thing.

Or maybe he just didn't want to believe Jack would do something like that. They'd grown up, not quite in sync, in the same pack. Whatever terms they'd parted on, how could Danny have missed the sort of sickness that did *that*?

A sigh heaved out of him, and he turned around, leaving his glasses off. There wasn't a lot of appeal in seeing the world clearly tonight. He sprawled out on the couch and flicked the TV on, falling asleep to a black-and-white rerun of *Doctor Who* and the faint whine of the shop alarm.

Sirens woke him up. He bolted upright, briefly befuddled at being in the wrong space for doing that. He groped for the bedside table and cracked his elbow on the coffee table instead.

"Shit," he said, rubbing his hand over his gummy eyes. After sitting up, he braced his elbows on his knees and buried his fingers in the tangled knots of his hair. His mouth tasted like groundwater and jasmine, and his dreams had been dog ones. That always left him feeling oddly unrested, like only part of him had gotten any sleep. After giving his face one last scrub, he picked his glasses up and put them on.

On the TV a stout man in a suit was signing along to Charlie Dimmock. Danny turned them off and wondered if—somehow—the police had tracked him from the bloody bin to here. It didn't seem likely, but it still took him a minute to get up. He ducked into the bedroom, grabbed a pair of sweats, and tugged them up over his long legs.

They felt vaguely damp against his balls, still chilled from him leaving the window open.

He opened the door and stepped out onto the landing, pausing in confusion when he found Jenny already there. She was standing at the wraparound windows, chewing absently on the collar of her shirt.

"Jenn?" he asked muzzily.

She didn't turn around. "Jesus, Danny," she breathed, her breath misting on the glass. "It's like the end of the world."

The echoed words made Danny flinch. He let the door click shut behind him and joined her at the window, peering out over the city. A building a few streets away was burning, a roaring pillar of flame and smoke ignoring the pounding rain, and fire engines and police cars were wailing through the streets. While they watched, lightning spiked down out of the sky at another location, sparking a smaller blaze.

It wasn't the end of the world that Danny imagined—there was more snow and blood in that, possibly a demon wolf eating the sun—but he could see her point.

"Maybe you should go to your sister's," he said. "The trains should still be running tomorrow. You could get to Devon."

"I hate her," she said.

Danny shrugged mutely.

"Maybe," Jenny admitted after a second. She pushed her hair out of her face, tucking it behind her ear. "My doctors are here."

"You had a doctor before you moved here," he said. "They have doctors in Devon."

She grimaced and hunched her shoulders, wrapping her arms around herself. "I'd be taken off the clinical trial. I'd be back to managing my epilepsy with diet and drugs that don't work. I can't do that, not unless I'm sure I have to. Besides, Brock doesn't want to go. His family's here."

There wasn't much Danny could argue with there, not without sounding like a jealous idiot. Instead he just stood with her in silence and watched the buildings burn.

Chapter Five

IT WASN'T really Danny's fault. The difference between a wolf and a dog was more than just skin-deep. Dogs saw the world for what it was, with only rare glimpses of the Wild that waited just under that.

Wolves....

Jack leaned against a parked van and watched a row of narrow red-brick houses burn, fire hopping along the roof and cutting through the garden fences. The firemen had given up trying to put it out, pulling back and soaking the houses yet unvisited in the hopes of sparing them. Bodies lay on the pavement, covered with dirty white sheets.

Where Danny would have seen a house fire and a tragedy, Jack saw something crackling and primal. A thing caught halfway between a forest fire unchecked and the gleeful maw of Surtr eager to lick the earth. He shouldered and spluttered at the storm that battered down his flames, eager to skip ahead to his turn in the end of things.

"Not yet," Jack muttered, smoke taste on his lips as he spoke. "There's a wolf winter and a god's death to come yet. We will have our pound and more."

The woman next to him, a see-through raincoat buttoned over pajamas and seal-short dark hair, gave him a curious look. Her eyebrows pinched together, and she leaned toward him, shoulder bumping his arm. "Sorry, what?"

A growl scratched at the back of his throat. He resented her intrusion into his space and her presumption of his attention. "I wasn't talking to you."

Her rain-chilled cheeks colored like she'd been slapped, and she tightened her mouth into an offended line. "I was only asking. You said something." She turned her back and moved away, muttering aggrievedly to the new group she fitted herself into. Jack watched her back sullenly as she was absorbed sympathetically, wishing it were that easy for wolves.

The fire finally gave up the ghost sometime before dawn, dying down into dully smoldering ashes and spitting cinders. It was hard to tell whether it was the firemen or the unrelenting rain that should claim that victory. The dead probably didn't care.

With the show over, the crowd started to drift away, gossiping clots still sticking together as they moved away from the smoke and roast-scrapings stink of the building. Jack stayed where he was, scowling at the listing walls of charred, cracked brick.

It would have been easier if Danny had been here. People liked dogs, even ones who looked human. It was some instinct for a soft mouth and a wet nose that made people easy in their company. It was one reason the Numitor kept them around, even with the prophets bitching and moaning about blood quantum and domestication. A couple of dogs in the pack, and the humans would deliver to the old farmhouse, come out to fix the generator when it creaked out its last gasp, or get the satellite back up and running before the Numitor missed his Netflix fix.

Except dogs liked people right back, liked their works, their cities, and their books. Loyal as Jack Russells and as stupid about picking fights half the time. If—*when*—the Numitor turned the wolves over to Gregor, he'd bring them south. Not right away; he'd wait for the winter and the north wind. Jack knew his brother—Gregor would want to hunt in Fenrir's shadow, nipping right at his heels. Eventually Gregor *would* come to glut himself, though, and if Danny was stupid enough to try and stop him, then Gregor would kill him. Knowing him, he wouldn't even realize that Danny was anything but another stray dog.

Jack wasn't about to let that happen.

During the chivvied run to the wall, Danny hadn't even crossed Jack's mind. Once the Wild put his scent under Jack's nose, though, he realized he should have. Danny had always made things easier, and now there was no reason Jack couldn't have him.

Two was a small pack, but it was still a *pack*. Jack wouldn't be alone, and Danny would be safe. Jack wiped his hand over his jaw, bristles scraping against his palm, and his mouth twisted wryly. Now all he had to do was convince Danny. The wolf in him grumbled that they shouldn't have let him leave earlier, but the man knew better. Bullying Danny was a short route to frustration; he gave in easily enough but then just did what he wanted when you weren't looking.

The rain finally eased up, the heavy sheets of water turning into a heavy drizzle that worked its way under his shirt and into his jeans. It tasted of pine and mountains, fresh and clean on his tongue, and of bleach and diesel. He licked the dampness off the back of his hand, curling his tongue around his knuckle, and wondered if the Numitor had been lying about the Wild weakening in the lowlands, or if this was new.

Down the street the woman he had not spoken to earlier was staring his way, eyes big and spooked as a flushed deer. Catching Jack looking back at her, she averted her gaze and nudged the man she was standing next to.

"So strange," she hissed. The effort at keeping her voice low made it more audible, the sibilants making Jack twitch. Her hand, fingers poking from under her overlong plastic cuffs, pointed halfheartedly toward either the ruined building or the corpses. "You don't think…"

Time to go. Jack pushed himself off the van, flashing a sharp-toothed grin toward the woman. She pinched lips together, drawing in closer to the other humans. Herd behavior. Safety in numbers was like the lottery—the more people involved, the lower your chances of your number coming up. The predator didn't care one way or another; he still got dinner.

Jack tilted his head to the fire, acknowledging the sullen old god as he faded into the embers, and walked away down the street. He'd bought a car in Newcastle, trading a handful of cash for a battered Ford that smelled of ten years of fish and chips and beer. It was somewhere to stash his clothes and the creased envelope of notes and identities the old man had given him as he left their den. Maybe Jack wasn't part of the pack anymore, but he was still a wolf, and he was still the old man's son. That got him something.

Not enough.

The car was parked up the curb in a narrow alley. The buildings around it were all boarded-up doors and broken windows, fly-struck glass shards glittering viciously in the predawn light. Paint peeled off the cracked walls in brittle green curls. Jack unlocked the car and popped the boot, stripping off his clothes with brisk impatience. He balled them up and tossed them into the back of the car, old trainers thumping against the muddy carpet. The road under his feet was gritty and cold; then he slammed the boot shut and let the wolf out.

Paws were tougher than feet, but to a wolf's nose the car stank of old grease *and* farts, unsatisfying sex, and the acrid stink left by years of passing dogs claiming ownership. He sneezed on the tire and shook himself, then turned and loped away into the dark. There wasn't much to hunt in the maze of walls and back roads, but he would find something.

He always did.

Later, stomach full of cat and scavenge, Jack dozed in the damp warmth of an abandoned shop. On some level he was aware that the shop was a Greggs and that stale cronuts were not wolf food, but the information didn't seem that important. Not when he could just sprawl out, stretching clawed toes against the cool tiles, and enjoy being the sleepy, sated wolf.

It would be better if there was another. Someone to watch his back, let him eat first, be warm and sated together. The thought settled in the seam of his mind, shared equally between wolf-want and man-want. Although, Jack thought with a flicker of humor, the wolf side was more interested in the fangs and play and less in fistfuls of dark curls and whippet-rangy shoulders. Probably best.

Peace gone for now, Jack scrambled to his feet. He shook himself, shedding fur and drool, and stuck his nose out the door. The rain had stopped, but a deep chill had taken its place. Jack's breath plumed from his mouth, spilling out of his jaws like smoke. The prickle of frost in it made him cough-bark in greeting, a rough hack of noise.

The snow he'd left in Scotland was coming to find him, chivvied on by Surtr's challenge last night. Winter did not care to have its toes stepped on.

He was glad of his fur as he shouldered the door open and stepped outside. Maybe his people didn't feel the cold, or the heat, as humans did. Although it was hard to tell if that was because wolves didn't dwell on things that couldn't be changed or because they were hardy enough that the cold had to be… colder… to hurt them. Either way, it didn't make the cold *pleasant*, just endurable.

During the hunt he'd lost track of himself in the maze of alleys and streets that made up a city. Tipping his nose down, he sniffed the cobbles, hunting for a familiar scent mark to orient himself. It was the lime-green cat fear that caught in his mind's map of the place, and he followed the fading spool of it. He stuck to alleys and shadows, cutting through back gardens and through empty, pockmarked car parks. Humans, like dogs, generally only saw the mundane, editing out things they didn't understand, but Jack saw no point in tempting fate.

Not when the Wild was so thick over the north he could taste it. Even the mundane could seem strange to someone in this weather.

"...dog attack last night. Northumbria Police have made no arrests as of—"

Jack stopped and doubled back. The flower beds that had been muddy the night before were now seeded with ice that crunched under his weight. He leaned against the side of the house and listened, but the news had already moved on to the cancelled football game.

It took him ten minutes to get back to the car and get dressed, giving a not-old woman in layers of rags and paper an eyeful as he hoicked his jeans up over inked hips. She laughed and whistled at him, sticking grubby fingers in her mouth.

"One way to get outta the walk of shame, laddie," she chuckled, shaking her head. "Tell you what, that sight's warmed up my old bones better than the shelter's tea."

Jack laughed. He'd been wolf enough the last few weeks that the sound rasped in his throat. After pulling the shirt over his head, the cotton damp and vaguely musty smelling, he tilted his head to the not-old woman. He could smell the juniper and malt-mash stink of her from where he stood, old booze sweated into her pores and clothes. Under that the bitter-apple smell of sickness, something more than a cold wrong in her gut.

Old, sick, alone. Easy prey. But she'd made him laugh.

"You should go south," he said, slamming the boot shut. "It'll be warmer there. For a while."

She opened her mouth to mock his advice but held her tongue. Old, sick, alone—and close enough to death that she could maybe taste the Wild. Her mouth compressed and she stared at him for a second, then hurried away, the worn soles of her trainers scuffing against the pavement.

Jack shoved the keys into his pocket, tugging the jeans low over his hips. She'd either ignore him and die, or listen and die later. That was out of his hands. He left the car and went looking for a newspaper.

Chapter Six

MRS. PATEL opened the corner shop on Monday as usual. She was wearing a woolly hat, mittens, and a knee-length, quilted puffer jacket in pink that she'd stolen from her daughter's wardrobe—but she was open. The only concession she made to the weather was that she opened an hour late, at 8:00 a.m.

Prices had gone up, though. Not on the staples, but a Milky Way now cost £4 and quilted toilet roll was a tenner.

"Do you have a *Northern Echo*?" Danny asked, rubbing his hands together and bouncing his feet from one foot to the other. It was bitterly cold outside, and dangerously bright. The sky was white as a sheet of paper. "Or the *Journal*?"

Mrs. Patel reached under the counter and pulled out a paper. It had been rolled into a tube and wrapped in cling film. She slapped it down on the table. "One seventy-five." He must have looked surprised. She shrugged and picked up her cup of tea, black and steam-ing, to take a drink. "Check the masthead. Production costs have gone up. They're still selling."

Danny shoved his hand into the pocket of his jack-et and groped for change, the coins unidentifiable to his numb fingers. He pulled out a handful and counted it out twenty pence by fifty pence. "The Internet is still down."

Mrs. Patel rolled her eyes. "I know, I know," she said, sweeping the money up in her mitted palm. "My boys won't stop going on about it. Adil trekked all the way into the university yesterday because he heard the computer lab had a connection stabilized. All to e-mail his girlfriend."

"Is she okay?"

Her mouth pinched, and she shrugged expressively in answer. Who knows, it said. It had become a familiar sight, that shrug, over the past few days. Danny gave in and bought a bar of chocolate and a can of corned beef as well, then shoved them both into the pockets of his jacket. Behind the counter, Mrs. Patel topped up her tea from her flask and shivered as he opened the door to let the cold in.

It had snowed and rained and then done it again, leaving the streets full of sharp clumps of gray, grungy ice and slush. Puddles had frozen in sugar-thin skins on the pavement, cracking underfoot when you stood on them. There had been falls, and the radio had told any-one who was vulnerable to stay inside, but that could only last so long.

Danny pulled the hood of his jacket up, ignoring the back of the neck tweak that didn't like muffling his ears, and wiped the condensation off his glasses with his knuckle. Once he could see again, he ripped the cling

film off the paper and stuffed it in his pocket. Despite
the precaution, the paper underneath already felt damp.
Or maybe it was just cold. He shook it out and tried
to remember the last time he'd bought a paper. It had
probably been back when he was in Scotland, fetch-
ing the news with the week's groceries from the village
shop/garage/pub. Until recently, he'd gotten most of his
news on his phone, packaged in headlines and helpfully
pinging to let him know it was there. Without the Internet, though, and with his 3G downloading one e-mail
an hour, it was back to paper and ink for now.

"Cold Snap Continues!" the headline announced,
over a picture of slushy icebergs washing up the Tyne.
Danny scanned it quickly, out of habit. There had been
tornadoes in Cornwall, the Met Office still had no expla-
nation, and Cameron had declared a state of emergency.
He flicked through the rest of the paper as he walked,
glancing up occasionally to make sure he wasn't walking into a lamppost or into traffic. There weren't many
cars about—roads had collapsed or flooded across the
city—but there were a few stubborn motorists crawling
through the puddles.

Roberta Blackman-Woods, the local MP, had released a statement encouraging everyone to stay calm
and use that "Northern grit" to get through the current
crisis. People in rural or isolated areas were encouraged
to stay safe and signal one of the police helicopters doing sweeps of the area if they needed help.

The wind yanked at the page as he turned it, the
cold reddening his fingers.

A Durham student in Greece reported to the paper
that rather than drowning, the locals were being baked.
An unprecedented heat wave had swept the country,

causing fires and leaving thousands of people in towns and villages short of water.

The sports section was winnowed down to retrospectives on last year's standing at this part of the year and to an interview with Magpies manager Steve McClaren about plans for next year. The For Sale section was full of blank spots.

The day after Danny found the body in the bin, it had been on the front page. Three days and two snowstorms later, it was relegated to seventy-five words and no picture on page eight: "The investigation continues into the tragic death of an unidentified woman last Tuesday night in Durham. Police have yet to confirm cause of death, but local resident Mark Franklin, who found the body, believes it was an animal attack. Since the onset of the current crisis, there has been an upsurge in animal attacks throughout the county. Police officers declined to comment on the theory, but have previously urged owners to behave responsibly with their animals."

The first report had included a low-resolution picture of a dog-shaped Danny's ass as he barreled through the fence. It hadn't been a photofit, but it had been enough to make Danny glad he'd not called the Numitor's attention to the situation. Murdering a human was a much lesser crime than exposing the pack. Although by not mentioning exactly where they'd found the body the press, or the police, seemed to be trying to keep the murder part under the radar.

He folded the paper shut and looked up as he turned the corner onto his street. There was a police car parked outside the flats, sitting fat and awkward-looking on chained tires. Danny stumbled to a stop, tripping over his own feet, and tasted the sour yogurt of a breakfast rerun in the back of his throat.

Run. The dog thought twitched the muscles in his legs. *Run and hide.*

Danny locked his knees against the trembling eagerness. There was no way they'd connected him—the him who stood on two legs and bought papers—with a scruffy dog seen a couple of miles away. They could ask anyone; dogs didn't even like Danny. He licked chapped lips, spit stinging, and stuck the paper under his arm before crossing the road.

The police were probably here about the car, still parked on the pavement and now wearing a toupee of iced-over show on its roof. The thought didn't *really* make Danny feel any better. He shrugged it off and headed into the building. The minute he pushed the front door open he heard the screaming.

"*You son of a bitch!*" It was Jenny, caught between rage and the snotty gargle of tears. "*You bastard. Get out.*"

Danny broke into a run, loping up the flight of stairs to the next floor. The hood of his jacket flopped down, balling up around his neck. He stopped on the landing, nearly bumping into the policewoman standing in front of Jenny's flat. The woman frowned at him.

"Sir? Is something wrong?"

Nerves made him stutter, shoving his glasses nervously up his nose. "No. I mean, I just heard my friend shouting, and I thought something was wrong. I didn't realize you were here—"

"You fucking, cheating asshole!" The tears were winning in Jenny's flat. "Get out of my fucking flat."

"Ma'am, please calm down," an unfamiliar man said. He sounded like Jack or the Numitor, the practiced calm of someone claiming authority. "This isn't helping."

"Listen to him," Brock snapped. "Crazy bitch. Keep her off me."

"Fine—let go of me, I'm not gonna do anything— Fine! I'm going. Fuck off before I come back."

Jenny stormed out of the flat, angrily jerking an old Durham University hoodie up onto her shoulders. Her face was pale enough her freckles stood out like ink, and her eyes were red and wet. She stumbled over her own feet when she saw Danny, face twisting around a couple of uncomfortable emotions.

"What do *you* want?" she asked, wiping her nose on the back of her hand. "What are you *doing* here?"

"I heard you shouting," Danny said, glancing uncomfortably at the policewoman. "I wanted to make sure you were okay."

She glared at him and wiped her nose again, sniffing fiercely. "I'm fine. Happy now?"

The policewoman cleared her throat. "Perhaps you should go with Mr....."

"Fennick. Danny Fennick," he said obediently.

"Mr. Fennick. We still need to speak to Mr. Davies about our inquiry. Once we're done, we can escort him out of the premises."

It took a second, but Jenny finally gave a jerky nod, hair falling forward around her face. She wrenched her sleeves down over her arms and stalked past Danny to the stairs. "Fine. Just… just get him out of my flat."

She stomped her way up to Danny's floor, then slouched against the wall as she waited for him to get his keys out. He shrugged an apology and gave the door a push, the unlocked door swinging open.

"For God's sake, Danny, when are you going to learn to lock the damn door?" she said. It was an old argument, from when they'd lived together. "This isn't whatever rural Ballykissangel hole you grew up in."

"Scottish, not Irish," he reminded her. He waved her in the door and closed it behind him. "Do you want—"

"No. I don't want a cup of tea or a biscuit or a cold drink or—anything. I just want to sit here and wait for Brock to piss off."

She stalked down into the main room and sat down hard on the sofa, elbows braced on her knees and head buried in her hands. Danny got her a can of orange from the fridge anyhow, sliding it onto the table in front of her. Water dribbled down the tin sides, puddling on the table.

"Oh, fuck off," Jenny said, voice wobbling back to teary again. "Don't be nice to me, okay? I can't—"

Her voice cracked, and she wiped her eyes on her sleeve, scrubbing impatiently. Danny flopped down next to her and waited it out. She finally straightened up and reached for the orange, popped the tab, and sucked down half of it.

"Go on," she said, stifling a burp against her tongue. "Say it."

"What?"

"I told you so," she singsonged acidly. "Brock was an asshole. I should have never let you go."

Danny unzipped his coat and shrugged it off, the weight of the corned beef tin dragging it off the sofa and onto the floor. He scratched the back of his neck, the curls sweaty despite the cold.

"Told you so," he said mildly. "By the way, what exactly did I tell you?"

She took another drink of orange and then balanced the can on her knee, frowning as she picked at the tab. The metal went *click click click* between her nail and the top. Drops of orange bounced out of the can and fizzed on the coffee table.

"The girl that was killed," she said, voice lilting up as if he might have missed it. "That's her car outside."

Danny wasn't a great liar. There'd never been much point growing up, not when the people around you could smell the lie on your skin. Luckily, Jenny was still staring at her soda as if the answers might be stamped around the rim, so his flimsy "oh?" went unchallenged. She gave a hard nod, chin bumping the collar of her hoodie.

"Yep, and apparently the reason she was here was to bang Brock." She spat the words out angrily and then hunched in on herself with a shudder. "Jesus, I can't even be angry. The poor cow's dead."

Old habits made Danny go to put his arm around her, but he checked himself. His hand dropped awkwardly onto her shoulder instead.

"I'm sorry."

"Don't be. I cheated on you right. This is my comeuppance."

Danny gave her a shake. "Quit that. It wasn't the same."

She looked up, pushing her hair out of red-rimmed eyes. "Why not? It feels the same. It feels like I deserve this."

He gave in and hugged her, pressing a quick kiss against her forehead. Her hair was dense and wiry against his lips. "Don't be daft. We weren't working is all, hadn't been for a while. You just had the courage to pull the plug."

Jenny leaned against him, her head on his shoulder. "We were okay."

"Nah."

She snorted. "God, Danny. Maybe my dad was right and I should have just let him set me up with someone."

He rested his chin on her head. "I don't think you and your dad have the same taste in men, hon. I never caught him giving me the eye."

Her shoulders hitched on a half laugh, and then she stopped, shaking her head. "I can't laugh. That poor woman. She didn't deserve to die just because she was screwing my boyfriend. Ex. Ex-boyfriend."

She sat up, sliding away from Danny, and tidied her hair back from her face. Her fingers worked distractedly at the knots she'd cried into it, picking them apart. "I suppose I should go and see if they're done," she said reluctantly. "Make sure he left."

"Want me to come too?"

Jenny took a deep breath through her nose. "Yeah," she said, pulling out a thin-lipped almost smile. "I'd appreciate that. Would you mind if I used your loo to clean up first?"

"Course not."

She gave his knee a grateful pat and got up, skirting the long way around the coffee table so she wouldn't have to step over his legs. It felt distant. Danny squashed the quick, anxious urge to do something about that, to topple her down into his lap for a cuddle until she relaxed, and let her go.

It wouldn't be fair. He loved Jenny, but he wasn't *in* love with her. Maybe it was because the prophets were right about humans and wolves not being able to live in harmony in the long run. It would be nice to think that, but he was pretty sure it was more about him having to hide so much from her. Five years they'd known each other, from friends to lovers to …this…, and Jenny didn't know where he came from, she'd never met his ma or his sisters—although that was more to do with them being horrible than them being wolves—and she'd never seen the dog him.

Even if he hadn't been worried about the Numitor finding out he'd breached the law, he wouldn't have been honest. It wasn't the sort of change to her worldview that Jenny would enjoy. Aliens, maybe. At a stretch. Gods, wolves and old Wild magic? Not so much.

"Oh God," she exclaimed from the bathroom. "I look like an angry panda. Jesus. You could have told me."

Chapter Seven

JENNY SHOVED all of Brock's things into a Tesco's Shop For Life bag: jeans, shirts, and a pair of old trainers that made Danny snort at the smell even in human form. She yanked the Xbox out of the TV and bundled it up, wrapping the leads around it roughly.

"Do you need a hand?" Danny asked, leaning against the door and shoving his hands into his pockets.

"No," she snapped, dropping the game into a half-empty bag. "I don't need any help. I'm not *sick*."

By the time the bathroom and kitchen were cleared out, it turned out Brock had moved in five bags worth of stuff. Jenny grabbed three of them and headed out onto the landing. Danny grabbed the ones left and followed her downstairs, pulling his stride so he didn't pass her on the steps.

"Did the police say anything else about her?" he asked. Jenny frowned over her shoulder at him, nearly losing her footing on the still damp steps. He grabbed her shoulder to steady her. "About what happened to her. Did they think that Brock had been involved?"

Her eyebrows twitched together. "What? No, of course not, nothing like that. It was a dog attack. The papers said so. They just wanted to know why he hadn't come forward. It turns out, it's because he's a cowardly dickhead."

It probably wasn't admirable to feel regret at that. Danny knew Brock hadn't done it, but it would have been reassuring to have the police looking that way. Just in case the truth wasn't something they wanted to know.

She reached the landing. Danny had been expecting her to leave the bags there. Instead she hip-bumped the door open and tossed them outside, clothes and Xbox games skidding out onto the muddy concrete.

It had started to snow, fat white flakes drifting down gently from the sky and melting on the cover of Saint's Row.

"You know he's waiting in his car," Danny said, nodding toward the battered Qashqai parked out on the street where the dead girl's car had been. The police must have come for that.

Jenny gave him a tight white grin and held her hand out. Danny shrugged and handed her the bags, then watched her toss them too. This time she got enough swing on them that they cleared the low wall, dumping their contents out into the muddy strip of dirt and shrubs.

"What the fuck!" Brock yelled, jumping out of the car. He ran across the car park, grabbed a pair of underwear from the prickly embrace of a winter-naked shrub, and waved them at Jenny. His pale skin had flushed, clashing with his ginger-blond cropped hair. "This is my *stuff*. What the hell do you think you're doing?"

"Getting it out of *my* flat," Jenny said, slapping his hand away. She jabbed her finger into his chest. "You're a cheating asshole."

Brock snorted. "Memory serves, so are you. Don't remember Danny boy here chucking your shit all over the car park." He glanced up at Danny and smirked. "Not that he'd have had the balls to—"

When he wasn't looking, Jenny hit him. Not a slap either—she balled her fist up and bounced it off his chin. Brock staggered back, caught off-balance, and grabbed his jaw with one hand.

"Whatever I did, at least I didn't leave some poor girl lying without a name," Jenny said, blinking snow out of her lashes. "Just go away, Brock, and don't come back."

One of the windows opened and a cue-ball head— shiny in a way that suggested a razor instead of nature was responsible—poked out. "What's going on down there!" he yelled, ignoring the companion trying to pull him back inside. "Shut up and take it inside."

Ignoring the advice, Brock grabbed Jenny's shoulders and shook her, dark hair flying around her face. "Like you give a damn about her, you selfish, whiny cow."

"Get off her," Danny growled, the dog crawling into his throat with his anger. He grabbed Brock's wrist and dug his fingers in, grinding the nerve down against the bone. Pain, and surprise, loosened the man's grip, and Jenny wriggled free. She stumbled backward, eyes huge and startled. Danny gave Brock an almost careless shove, sending the man sprawling the length of himself on top of his clothes. Anger was a raw, gray space in his head, his teeth aching in his gums until he had to clench his jaw to stop them lengthening. The dog thought Brock didn't need his throat. Clenching his fists, Danny dug his knuckles into his thighs and pushed the shift down. He clenched his teeth, refusing to let them crack into fangs. "You heard Jenny. Get lost."

Brock stared at him, face blank as he tried to work out how he'd gone down so easy. Then he laughed and scrambled to his feet, wiping his hands on his jeans. He swaggered up to Danny, all shoulders and the stink of aggression. "Or what?" he asked. "You think I'm scared of you, you lanky streak of piss?"

He slapped Danny, the flat of his hand cracking against Danny's cheek. The blush of heat made Danny realize how cold it was. He reached up and straightened his glasses, deliberate movement thwarting the bunched muscles in his shoulders and arms.

"Don't!" Jenny yelped. "Brock, don't hurt him."

Annoyance twitched up Danny's spine and out his mouth. "Touch me again, and I'll break your fingers."

Something flickered through Brock's eyes, some fleeting "bad idea" instinct. It didn't last. A grin pulled his lips thin over his teeth, and he lunged at Danny, ducking to ram his shoulder into Danny's gut. This time they both went down, scuffling in the dirt. Danny pulled his punches, absorbing most of Brock's without a flinch.

He'd grown up scrapping with people who didn't hold their punches and thought that him being a dog made him their punching bag. A couple of rabbit punches from a cocky asshole like Brock weren't going to slow him down.

Then Brock got a handful of Danny's hair and smacked his head against the concrete. Pain splintered through Danny's skull, red fringed with black, and his control of his temper slipped. Fingers tightening,

Brock did it again. It was satisfying to let the leash slip through his fingers.

"Fucking loser," Brock hissed in Danny's face, spit warm against cold cheeks, as he cocked his fist back to his chin.

Blinking the dots out of his eyes, Danny grabbed hold of Brock's fist as he threw a punch. He wrapped his long fingers around the man's hand, feeling the impact as knuckles dug into his palm, and squeezed. Flesh bruised and bone creaked, making Brock's anger-red face blanch.

"I told you," Danny said. "If you didn't leave, I'd break your fingers."

He squeezed tighter, feeling the protest of joints pushed out of true, as Brock yelped. Before he could make good on his threat, someone yanked Brock away from him. Danny snarled in frustration, shoving his glasses back on roughly, and scrambled to his feet, finding himself face-to-face with Jack.

The habit of old hierarchies jerked at him like teeth in the scruff of his neck, but he pulled against it resentfully.

"I didn't need your help," he snapped, twisting away from Jenny's fussing at his elbow.

Jack shrugged and let go of Brock, leaving the man slumped against the hood of a silver car. Livid blue-black fingerprints stood out against his skin, although the bruising was slowly smearing out over his knuckles.

"Don't think of it as help," Jack said. "Think of it as not wanting to stand in the cold while you two roll around in the mud. When was the last time you threw a punch? That was pathetic."

Brock made a groaning noise that turned into a curse. "That fucking asshole broke my hand."

"Good," Jack said genially, slapping Brock on the shoulder hard enough to stagger him. "I mean, I'd have broken your legs, but at least he's not forgotten how to fight completely."

"Fuck you," Brock said.

Jack looked him up and down, a low drag of attention. His mouth curled with contempt he didn't even bother to hide. "I don't think so."

He turned his back and dragged Danny into a rough hug, ignoring the nervy twitch of tight muscles. Jack's hand cupped the nape of Danny's neck, thumb finding the tender hollow under his ear, and he rubbed his stubbled cheek against Danny's throat.

"It's always good to see you, Danny," he said. "Still picking fights you can't win?"

The growl stayed in Danny's throat, but he knew Jack could hear it. Feel the buzz of it against his cheek.

"What are you doing here, Jack?" he muttered. A need to do something with his hands—or real old habits—hooked his arm around the solid shelf of Jack's shoulders. It felt good, lean and hard enough to bruise on. Wolves weren't *comfortable* to have around. "I told you, I don't need a pack."

He felt the quick scrape of teeth against his throat, sharp as a knife, and his balls clenched in reaction. "And I told you, you do," Jack said. He didn't bother to try not sounding smug. Letting go of Danny he stepped back, one arm still hooked casually up on Danny's shoulder. "So, are you going to introduce me or not?"

It was stupid to let himself be charmed, but he was. Irritated, too, but it was Jack. Arrogance and cockiness were as much a part of him as the ash-gall ink work on his skin or the green of his eyes. Danny glanced at Jenny, who had her arms crossed and was frowning at them both. The snow was coming down in flurries now, their breath white and chilly as it left their mouths, and she was shivering. Danny—belatedly—supposed he should be too. Instead he grinned crookedly at her.

"Jack, Jenny," he said. "Jack's an old friend. From—"

"Scotland," Jenny said. Her voice was wobbling with the cold. She rubbed her arms as she talked, trying to stay ahead of the goose pimples. "I guessed from the accent. Look, Jack, as you can see, this isn't a great time."

Jack flexed strong fingers around Danny's shoulders, digging down into the knot of tense muscle, and the distinct cold-ozone smell of snow was pushed away by a rush of sticky green Wildness.

"You mean pulling that loser off Danny?" Jack said, voice gone dark and thick as fur. "I suppose I could have been interrupting something, but he could do better. Hell, darlin', better's done Danny."

The implication wasn't subtle, but Jenny just looked confused. Danny felt a pinch of that old guilt about just how much of him she didn't know. He gave Jack a shove, sliding from under his arm. The snow was still melting as it hit the wet concrete, but damp little drifts were building up on the clothes tossed on the ground.

"We should go in," Danny said. "There's a storm coming."

"It's winter," Jack corrected him, glancing up. "And it's already here."

That wasn't something Danny wanted to argue here and now. He turned to Brock, absently straightening his glasses on his nose again. "Get out of here, Brock."

Flexing his fingers gingerly, Brock used his hips to push himself off the car. He looked over Danny's shoulder at Jenny.

"You think about this, Jenn," he said. "I go, I ain't coming back."

"Good," she said briskly.

Ugly emotion twisted Brock's face. "Fuck you, then," he said. Pale eyes flicked to Danny. "You think she wants you back, you sad ballsack? When we were fucking behind your back, we used to laugh at what a limp-dicked, four-eyed loser you were."

Danny's hands twitched, but he held on to his temper this time.

"Maybe if you'd focused more on fucking her and less on jokes," Jack said, "she'd not be dumping you."

Brock jabbed a finger at Jack. "I'll remember your face, you Scottish prick."

"Yeah?" There was nothing human in Jack's smile; it was just hunger and wolf behind his teeth. "Well, don't worry. You won't see it coming."

Brock backed down. He might not know why, but some part of his hindbrain that hadn't bothered to wake up for a confrontation with a peevish academic was telling him to run. It didn't even require him to make the smart choice, just the one that had kept his monkey ancestors from getting eaten before they could knock another monkey up.

"You'll regret this!" Brock snapped, grabbing his Xbox and an armful of clothes. "I hope you all fucking freeze."

He walked away over the car park, boots sliding in the slush. Danny hadn't realized how thick the snow had gotten until Brock disappeared into it, just a shadow and the spluttering growl of an engine.

"Come on," he said, rubbing a hand through frosty hair. "No point in obliging him."

Chapter Eight

JACK SPRAWLED out along the sofa in Danny's living room, one booted foot balanced on the arm. Worn denim and faded cotton clung to the slopes and hollows of his body. Danny dragged his wandering attention away from the slice of skin visible between jeans and T-shirt. It was more distracting than if Jack had been naked.

The tight, tawny memory of naked, tattooed wolf smirked out of his subconscious. Danny's breath caught in the back of his throat, hot and scratchy with awareness. Okay, maybe he should just stop thinking about Jack's body or the fact the bed was six steps, a door, and a stumble away. He glanced over at the window, the glass a field of white from the snowstorm, as if the cold outside would chill his lust.

It didn't work. Danny gritted his teeth and cleared his throat, waiting until Jack yawned, stretched lazily, and opened his eyes a crack. "What do you *want*, Jack?"

There was a pause as Jack looked Danny up and down, his mouth curling in a crooked, suggestive line.

"I can think of a few things," he said, eyes finally making their way back up to Danny's face. "A thank-you would be nice, to start with."

The request made Danny bristle resentfully. He hadn't needed help; he hadn't *asked* for help. Not to beat Brock up, anyhow, although Jack had stopped the fight before Danny lost control and killed the other man. Taking a deep breath, Danny forced his shoulders down. Tension twisted into a hot knot at the nape of his neck as he bent his head stiffly. He'd already fallen back into the old habit of avoiding eye contact, his attention on the scruffed line of Jack's jaw.

"Thank you," he said, trying to sound like he meant it. "How did you find me?"

Jack shrugged. "Wet dog is pungent."

Annoyance pinched at Danny's mouth, but he supposed he'd left himself open to that. Besides, he was a dog. It had been a long time since he'd bothered trying to pretend otherwise. That took some of the sting out of the jabs.

"Fine," he said. "*Why* are you here?"

Jack shrugged from where he lay, only his shoulders moving. "I told you. You're pack."

"That's not it."

Jack rolled off the sofa and to his feet in one smooth move. He closed the distance between them with two long strides and was suddenly very much in Danny's space. It made it hard to pretend that Danny wasn't *very* aware of all that hard muscle and inked skin. Jack closed a rough hand over Danny's throat, pressing his thumb against the pulsing bubble just under the jaw. Danny tilted his head back on instinct, swearing to himself as he realized he was showing throat. Why didn't he just drop to his knees and lick Jack's stomach? It would be more subtle.

A low, pleased growl escaped Jack at the show of submission. "Good boy."

Danny jerked his chin down, heat scorching over his cheekbones, and glared into green eyes. "Sod off."

"You have a mouth on you," Jack said. His mouth firmed into a straight line, and he carefully pushed Danny's glasses up the bridge of his nose with one finger. "You always did, though, didn't you?"

When Danny swallowed, he felt his Adam's apple bump against Jack's palm. He leaned back against the wall and looked down at Jack. It felt odd—it always felt odd—to realize he was taller than the wolf prince. Back in Scotland, he'd always felt vaguely like his extra inches were some sort of treason.

"Come on, Jack," he said. "What's going on? What the hell is the wolf prince doing in Durham?"

"I like you, Danny," Jack said, pressing his thumb down on Danny's pulse point. Heat curdled through Danny, pulling tight low in his gut. Or, if he was to be honest, his balls. A spare smile ticked over Jack's face—there were knives in the corner of it. "But it's been a *long* time since you had the right to question me."

Danny rolled his eyes up, catching Jack's eyes. "I'm a dog, Jack. I never had the right to question you; I just did anyhow."

Something wicked flashed through Jack's eyes, and he slid his hand round to the back of Danny's neck. If anything it was more controlling than the throttle grip he'd had before, just a clench away from scruffing him like a puppy. Danny started to growl, but the sound got lost in his throat as Jack tugged him down the few inches into a kiss.

His lips were full and slightly rough, chapped from the weather, and the kiss was hard and almost impatient. The frame of Danny's glasses dug into his cheek, the lenses clouding with their breath. Danny made a low noise—with a knife to his throat, he couldn't have sworn if it was startled or hungry—as Jack tangled blunt fingers in his hair.

Heat had just started to coil in his gut and balls when Jack used the handful of hair like a leash, yanking him back out of the kiss. Danny bit the inside of his cheek, choking back a string of frustrated swearwords.

"The Numitor is standing down," Jack said. His voice was rough, anger scratching at the words as he spoke them. He kept his fingers tight in Danny's hair, pulling his head back and neck tight. Danny set his jaw, feeling the strain in his tendons. "He's chosen his successor, and Gregor will be the wolf to take our throat and title."

"Oh." Danny tried to wrap his mind around that. Around all of it. It meant the Numitor *really* believed in the wolf winter. Numitors didn't retire; they died. And Gregor… he'd almost made Jack look human by comparison. Not that Jack would find that flattering. Then there was the aching lust that felt like it was in his *bones*. "Shit."

It made Jack laugh, a startled bark of sound that banished the sharp edges of rage from his face. He loosened the punishing grip on Danny's hair, letting him lower his chin, although he was close enough that Danny could *feel* him breathing.

"Yeah," he said. "Shit. That sounds about the right word for what it is."

Now that the information had settled in, though, it didn't make sense. The twins had been in competition since their race from the womb, but Jack had always had the race by a nose. Gregor was meaner, bloodier, but he was a loner, and he resented having to control *himself*, never mind a pack. The wolves admired him, but he wasn't an easy creature to *follow.*

If it had come down to a challenge, Gregor *might* have won. He'd have sent Jack to Hell, though, not to Durham.

"How? Why?" Danny asked. "The Numitor favored you. Everyone knew it."

This time the grin showed teeth. "That's for me to know and you to find out, Danny Dog," he said. He stepped back and dropped onto the sofa, swinging his boots up onto the coffee table. He slung his arms along the back of the sofa, T-shirt pulling tight over his shoulders. The sprawl of his legs made it obvious he hadn't just been playing dominance hump games with Danny, his erection pressing its outline against his jeans. The humor slid off his face, and he tilted his chin down, grimness settling around him like a mantle. "What does it matter, anyhow? It's done and gone and what the old man wanted. I'm not going to thwart his last wish."

Danny had gotten caught in a trap once or twice— his mother trained her litters hard. This felt the same— the jerk, the confinement, and the hollow acknowledgment that you were not currently in control of your "next."

For the past ten years, Danny had been running from the pack, whittling down the ties that bind to a biannual phone call to his mother and a monthly direct debit that sent his stipend to the Numitor's account. It had been his choice, and dogs weren't nearly the pack animals that wolves were, but it had still nearly broken him.

Now the only thing between Jack and that terrible *lack* was Danny.

He dropped into a crouch, resting his forearms on his knees. It put him lower than Jack, another old habit of submission.

"The rest of the pack could—"

Jack shook his head. "No. Now shut your mouth about it, Danny." He scrubbed his hand over his short-cropped hair, making it stick up like hackles. "If you've got to bump your gums, what was that about with the redhead?"

He didn't want to drop it. If only because he'd played human long enough to resent being told to shut up in his own house. Giving in to the urge, though, would just end up with the two of them growling at each other until they ended up fighting. Or fucking. Or both.

Danny shook the rough, sweaty memories out of his head and lowered himself the rest of the way to the ground, crossing his legs.

"Long story."

"Good." Jack tilted his head back against the cushion, eyes half-closed as he waited.

Danny rubbed his thumb over the knee of his jeans, picking at the dirt he'd ground into the denim. "He was pissed off that Jenny was throwing him out because he screwed someone else."

Jack lifted his head and gave Danny a skeptical look. "That's a long story?"

The corner of Danny's mouth tilted with a rare moment of easy nostalgia. In the pack, a "long story" was the meat and drink of a dark, cold winter, eked out in dribs and drabs. Danny's sister had once dragged out recounting a fight with her human boyfriend over how rare to eat your meat for three days.

"The someone else was the woman they found in the bin," Danny said.

"*They* found?"

Danny blinked, remembering the rancid-meat smell and open dead eyes of the girl. He hesitated, biting at the inside of the cheek.

"I thought about calling the Numitor," he admitted.

Jack waited.

"I didn't."

"So why bring it up?"

Danny shrugged and ducked his head, rubbing nervously at the back of his neck. "Should I have?"

It was a question that would have put a strain on most of Danny's relationships. His human relationships, anyhow. Jack just snorted. "If I'd killed the woman, you wouldn't have found her bones."

That shouldn't have been reassuring. Somehow, though, the bluntness of it was. If Jack had killed someone, he wouldn't bother to lie about it. Danny looked up. His gaze caught on Jack's cheekbones, studying the spray of soft brown freckles and the thick rim of his lashes.

"You going to ask if I did it?"

"You?" When Jack grinned, his eyes creased at the corners. The wrinkles were wear instead of age, but they hadn't been there before. "You're not a killer, Danny. Besides, when you feel guilty you look like a sad retriever."

Danny wasn't entirely sure how he felt about that. Somewhere between reassured—Jack might not be part of the Numitor's pack anymore, but he might have felt obliged to still contact him over a murder—and vaguely insulted. He could have killed someone. If he wanted to. He might be a dog, but he wasn't some toothless purse Chihuahua.

"Really?" he said. "I could have—"

The sound of footsteps on the stairs made him stop, tilting his head. Jack's lazy sprawl on the sofa shifted, the loose muscles going tight and wary as he sat up. He sniffed the air and grimaced.

"The girl's sick," he said, not bothering to hide the distaste in his voice.

Danny unfolded himself from the ground, deliberately claiming all his inches as he frowned down at Jack. "She's my friend."

Instead of the aggression Danny had braced himself for, Jack just narrowed his eyes. "That all?"

"Yeah."

"Not what the dickhead thought."

"That's because he's a dickhead."

A grin sliced over Jack's face, and he inclined his head in acknowledgment, just as Jenny rapped on the door. Leaving Jack to sprawl, Danny went to answer it.

"You okay?" he asked, leaning his shoulder against the jamb.

"I… yeah," she said, tilting the corners of her mouth in a pinched smile. "He was an asshole. I always knew that, I guess. Do you want to come down to dinner? It's nothing much, I just wanted to say thanks for earlier."

Danny rubbed the tip of his nose. She smelled like nerves and chili. "I don't know," he hedged. "It's not—"

A heavy, warm arm dropped over his shoulder, thumb hooked in the collar of Danny's shirt. "I could eat," Jack said, leaning against him. His cock nudged at Danny's hip as he shifted. "What you got, chili?"

Reserve tightened Jenny's expression as she folded her arms across her chest and tucked her fingers into the crooks of her elbows. She was still smiling, but it was all shine now. Her "give me your money, we'll do good things with it" work smile.

"I didn't realize you were still here," she said. "You're welcome, of course, but I only made enough for two."

Jack shrugged. "That's all right," he said. "Danny'll be happy with the leftovers."

Jabbing his elbow back into Jack's stomach, forcing the amused wolf to step back, Danny shrugged an apology. "Ignore him. He's got the manners of a goat. We don't want to impose—"

Jenny shook her head. "No. No, come down. I'll just make more rice. Jack's more than welcome. I'll... see you down there."

She gave Jack a last, doubtful look and left, scuffing her feet down the stairs. Danny closed the door and turned around.

"Leftovers? It's dinner; we're not picking over a kill."

Jack rubbed his thumb over the short scruff of gilt stubble on his jaw and looked amused. "Want to fight me for the wolf's share, then?"

No. No, that wasn't what he wanted, because he wasn't an idiot. Danny leaned back against the door and rubbed his hands over his face. Jack might need him right now, but he didn't *need* Jack. He never had, it was just that Jack made that hard to remember sometimes.

"Just don't piss on anything in my friend's house, okay?" he said.

Jack gave a smile that had enough teeth to do Red Riding Hood's wolf proud. It wasn't a threat, but it wasn't *safe* either. "Me? Maybe you should tell *her* that."

Chapter Nine

THE SPOON scraped the bottom of the bowl, chasing the last smear of chili. Danny hadn't realized how hungry he was until he'd sat down. The last few days he'd been eating cold cuts and tinned meat. It was good enough for the dog's stomach, but a hot meal in company fed something else.

Jack sucked Dorito crumbs off his fingers, and Jenny watched him with an uncertain mixture of fascination and distrust. When she caught Danny looking at her, she looked flustered and popped to her feet, busying herself with clearing the table.

"Don't you dare," she told Danny when he went to get up and help. "You're a guest. Sit."

Danny hesitated, hovering half in and half out of the chair. The memory of his mum's hand skelping him around the ear was at war with her order. After a second he grimaced and made his knees drop him back into the seat.

"So," Jenny said, trying to sound casual as she piled dishes in the sink. "You grew up with Danny, Jack? He's never mentioned you."

Sometimes—living amongst humans, pretending he *was* human to everyone he knew—Danny was able to shove the stranger aspects of being a shifter to the back of his mind. It wasn't part of his life. Turning into a dog was the weirdest thing *he* did. For most wolves—even those that ran with the Numitor's pack—it was the weirdest thing they did.

Jack wasn't urban or civilized. The wolf lay close to his skin, and fur side or skin side, his eyes were the same. He brought the Wild with him—dark and raw and sharp—and he *was* the stranger side of being a shifter.

It was impossible for him not to be the center of attention. Even if you weren't entirely sure if you liked him or not.

"Really?" Jack said, hanging his arm over the back of the chair and stretching his feet under the table. "His mum is usually full of stories about him and me growing up."

"Not that I've ever heard," Danny said, kicking Jack's ankle under the table. "Mam's stories were always about Bron."

Water gushed from the tap, splashing noisily over the plates. "Bron?" Jenny queried over it.

"His sister," Jack said, kicking Danny back hard enough to make tears start to his eyes. He stifled a yelp behind his teeth and leaned down to rub his shin. "Don't tell me he didn't mention her either?"

There was a pause, and then the water was turned off. "No. I guess not."

"Me and Bron aren't close," Danny said, straightening up. She was his little sister, the pure wolf pup that disproved the prophets' theories that his mum had bred out of wolves and only had dogs left. "I'm not close to any of my family."

Jenny didn't say anything. He supposed she didn't need to. When she came out of the kitchen, she was still smiling, and her attention was focused firmly on Jack.

"So, what do you do, Jack?" she asked, offering him a beer. "You in academia as well?"

Jack laughed, a rough scrape of noise. "Me? No, only reason I ever read a book was to see what speccy four-eyes here saw in them. Never did work it out."

"So, you're a mechanic? A driver? No shame in it." Jenny leaned against Jack's chair, hand on his shoulder. "Danny can't even put together an IKEA wardrobe."

"I'm a.... Jack of all trades," Jack said, mouth tilting at his own joke.

Irritation pricked at Danny's nerves. It was stupid. He wasn't in love with Jenny anymore, and if she and Jack hooked up, it would get Jack off his case. The bit of his brain that was stuck dealing with things he didn't want to deal with let an old hunch almost slip out, a mutter of "not really going to happen?" He ignored it.

"His dad owns the village where I grew up," Danny said, voice sharp with irritation. "If he ever dug a hole or fixed an engine, it was because he wanted to. Not because it was his job."

Jack raised his eyebrows at him over the table, looking too amused for Danny's peace of mind.

"So, what?" Jenny said skeptically and a bit disapprovingly. She was a born-again socialist, rebelling against her parents and their adopted middle-class values. "Your dad is landed gentry or something?"

"Or something," Jack agreed pleasantly. "We've just been in the area a long time. My family can be traced back to when the Romans got here. Apparently."

He added the *apparently* with a hint of an eye roll, inviting anyone listening to disbelieve the truth. He had always been a better liar than Danny. Jenny snorted agreeably, seeming to find it easier to go along with Jack than not.

She got up off the arm of the chair and went through the habitual process of clearing the placemats from the table and putting the orchid she was trying not to kill back in the middle.

"Did you all evacuate?" She waved a hand at the white-out outside the window, the frost scrawling graffiti on the glass. "To get away from the weather?"

"No," Jack said, sounding vaguely distracted. He watched the window with sharp eyes, like he saw more out there than just snow. "They'll come down later. Soon, though, I think."

"Because that's something to look forward to," Danny muttered scathingly.

"Danny!" Jenny protested, whacking his shoulder. She pulled an apologetic face at Jack. "Ignore him. Sometimes he thinks he's funny."

"Yeah, I've noticed that too," Jack said. He gave Jenny a slow, dangerous smile, and his voice dropped to a rasp. "I've always liked his mouth, though. I just need to find him something more useful to do with it."

Jenny choked, coughing over the words caught in her throat. Maybe it could have been passed off as banter, but there was no subtlety in Jack's voice or the way he was looking at Danny. After a bewildered second, Jenny excused herself stiffly and fled back into the kitchen, muttering tightly about coffee.

"What the hell?" Danny hissed through clenched teeth. He checked the kitchen door and dropped his voice lower. "I asked you *not* to piss on anything. That includes me."

"What? Did she think you were a virgin?" Jack asked dryly. He got up and wandered around the room, poking into corners and behind cushions. "Now she'll stop asking questions about how we know each other."

Cups rattled in the kitchen, and the bubbling of the kettle turned aggressive. Danny grimaced at Jack. This wasn't over, but there wasn't time to argue about it. He nudged the chairs back in and went over to turn the TV on, habit scrolling the channel down to BBC One.

A squint-eyed man turned square by layers and a heavy waxed jacket stood on a pier in front of an eerie seascape of ragged ice. The waves had frozen midcrash, jagged and glittering in the pallid sun.

"…you can see behind me," the reporter said, his voice shaking with the cold. His breath puffed around his lips as he breathed, turning his words visible. "The sudden cold snap, which has seen temperatures drop to below minus ten Fahrenheit, has actually done what Canute could not and stopped the tide. Further evidence that this unusually bitter weather isn't done with us yet."

Jenny left the kitchen just in time to catch the last panning shot of the flash-frozen water. She made a soft, shocked noise as she pressed a cup of coffee into Danny's hands, handing the other to Jack.

"I guess climate change isn't up for debate anymore," she said. "I mean, that doesn't even look real. It looks like something you'd see on *Star Trek*."

She perched on the arm of the sofa, watching as the anchor back in the newsroom talked about the situation in other parts of the UK. According to him, the brutal cold was actually in the north's favor in some ways. It was too cold for the meteorological oddities that were battering the rest of the country, like the tornado that had touched down in the middle of London and left a double-decker bus thrown through the window of Harrods. The queen was still in Buckingham Palace, but the rest of the royal family had been evacuated along with the politicians and Boris.

The rest of the world wasn't doing any better. Russia was frozen over, the storms there making the snow-laden Scotland look tropical; America had weathered a scorching summer only to find the storms that waited at the far side of it.

Jenny got quieter, her mouth pinched and worried as she drank her tea. It smelled strong and green, herbal to avoid the caffeine.

A prerecorded interview with Nicola Sturgeon saw the Scottish MP packing herself into a truck with boxes of rations and medical supplies. "We're Scottish. It'll take more than a few bad blows to get us off our land. Hell, I happen to know it's not even got any Highlander out of their kilts. The Scots will not be evacuating to the South."

"She's right. It can't last much longer," Danny said, wanting to comfort her. "It'll blow itself out."

He didn't look at Jack; he didn't need to. The still presence of the wolf in the room, the weight of his attention, was enough to make Danny feel like a liar.

JACK SPENT the night. He wasn't actually invited, just made himself at home on the couch. Danny supposed he should have been grateful he got to keep his own bed. If it had been Bron, he'd have had to fight her for it.

Lying on his bed in the dark, Danny stared at the ceiling and thought about his little sister. They'd never been close—she'd been a brat and a biter—but he worried how she'd do under Gregor's paw. She'd cut her own nose off if you told her not to.

He hadn't seen her in years. Hadn't even thought about her beyond a rote "how is she?" to his mum during the biannual call. Jack had brought her up earlier, but Danny thought it was the silence that kept her in his head. The last time he'd heard a night this quiet—all the buzzing and banging noises of the city gone or muted under a blanket of snow—it had been in Scotland.

His last night in Lochwinnoch. It should have been… something. Bitter. Sweet. Nostalgic. It hadn't been anything in particular. He'd eaten dinner, watched TV, and gone to bed. In the morning he'd tossed his bags in the back of the car and headed south.

It had taken a week before anyone called to find out where he was. That had been Bron, he recalled with a flicker of surprise. She'd wanted to borrow the van and cursed him like a sailor when he told her where it was.

Brat or no—he rolled onto his side and punched the pillow into shape—he hoped she had the sense to shut her mouth and keep her head down. If she did, their mam's reputation would protect her. Even the Numitor hadn't relished crossing fangs with her.

He dozed off finally, sliding into dreams of snow and hunting. Except in the dream he wasn't sure if he was the hunter or the hunted. His mouth watered with the taste of blood, but he could feel the muggy huff of… something… panting behind him.

A cold hand on his stomach, warm breath on his shoulder, woke him up. He sucked in a startled breath and tasted cold on the way down, prickling at the back of his throat and down into his lungs.

"Shit," he muttered, registering the chill that numbed his toes and made his balls ache.

"Your heatin's bollixed," Jack mouthed against the nape of his neck. His accent was thicker than usual, sleepiness blurring the words.

Shit, again. Danny knuckled the sleep roughly out of his eyes and propped himself up on his elbow. Cold air slid under the blankets, a shock against his skin. Without his glasses the room was a dimly lit blur, all gray shadows and vague, curtain-filtered light.

"What time is it?"

He felt Jack shrug. "Don't know. Not dawn yet."

Danny hesitated, jaw creaking as he tried to stifle a yawn. It felt like something he should deal with, but he felt logy with dreams, and the sheets still held some warmth. He let his arm fold under him, dropping him back onto the mattress, and Jack dragged the blankets up over them both.

"It's just weather," Danny said. His voice lacked conviction.

Jack breathed heat on his neck. "And we're just wolves."

If there was an answer to that, Danny didn't know what it was. He was a dog—born to run in parks and pee on street corners. The human world was where he belonged, and it was impossible to imagine it… overshadowed.

Or it had been. Maybe his imagination was getting better.

He closed his eyes and tried not to think about that. It was easier than he'd like to admit. The smell of their bodies, the damp fug of shared heat and breath, felt… right. Dammit.

"So you know," Jack mumbled, stubble scraping Danny's back as he yawned. "I'm still gonna fuck you. I just don't wanna stick my ass out into the cold now it's started to warm up."

Danny nearly choked on a surprised laugh. "You're sure of yourself."

Silence for a second as Jack considered that. "Yeah," he said agreeably. "I am. Go to sleep, Danny Dog."

The old nickname would have made Danny grumble, but there was a layer of command under Jack's words. It dropped Danny into a heavy sleep, wrapping him in toe-twitching, pine-scented puppy dreams of warm grass and fat, stupid rabbits.

Chapter Ten

HE'D BEEN wrong. It wasn't the heating that was bollixed, it was the power. The storm had taken the city's throat out, letting it bleed out in a night. Two days later it was a carcass, concrete bones moldering under a coat of snow and frost.

Jack waded through a drift of hip-deep snow, jeans sticking to his balls like a rough, chilly hand. He caught the echo of Fenrir's bark on the wind. It was a reproof for the prophets who'd thought catechism would catch a god, that The Wolf would need his wolves to chase the humans out of their dwelling places into the Wild.

Instead Fenrir had brought the Wild to their dwelling places. Without light and heat, without TVs and Internet, a penthouse suite was just a cave with a nice carpet on the floor. Why harry them out to the valleys and woods when you could kill them where they lived?

"Smart enough, but Gregor won't like it," Jack told the wind. "He's not got the patience to hunt through a warren."

The wind spat a gust full of icy snow into his face. Apparently Fenrir did not care what Gregor liked or didn't like.

Jack wiped his face on his sleeve. It would be easier if he could put the wolf's skin on, loping across the snow instead of laboring through it. Jack glanced sidelong at the man slogging along next to him, sharp brown eyes hidden behind a pair of misted-over glasses. Easier in one way, but there was no point in reminding Danny that a wolf could survive easily in this cold. So far Danny hadn't questioned that Jack needed a place to stay. Jack wanted to keep it that way.

Maybe it had occurred to him that Danny might know why he was there, that he needed Danny more than the roof. If it had, he'd shoved the idea so far down in his brain that it might as well have never happened. It wasn't a notion he was willing to harbor. Even in exile he was the Numitor's son, a Wild-touched wolf. It was bad enough to be weak; he'd be fucked before he let someone see it.

So he stuck to feet instead of paws and broke a path down to the salted and gritted main road. It smelled of chemicals, spilled oil and fear, the humans marking their territory as if they could warn Fenrir off if they could just piss far enough.

Jack stopped on the curb and wiped his dripping nose on the sleeve, his breath steaming on his lips and the sky overhead white as wedding linen. There was another storm building—he could taste it on the air. All in, he thought Fenrir was winning the pissing contest.

"Where did you say you'd left your car?" Danny asked, stamping his feet to shed clumps of stained snow. He took his glasses off and wiped the lens with his thumb, squinting at Jack as he went out of focus.

Jack shrugged and jerked his thumb toward the river. "Down there."

The glasses went back on, and Danny shoved his hand through his hair, raking it back from his face. It was longer than he'd worn it in Scotland, when it had been as likely to be shorn short by the sheep shears as cut by a hairdresser. Jack liked it, liked the way he could clench his fist in it like he was scruffing Danny.

The wave of lust that went through him banished some of the chill, curling heat through his gut and into his thighs.

"Did you get a street name?" Danny asked, his voice sliding toward the sardonic. "Landmark? Tree you pissed on?"

Given the excuse, it seemed like a waste not to scruff Danny again. Jack grabbed a handful of dark curls and dragged Danny down a few inches.

"I know I said I liked your mouth, Danny," he said, angling Danny's head back so he could see the long plane of his cheek and the stubborn jut of his jaw. There were specks of blood on his face from the cold water and soap shave he'd sworn his way through that morning. Jack let his voice drop lower, the rough edge of a growl under his words. "Go too far and I *will* put you in your place. I've done it before. Remember?"

He did. That memory flickered over Danny's face, darkening his eyes, and then was gone. It left a frown and the spent-match smell of old lust in its wake.

"I made a lot of bad decisions back then," Danny muttered. He shoved at Jack's shoulder. "Get off me before someone calls the police, you idiot."

Jack snorted and bent Danny back further, catching the weight of lean muscle and bone on his forearm as Danny's knees folded under him. Danny gave up shoving at his shoulder and grabbed him instead, hanging on to Jack for balance.

"Don't know if you've noticed, Danny," Jack drawled. "Police are busy, and people got other things to worry about than me kissing you in the street."

It probably wouldn't have mattered what Danny said, but Jack still felt a slow coil of satisfaction when Danny challenged him. "You *aren't* kissing me, though."

The corner of Jack's mouth tilted in a smirk, and he fixed that, covering Danny's mouth with his. It was rough and impatient, all cold lips and hot tongues. Danny stopped trying to push Jack away, grabbing the back of his neck to pull him closer instead. His breath felt hot against Jack's cold skin, almost painfully sharp.

Hunger cramped in Jack's groin, the ache of it spreading into his muscles. He *wanted* to shove Danny down, fuck him in the snow until the stubborn git forgot about playing human and protecting his little, spiky human friend. Fuck him until all he cared about was Jack.

It wouldn't work. He knew that. There had been plenty of times, back in Scotland, when he'd tried to fuck Danny into being a good dog. It worked, for about as long as it took Danny to get his jeans back on. He'd never been sure if Danny was stubborn or just oblivious.

He bit Danny's lip hard enough to draw a dribble of sharp copper-salt blood and pulled out of the kiss.

Dull color stained Danny's cheekbones in stripes, and his glasses were resting crookedly on his nose. Jack licked blood off his lips and straightened up, pulling a panting Danny up with him.

"See?" Jack said, cuffing Danny's head. "Better things to do with that mouth than smart off to me."

Annoyance narrowed Danny's eyes, and he ducked away from Jack's hand, scruffing his hands through his hair self-consciously. It was a gesture Jack had seen Danny do a hundred times before, even before he'd been paying any attention to the lanky dog. It was the way his head dipped and his shoulders hunched, like he was trying to fit into a space too small for him.

Feelings were visceral. They caught in Jack's guts like a hook and wrenched at things he didn't want to admit he had in there.

He looked away from Danny, working his jaw to make the hinges pop. He saw a man and a child making their way up the wood, skating on the ice in badly chosen wellies. He watched them, letting the wolf peek through his brain to whet its hunger.

"Don't," Danny said. "They're people, not prey."

"They are to us," Jack said, watching the man slip and pitch forward. He broke his fall with hands, hurting his elbows. That would be an easy hunt. "We're wolves. If the humans wanted to claim us, they wouldn't have banished us over the wall."

"That was nearly two thousand years ago," Danny said. "*If* it happened the way we've been told. It's a long time to hold a grudge against a dead Roman, on the word of the prophets. Maybe we shouldn't just take what they say at face value?"

Jack coughed out a laugh, his chest aching as the cold air hit his lungs. He dragged his attention from the humans back to Danny. "Trust me, Danny, I don't believe *everything* they say. If I did—"

He stopped, clicking his teeth on the bitter words like they were living.

Danny cocked his head to the side. He'd shoved his hands into his pockets, hunching the heavy jacket around him. "What?"

His face was open, his gaze intent behind his glasses. The expression was practically an invitation to trust him. Jack ignored it.

"Pack business," he said. "Nothing to do with dogs."

Danny's expression closed over, and he leaned his weight back on his heels. He pushed his glasses back up onto his nose with the back of his hand. "Of course not," he said, mouth twisting. "Look, I'm going into town to try and get a radio. With the power out, that's probably the best way to find out what's going on. You go find your car and your stuff."

He started toward the road, habit making him look both ways even if there hadn't been a car out in days. The lack of an invitation to meet back at the flat was pointed. Not that Jack planned to pay any attention to it, but it still stung. He watched Danny slide up next to the struggling man, offering him a hand up, and wondered if Danny had any idea how *inhuman* he looked. Sure-footed on the slush, confident that his body would accommodate what he needed from it.

The memory of that body—the long, lanky sprawl of it under him in the Scottish grass years ago, the solid sprawl of muscle and bone in the bed the other night— made Jack's cock harden. He reached down and tugged his jeans, adjusting himself. That could wait until later.

Right now he had things to do. Unfortunately, he needed his jeans later, so he'd have to keep his skin on.

JACK RIPPED the overlaid strips of duct tape off the backseat, balled it up, and then tossed it aside. His hands felt clumsy and raw as he worked. The car was where he'd left it but half-buried in snow. He'd had to dig a path to the door, and even wolfish hardiness had felt the cold of that.

The tear in the seat gaped open, the edges fraying and foam popping out. He reached in and pulled out the stuffed envelope, folded it in half, and jammed it into his back pocket. There was a sense of eyes on the back of his neck, the cropped hair prickling like it aspired to be hackles. He wasn't worried. Skin or fur, he could defend himself against humans.

And what if it's not a human? If a wolf did kill that girl?

He curled his lip at the thought, a snarl scratching at his throat. Most violence against humans was done by humans, but the timing of this was too perfect. Just on the tail of him arriving in Durham, just outside Danny's den, when everyone knew Danny belonged to Jack. It didn't matter. If it was a wolf, let them come. He hadn't held his rank just because he was the Numitor's son—he'd fought for his ink just like any other wolf.

And what if it's Gregor?

He let the snarl out past his teeth. Maybe he'd been spending too much time with Danny, and questions were catching. He grabbed a duffel bag—stuffed with spare clothes and a pay-as-you-go phone he'd not needed yet—and slid out of the car. If it was Gregor, let him come. That was one fight that had been brewing long enough. It was time to see who'd win. Time for there to be only *one* of them.

There was one last question he wanted answered, gnawing at the edge of his attention like a pup with a bone. *What if the prophets made Gregor the same offer they made you?*

He kicked the thought away, stamping it down until he could ignore it, and left the car where it was. If anyone in Durham wanted it enough to dig it out, they could have it. He didn't need it anymore; he had a den now, and a pack.

Well, a flat and a snappy dog. Close enough— for now.

The wind blew snow down the street, spinning the scents of the city in riptides and eddies. Jack paused, lifting his head and casting around to try and catch the shred of smell. There it was: salt and metal and the fading, distinct smell of sickness and liquor. Jack ducked his head through the strap of the duffle, crossing it over his chest, and followed the smell down the street.

It didn't take him long. This time they hadn't even made a cursory effort to hide the body. Her foot, still in its cheap trainer, stuck out of the open door into the street. Tugging his sleeve down over his hand, Jack nudged the door open. The old homeless woman he'd spoken to before going to Danny's flat lay dead in a puddle of her own organs on the beige sea-grass carpet in the hall. Her arms were thrown out to the sides, callused hands cupping frost, but there were no injuries there or to her legs.

Between death and the bitter cold, her skin had gone blue and tight. It gave her face a strangely ethereal cast, pulling out the wrinkles and smoothing out the red of broken veins in her cheek and nose. She looked surprised, but the dead always did. It didn't matter if they died screaming or midfuck, the corpse was always taken aback.

Still, sick as she'd been—sick enough Jack had smelled it, sick enough that whatever killed her left her uneaten—maybe she'd died before it hurt too much.

He knelt down between her knees and bent over the body, catching the duffel in one hand before it could swing into the mess. The open wound was clotted and crusted. Death had come before the last big frost. Still, he should have been able to smell something on her. All he smelled was soap—lye and vanilla and the flat, tin taste of tap water. When he poked the woman's arm with his cuff-covered thumb, a skin of ice cracked and crumbled.

They'd washed the body, or at least tossed a bucket of water over it. Jack frowned and sat back, rubbing his hand over his mouth. Why bother? This was obviously done to taunt him, so why not piss on the walls in challenge?

First someone on the periphery of Danny's life; now someone on the periphery of his.

It didn't make sense, and his head ached with the stupidity of it. Why kill a woman who was already dying? Jack hadn't cared for her. The death had cost him nothing but a moment of annoyance and a slight stirring of pity. Finding the corpse had bothered Danny more—he was a dog, he was soft—but not that deeply.

This was stupid, and Gregor wasn't that. Sullen, cruel, and sometimes a fool, but not stupid.

Jack pushed himself to his feet and backed out of the hall. He let the door swing shut on the dead woman's leg, her trainer jerking at the impact.

"I said you should leave," he said. "Maybe you should have listened, but this might have been kinder. In the long run. Hope your afterlife is warm, old woman."

He turned and loped back up the road, adapting his stride to keep his body loose and his feet landing under his hips. The air was bitter, scraping his lungs on the inhale and steaming against his lips on the exhale, and the streets were empty.

It was a different world than it had been a year ago, and he was *fit* for it in a way he'd never been for the old one. Or maybe it was finally fit for *him*. Either way, he wasn't going to let anyone take him away from it.

Chapter Eleven

THERE'D BEEN three more dog attacks, and Durham was scheduled to receive a delivery of food rations in two days' time for anyone in need. People were urged not to panic, that this climatic anomaly would soon pass. According to the Met Office, once the atmospheric instability evened out, it would be a cold winter but nothing statistically abnormal.

Danny thought that was the first time in five years they'd *not* predicted it would be the "coldest winter for fifty years."

He trudged home through the snow, the windup radio he'd borrowed from Professor Sorley's office wrapped up and tucked under his arm. It took five minutes of enthusiastic cranking before it worked, and they'd all taken the mickey out of Sorley when she bought it. She'd been on holiday when the weather started going crazy; when she got back he'd have to apologize.

Abandoned cars lined the road, some of them half-buried already while others sat in slowly filling up ruts. As Danny crossed the road, he saw a car slide in slow motion through the pedestrian crossing opposite St. Nicholas's. The smell of hot brake fluid filled the air, smoke farting out of the tire wells, and the car slid inexorably toward the railings.

Danny's stomach squeezed tight, but he didn't really have time to *feel* anything. The driver flung the door open and rolled out, snow flying up in a cloud where he landed. A second later the car hit the railings, and they cracked out of their moorings, letting the car tip over the edge in slow motion.

The impact of it landing sounded different than Danny would have expected, less solid thump and more ripping metal. He jogged over to the driver, who was still lying in the snow, swearing and flailing as he tried to get up.

"You okay?" Danny asked, offering a hand. "Was there anything in the car?"

Not anyone, he hoped. The man grabbed his hand with clumsy, ski-gloved fingers, and Danny hauled him easily to his feet.

"Did you see that?" the man asked, wiping his face nervously. "God. How am I meant to get home now?"

He asked for Danny's name and contact details. "For the insurance claim."

"Do they pay out for storm damage?" Danny asked, pulling a glove off with his teeth. He took the pen and scribbled his name and address down on the back of a Morrison's receipt. "Or is it an act of God?"

Gods. He flinched from the quiet, confident correction. It would have been nice to blame it on Jack, but he wasn't sure that was true. He didn't want to believe in gods, but he wasn't sure of the weathermen either.

"That's just houses, mate," the man said confidently. He grabbed the receipt and fumbled his coat open, then stuck the details into an inside pocket. "I've claimed for storm damage before."

Smoke was leaking up from the car below, black and oily. The snow melted around it, a damp funnel of ash forming.

"Here," the man said. "Give me a hand getting my stuff out of the car?"

Danny shook his head. "I have to go." He tugged his glove back, fingers sweaty and the wrist damp where he'd drooled on it. "So should you. The snow's going to get worse."

Instead of listening, the man stubbornly shook his head. "I heard it will thaw soon. Warm front coming in from down south. Going to be wet for a bit, but this will clear up."

The confidence in the man's voice was unassailable, even with the snow billowing around them in sheets. Danny hesitated, guilt pinching, but it was getting colder, and even the dog didn't like the idea of being out once it got dark. He made one last try at talking the man into heading home, even offering to walk him that way, and then gave up.

He glanced back as he passed the Gala, catching a last glimpse of the man slip-sliding his way down the on-ramp.

"Idiot," he muttered.

Hitching the radio up under his arm, he tucked his chin down and refused to feel guilty. A little paranoid—when he wondered darkly what would happen if the police found his name and number on a frozen corpse—but not guilty.

Those thoughts faded too as he left the city center and stumbled into the ungritted streets again, sweating into his parka as he waded his way through deepening snow. It got down into his boots, wicking its frosty way down his socks, and stuck cold needles under his toenails. He tripped twice, ending up on his knees in the snow, and the only things going through his brain were his next step and every ripe Roman curse he'd learned from the pack elders.

One good thing about the blackout, he supposed as he headed into his neighborhood, was at least the co-op's alarm had finally given up the ghost.

He glanced at the space where the dead woman's car had been. Her body was probably still in the morgue, Danny realized. They could hardly bury her in the middle of this.

After a couple of days with no heating, the old building was freezing, the cold sunken into the old stone. Danny checked his mailbox out of habit, finding a note from the police saying they'd been out but nobody was home. He stared blankly at the crest for a second, then balled the paper up and shoved it in his pocket.

It was more likely to be about the fight with Brock than the murder, and he doubted they'd bother to come back.

When he got up to his flat, Jack was already there. He was sprawled out on the floor, muzzle resting on his paws, while his wet clothes dried on the sofa. Indoors the wolf looked even bigger, something that hadn't comprised down to fit the modern scale of living. Danny left the radio on the kitchen counter and stripped out of his layers, shedding the parka and his sweat-damp jumper.

"Did you find your car?"

The wolf opened one leaf-green eye, yawned, and rolled on his back. His tail whisked over the floor in a lazy wag. It spoiled the intimidating effect a bit. Danny crouched down, balancing on the balls of his feet, and tugged Jack's ear.

"Very cute overload," he said dryly. "Did you find the car?"

Jack sneezed on him and scrambled to his feet. He shook, shedding a cloud of dander and hair, and pointed to the corner with his nose. A battered old duffel bag lay against the wall, sliding sideways like a drunk man. Something tickled Danny's nose. He sniffed the air.

"Is that blood?" he asked, glancing back at Jack.

Jack'd shrugged his skin back on, sitting cross-legged on the rug. Black inkwork ran over his skin, curving over the tight lines of muscles. His feet were bare and oddly new. Wolves' didn't callus or scar, not easily.

"I spoke to a woman the other day, before coming here," he said. "She's dead now."

"How?"

"Winter."

"She died of 'winter'?" Danny said dubiously. "You mean she froze to death, or died from exposure?"

Jack scratched his thigh absently, dragging his fingers up to his balls. "She died because it's winter," he said. "Does it matter if it was Fenrir's fangs or ours?"

"Yes!" Danny said, his hands getting away from him in a frustrated gesture. He shoved both through his curls, fingers catching in the damp knots. "Fenrir didn't kill the woman in the bin, Jack. One of us did, with fang and claw. And there was something *wrong* with them, Jack, like humans go wrong."

The muscles along Jack's jaw tensed. "I know," he admitted, voice raw with reluctance at having to spit the words out. "Whoever it is, I'll deal with it."

"What if you can't?"

He lifted his chin with the question as if it was a challenge. That's because it was, if only a small one. Danny was expecting the lunge that pinned him to the ground, Jack's body heavy on top of him. Green eyes flashed as Jack leaned down until Danny could feel his breath on his jaw.

"Then when I'm dead, you call the Numitor," Jack said. "He always liked his dogs, did my da. Maybe he'll listen."

That wasn't expected. The crack, however small, in Jack's self-assurance chilled Danny more than the snow. It sent a shudder down his spine, shaking his bones, and Jack's grim expression cracked with a half-hearted smile.

"I'm the one who's naked," he said. "Why are you cold?"

Danny swallowed and lied, "My clothes are wet."

Jack snorted and kissed Danny's neck, scraping his teeth over the thin skin covering his pulse. "I could warm you up."

He *should* have pushed Jack off, pushed for more details about the dead woman. Instead he curled his hand around the nape of Jack's neck, clipped hair prickling against his fingers, and pulled him down into a kiss. It wasn't even anything to do with the pack and old habits, he just preferred Jack to be cocksure and confident.

For a second he was in charge, flexing his hand possessively and his tongue in Jack's mouth. Then Jack shifted on top of him—burying his hands in Danny's hair and tilting his head back—and took back control of the moment. He scraped his mouth roughly over Danny's, crushing his lips against his teeth and pinning Danny's glasses awkwardly between their faces. Danny ran his hands down the taut line of Jack's back, tracing the lines of ink from memory. He ran his thumbs over the muscle-sheathed slats of rib bones, down to the hard dip of his waist. Under his damp jeans, Danny's cock pressed with uncomfortable eagerness against the zipper. He arched up, eager for the hard press of Jack's body against him.

Letting go of his hair, Jack reached down between their bodies and tugged Danny's jeans open. He peeled the wet denim away from his stomach and slid his hand under them. Jack's hand was hot around Danny's cock, dragging a ragged, begging sound out of Danny's throat. Jack swallowed the sound and squeezed, making Danny's blood thump in his ears.

Or….

He twisted his head away from Jack, licking the taste of the other man off his lips. Someone rapped on the door again, Jenny's voice hesitantly repeating, "Danny?"

Jack tightened his fingers. The jolt of pleasure made Danny jerk, lifting his hips up off the ground. He had to clench his jaw, stifling the yelp that nearly got out.

"Answer her, I will bite you," Jack said in his ear, proving his point by nipping the lobe between sharp teeth.

Danny dropped his head down against the floor with a thud, trying to drag his brain out of its orbit

around his cock and the hand on it. He distractedly
straightened his glasses, hooking them back over his
ears properly and straightening them on his nose. The
sound of rattling metal gave him the feeling that there
was *something* he should remember. "She's got a key,"
he managed to dredge up after a second.

"Why?"

"She's my friend. That's what you do," Danny
said. He propped himself up on his elbow and raised
his voice. "I'm here, Jenn. Sorry. Just give me a second,
okay?"

Jack gave a disgruntled growl and rolled off Danny, then pushed himself easily to his feet. His cock was
heavy and aroused, lifting up toward his stomach. It
twitched with his heartbeat. Lust cramped through Danny's gut, the ache of it starting in his balls and spreading
down into his thighs until it felt like he'd been running.
He closed his eyes and took a deep breath. It didn't
help. The air smelled like Jack and fucking.

He scrambled awkwardly to his feet and prompt-
ly got shoved against the wall. Jack pressed his hand
against his chest, the spread of his hand from thumb to
fingers touching Danny's collarbones. Leaning in, the
hard weight of his body pressed against Danny, Jack
kissed him. It was quick but thorough, leaving Danny
flushed and breathless.

Lifting his head, Jack stepped back and patted
Danny's cheek roughly. "Get the keys off her."

Danny grimaced at him, reached down and adjusted his erection until he could get his jeans buttoned up.
He made it to the door just as the key scraped in the
lock, opening it to Jenny frowning up at him.

"I thought you'd got stuck in the toilet," she said,
propping her hand on her hips. "What were you doing?"

It felt like that was obvious. He tugged his T-shirt self-consciously and shrugged. "I'd been out. I was just getting cleaned up."

Jenny sniffed at him, wrinkling her nose. "Give that another go," she said dryly. "Look, I was talking to Bill."

He blinked at her. She rolled her eyes.

"Bill. Lives here. Called the police on Brock after the fight the other day, moved in last year? Really, Danny, talk to people sometimes. It won't kill you. Anyhow—"

She stopped, staring past Danny's arm with wide, startled eyes. After a second she made a strangled noise, red surging up her cheeks, and spun around to stare at the windows. "I see your friend Jack is still here, then."

Danny glanced around and saw Jack leaning against the door to the living room, arms crossed over his chest. He was naked and still lazily hard.

"Fuck's sake," Danny muttered. "Put your jeans on."

Jack shrugged the shoulder that wasn't propping him against the door. "They're wet."

"Borrow mine," Danny said, waving a hand at his bedroom. He stepped outside, tugging the door shut behind him. Jenny was still staring ferociously at the skyline, her face scald red all the way to her temples. "Sorry about that. Jack's... naked."

"I noticed," Jenny said, voice full of slightly poisonous sweetness. "He made *sure* I noticed."

Danny put his hand between her shoulder blades and absently nudged her away from the door. Not that it would stop Jack hearing them if he wanted to bother. They stopped in front of the window, the chill from the frost-laced glass biting at their arms and face. Looking out the window, Danny was caught by how ugly the city looked from an elevation. The snow was stained gray where it lay over the houses, full of ashes and smog. The few cleared streets were full of gritty, gray slush, like a sad canal.

Hardly the clean, untouched wilderness the prophets conjured whenever they preached about the wolf winter.

An elbow bumped his arm. "Earth to Danny."

He glanced down at Jenny, quirking his mouth in an apology. "It's only September. This time last year there were kids sunbathing outside the castle."

She nodded and hugged herself, burying her fingers in the loose knit of the oversized sweater she was wearing. "At least *they* weren't naked."

Danny snorted, muffling a laugh behind his hand. "Don't let Jack get to you. He's just a bit rough around the edges sometimes."

When he wanted to be.

"You'd know. Old friends and all," Jenny said. She hesitated, lips pursing around something she wasn't ready to let slip. Danny shoved his hands in his pockets and regretted it, the denim pulling tight over his aching balls. He shifted and leaned against the glass wall, waiting for the chill to cool him off. Maybe Jenny noticed, or maybe it just seemed like the time to ask. "Is that *all* you were?" she asked quickly. Then she didn't wait for an answer. "I mean, I know you left home and never went back; I know you don't get on with your family. I didn't know you had a sister, but you only sent duty cards to your mom. Was it that way because you were… with Jack?"

She finally wound down, chewing her lips and staring up at him with tight, anxious eyes.

"My family loved Jack," Danny said. "They're all *like* Jack, so they would."

"Not what I meant. Are you gay?"

Danny hesitated. Wolves didn't care. His mam would have chewed the face off anyone who told her who she could or couldn't fuck. That didn't mean there weren't other things that they cared about. It got complicated, because it wasn't human. "I had a thing with Jack before I left Scotland, but—"

Jenny shoved him, small hard hands punching his chest.

"I felt so guilty for what happened with Brock," she said. "You *know* that. I thought that it was all on me, that I had screwed *us* up for some stupid hookup. Except there was never an 'us,' was there? There was always this distance, and I seemed to be the one who noticed it. You always said that there was no problem, that there was nothing wrong. Only there *was*."

She thumped him again. He let it push him back a step, giving way to anger. "Jenny, it's…."

What was he going to say? That it wasn't like that? Except it had been, in a way. The distance had been there, except it hadn't been because of her gender but her species. Trying to work out how to explain that, if he should explain that, took too long.

"I wouldn't have *cared*," she said. A laugh spluttered between her lips, and she rubbed her hand over her forehead. "Okay, I would have cared, but I'd still have been your friend. You could have told me. You should have told me."

The hurt was naked on her face, and Danny felt like shit. He just didn't know if explaining would make it any better. Especially since he couldn't *really* explain.

"It's not that simple," he said. "I thought it was okay. I thought it could be."

Jenny looked down, biting her lip hard. "I guess you were wrong, but that's... um... that's not what I came up for."

Danny reached out, cupping his fingers around her elbow. "Jenny...."

She shook her head, tongue wetting her lip, and squirmed away from his touch. "Don't, Danny. We'll be okay, just don't. Like I said, I didn't come up to talk about this. It's not even my business, is it? Not now." Jenny took a deep breath and let it out, lifting her chin. "Bill and a couple of the other residents are going to the food drop so they can help carry the food back. I said you'd go. I was... I still need to ask you a favor."

He spread his hands, trying to look helpless. "Of course. Anything."

The promise rang false, not that Danny meant it to be, and Jenny gave him a sharp bitter look for it. She reached into her pocket and pulled out a folded-over green scrip. "They are meant to have some emergency medicine at the drop, for people with chronic conditions. If they have any of my meds, if you could pick them up for me? I would appreciate it."

Danny took the stiff fold of paper off her. "I'll do my best. Your meds from the hospital, are they—"

"Out," she said, folding her lips in a dismissive smile. "Maybe I should have gone when you said."

She turned and took the few brisk steps to the stairs.

"Jenny, I did love you," Danny said. It sounded weak. "It was never that."

She didn't look around at him. Her shoulders hitched awkwardly. "No, it wasn't," she said. "It was about you not trusting me."

There really wasn't any way to argue with that.

Chapter Twelve

THEY'D BROKEN up over a year ago, Danny's things shoved in boxes borrowed from the library and Jenny smelling of other men and sex. He'd been sad, but it passed. This felt worse. It felt like it might not be fixable. There was a churn of emotion in his gut he couldn't have put a name to if you paid him: loss, anger, resentment. A bit of frustrated lust and a wedge of self-loathing at the idea.

He wanted Jack. That had been a compass point of his personality since he was sixteen and the fifteen-year-old pup prince had scruffed him to drag him off to bed. Right now, he felt too shit to get anything he wanted. Especially that, like it was a reward for hurting his friend.

So instead of going back into the flat and taking off whatever jeans Jack had put on, Danny swore under his breath, putting as much viciousness into the soft word as he could manage, and followed Jenny downstairs.

He hesitated outside her door, smelling salt, roses and sugar. That meant she was crying and had broken out the box of Turkish delight she'd gotten in Tynemouth market the last time they went.

He rested his forehead against the door. Nothing rattling around his head right now would make this right. All he had was more lies, or a really bad idea: truth. Danny squeezed his eyes shut in frustration and pushed himself off the jamb, stripping his shirt off as he headed down the next flight of stairs. There was a green door with a red Do Not Enter sign on it under the stairs on the ground floor; it led down into what a generously minded letting agent might call a basement. It was actually just a large utility room that smelled persistently of vinegar and old books, a bank of electricity meters on the wall. Usually ticking away efficiently, now quiet and inexpensive.

Residents were allowed to keep their bikes down here if they had them. There were four bikes parked in the installed rests, but Danny had only ever seen them move once. Generations of spiders had been born and died on the back spokes of Jenny's. No one ever came down here but Danny.

He stripped down to his skin, the cold pricking goose bumps over his thighs and forearms, and folded his clothes over the handlebars of Jenny's bike. His breath was steaming as he padded over to the old coal hatch and unhooked the combination lock.

The hinges grated and creaked as he lifted the heavy iron panel, propping it up with a stick. Danny wrinkled his nose at the itch of old coal dust in his nose and boosted himself up into the short tunnel. It was just wide enough for his shoulders, old screws scraping at his ribs as he squirmed into position. Then he pulled his fur on, and the dog's paws slid on the metal.

It snorted coal dust out its nose and scrabbled, nails scraping, up the slope until it could squirm out the other end. Dropping into the snow on the other side, it sneezed and shook itself, scattering bits of old coal over the pristine white around it.

Everything smelled clean and starched, like something new. Bitterly cold but otherwise still compared to the storms and batterings of the past weeks. The dog grumbled happily to itself—ignoring the twitch of human dread and the idea of "the calm before"—and scrabbled out of the garden to run, sticking its nose under things and getting snow in its ears. Runoff dribbled from melting icicles on a van mirror down into its ear canal, and it shook its head as hard as it could, twisting in circles as it rubbed its ear on its shoulder.

Complexities of emotion were impossible in dog form. It lacked the structures to support them. It had felt bad about fighting with the human that was sort of pack, but there was nothing it could do to fix it. Even if there had been, the human that was sort of pack wasn't even there right now, and dogs didn't really do object permanence with emotions.

Besides, there was a stick under a fence.

Digging down into the snow, the dog wedged its head under the fallen tree branch until it could lever it up enough to get its jaws around it. Sharp teeth dug into the wood, still fresh enough to taste green with sap, and dragged it out.

Put his skin back on, and he was never entirely sure what he wanted with the stick. It was just enough it was a stick. The dog struggled back up the hill, the ends of the stick fouling in the snow, feet cold and prickly with ice. The bitter wind whistled around it, blowing its fur in the wrong directions. Reaching the top, it dropped the stick and looked at it with satisfaction.

Definitely a stick.

The attack caught it off guard, tawny fur and muscle ramming into its side and bowling it back down the hill in a flurry of snow and hair. Shop fronts and snow-covered cars spun by on either side.

The stink of a wolf filled the dog's nose, fear of a bigger predator pulsing adrenaline through its muscles. The seed of character, the bit of him that was the same whether "Danny" or "Dog," stalled the panic. Wolf, but not *just* a wolf.

Jack. Heather, stone, and the Wild—wolf or human, that was Jack.

They landed hard at the bottom with the dog on his back and the wolf on top. White teeth snapped just shy of the dog's nose, and then the wolf jumped away from him, tail up as it leaned down on its elbows.

Come play. Wolves and dogs didn't need words.

The dog woofed back, plumed tail sweeping the snow as it scrambled to its feet. Except... human stuff? Human stuff. It clamped its tail between its legs resentfully and let the human out to deal with that, sitting on his knees in the snow with a sour pit in his gut.

Danny took a sharp breath through his teeth as the cold bit at him. Feeling the cold less than most didn't seem to mean much when his balls were swinging free in the breeze. That would give anyone a shiver. He should have thought that through better, but the dog never did.

"Fuck," he muttered, cupping himself with both hands—they were cold too, so didn't help much—and adjusting himself into an awkward squat. The bitter wind found every crevice, every tender spot, to stick cold fingers in. "Shit. Not now, Jack. I need… space."

The wolf snorted at him and used his nose to toss snow at Danny. He flinched back and nearly went ass-first in the snow, barely catching himself. His fingers crunched down into the snow, disappearing almost to the knuckle. Even half-blind without his glasses, he could tell when the wolf laughed at him, ears pinned and tongue lolling. He gave it the finger and tried to find the sweet spot between freezing valuable bits of himself off in the snow and flashing Mrs. Patel and half of Durham his naked bits.

"I'm not used to having people *around*," he said. "Not anymore. Not *all* the time. I needed to think, not fuck or play in the snow."

The wolf play-pounced at him, nipping at his knees and elbows. Danny slipped and ended up on his back in the snow, a curse squeezed out of him as the shock of it stole his voice. The wolf poked a cold nose behind his ear and then deliberately sneezed in it.

"If my balls fall off from frostbite, you'll be sorry," Danny muttered, shoving at Jack's heavy shoulder. Under the thick fur, he could feel the heat of Jack's wolf body. Then the fur was gone, and his hand was pressed against bare tanned skin. His thumb brushed over the crown inked and scarred into the skin just over Jack's collarbone, rough and raised.

"You feel bad you hurt your friend," Jack said, bending down to the angle his face came into focus. "You didn't want to fuck me because you know she was right. You want me more than you ever wanted her. Now you want to sulk out here until you convince yourself that the only fair thing is that you never get fucked again. I know you."

"You knew me."

"You're a stubborn idiot that likes humans and books too much," Jack said, a growl threatening around the edges of his voice. "And you *are* gonna need your balls."

It was enough to win a rusty snort of laughter from Danny. He was about to give up and head back to the flat with Jack when someone screamed out in the cold. It was a ragged, echoing sound, suddenly torn off by silence.

Jack lifted his head sharply, eyes glittering and nostrils flaring as he smelled the wind. Then he was gone, and Danny grabbed at the wolf, twisting a hand in his ruff.

"Wait!" he said. "They're looking for killer dogs, remember? What do you think they'll do if they see a *wolf*?"

A black lip curled, flashing a sharp, white fang to his opinion of that idea. Jack shook himself and lunged away, Danny losing his grip on him. So cold now that he would swear his balls were turning blue, Danny shifted back into the dog and took off at a run. He'd meant to head back to the flat first, grab his clothes, and then investigate; instead it went after Jack.

THE BRIEF respite from the weather was over, as the wind scoured viciously through the streets. It came from the north, from over the wall, like the wolves, and carried ice in it. Drifts of fallen snow toppled over as it hit them, frozen lumps of ice picked up and skipped like stones across the road.

A chunk of it caught the dog in the side and sent him sprawling, rough paws losing their purchase on the ice. It took a second to struggle back to his feet. Its hip ached dully from impact, and there was blood and hair scraped onto the hard-packed snow.

Huffing steam between its fangs, the dog shook itself. The wind flipped its ear inside out, digging icicle fingers down inside, and tugged at its tail. The dog hobbled, hindered as it worked back up to a lope, gusts nipping from side streets to push at the dog's ribs or suddenly letting up so the dog pitched forward onto its knees and nose in the snow.

It gave the human shadow in its brain an atavistic chill, the fear of a spiteful hand behind every bad fall or the judgment in a disaster. The dog didn't worry about the meanings behind things much, just the reality of the thing itself. Still, just in case the human was right, it snapped at the wind as if there was flesh to tear.

The screaming had stopped, but if the dog strained its ears it could hear a rattling whine. It sounded like a rabbit just as your teeth closed over its throat. His brain gave itself whiplash as half of it went "prey" and half went "help." Both drives made him move faster, sending him after whoever made the sound. Only one flooded his mouth with saliva.

It followed the sound down the street, through a barren lot, and across its fence. The plan hadn't been to go back to its den, but the scentscape of the neighborhood was drawing it in. Every turn it took narrowed the map in its head, until it squeezed under an abandoned truck, sniffing the sharp stink of fox against the rubber, and came out the other side in front of where it denned as a human.

The dog stopped, tail clamping against its hindquarters for all the wind's efforts to wave it. A nervous growl whined out of its throat, leaking up into his nose. It didn't like that the Other had come hunting here again, didn't like that it hadn't smelled it on any of the boundary trees. What wolf claimed a hunting ground and didn't piss its ownership over every branch?

A window on the den opened, and one of the people the dog had to put up with leaned out. "I've called the police," a man yelled the lie out his window. His teeth were chattering with more than the cold. "They'll be here soon!"

Other faces appeared at windows, pale smudges through frosted glass as they squinted out. The dog left the shadows and slunk across the road, trying to avoid notice. There was blood half-buried in a mound of blown-about snow by the big gate. When the dog sniffed the spot, it could smell the soap and salt of freezing blood, the satisfying reek of fear, and nothing else.

"I see it!" someone yelled, leaning out of their window. "Big bastard of a thing. Go on, get away from there."

Something smashed against the wall, scattering bits of glass all over the snow. Too far away to make it worthwhile for the dog to even flinch. It sniffed the snow again, not that it needed a scent to follow the churned-up snow. Every few feet there was another splodge of pink, ground into the snow by sneaker-shod feet.

The dog loped along beside it until it reached the broken window of the now silent co-op. More blood, smeared on the frozen spikes of glass. The dog hopped over the low wall, cocking its head from one side to the other to adjust to the echoes off the bare shelves. Brock hadn't made it any further. He lay on the tiled floor, blood crusting around him. The smell of fresh blood and raw meat made Danny's mouth water again. Drool spilled between his teeth, sliding over his black lips.

A single blue eye stared glassily at the roof, blinking with shocky slowness, while the other was glued shut with blood and swelling. His breath rasped through a matted sieve of blood and torn skin. One arm was broken and twisted, bent all the wrong way, and there was a huge bloody bite in his thigh. That was where most of the blood was coming from.

Still no scent of anything but blood and pain on him.

The dog stepped closer and poked its nose against Brock's shoulder. The contact made him start screaming again, torn lips spraying blood as the air hit them, and flailing weakly on the floor. His feet kicked and slid on the tiles—one shoe on, one gone—and he tried to drag himself away, smearing red behind him as he went.

The acrid smell of piss joined the blood and meat.

Whining apologetically, the dog backed off. It flopped down on its belly, chin on paws, and dragged the human up over it. The dog was good at running and tracking, at being a dog. This had the sort of corners the human could follow around better.

Chapter Thirteen

DANNY WAS getting sick of going skin side with his cock on something cold. He scrambled to his feet, spitting out curses and wishing he'd had the knack of bringing clothes with him when he changed. There were a few in the pack who could—the Numitor, his mam, a few of the elders—although they never bothered much. Even if any of the local humans saw them running around naked, they'd not complain. The laird up the hill and his folk were always good for a gossip.

But when you were a not-yet-tenured professor of religion, being caught with your balls out anywhere wasn't so tolerated.

"Brock," Danny said. "What happened?"

Instead of answering, Brock just wedged himself against a rack of empty shelves. His torn lips were moving, drooling blood down his chin, as he muttered prayers. It was a mangled version of a Hail Mary, mouthed again and again.

"Hail Mary, full of grace, pray for us now and at the hour of our death. Hail Mary, full of grace…."

"Did you see who did it?" Danny asked. He detoured around the smears of blood. It was freezing visibly but was still wet enough to leave prints in. He crouched down, reaching out to offer some sort of comfort to the man. He hesitated, uncertain of where to touch that wouldn't panic the man further. "Brock. Brock, listen to me. Did you see who did it?"

"No."

Brock's lips were still moving through the bits and pieces of prayer he remembered. It was the wrong gods to have any effect, but he was trying. Danny looked up. Jack stood in the middle of the aisle, wiping blood lazily off his fingers. For a second Danny wondered where Jack had found the clothes. Then his brain caught up. The ink crawling down his body was the same, but the hair was too long and a shade darker from never seeing the sun, and the stubble on his jaw was a scratch away from being a beard. His eyes were the right green but too detached. Jack wouldn't have cared, but he'd at least recognize that Brock was a living thing in pain.

"Gregor," Danny said, straightening up. He stayed half-crouched, balanced on the balls of his feet. "Why?"

"Because humans are dim and notice little." Gregor shrugged. He stepped forward, foot squelching in the blood, and Danny stepped back. The wind shoved at his back, trying to hem him in. Gregor cocked his head to the side. "Do I know you? I know you, dog."

"I don't think so," Danny said. His legs trembled with the need to step back again, but he could *smell* the arousal in the air. If he ran, Gregor would chase him.

Gregor slowly tilted his head to the other side, as if the different angle would jog his memory. A shudder racked through Danny, making him hiss and struggle to keep his hands steady. It was mostly the cold. Gregor had always been... unpredictable. He spent too much time fur side, and that could cause the edges of things to... blur.

"You were my brother's dog," he said, green eyes narrowing. He held his hand up and snapped his fingers, like he was calling a sheepdog. "I remember. Came running when he called."

"I don't belong to anyone."

When he smiled, he didn't look so much like Jack. It was a ghost of a thing, barely bothered with, and didn't reach his eyes. "So you're a stray? There are rules about strays. Come here."

"Fuck you."

Gregor looked him over, shoulders to balls. "I might, if you didn't stink of my brother. Dog, where's Jack?"

"Don't know."

Gregor growled, an animal noise coming out of a human throat. His lip curled, and he shook his head, shedding the anger. Brock's ruined arm was in his way. He kicked it to the side, making the injured man squeeze out that dying rabbit whine again.

"Where *will* he be?"

"Not telling you."

Gregor laughed, a rough scratch of noise. "Good dog. Maybe I'll just scrub you down and fuck you after all."

Danny tensed, clenching his fists and hunching his shoulders. He was already taller than Gregor—the exact same amount he was taller than Jack—but it didn't feel like *enough* bigger. Because he wasn't. If it came to a fight, Gregor would peel his skin and wear it as boots.

"Why do you even care?" Danny asked. "You won, Gregor. The Numitor picked you, not Jack. That's what you wanted."

Gregor closed the distance between them in two long strides, closing his hand around Danny's neck. His fingers dug in, finding the nerve bundle that jabbed ragged fingers of pain up into Danny's brain. Despite his clenched teeth, a yelp scraped up Danny's throat, and he folded reluctantly into Gregor's grip, trying to ease the ache of it.

"My da picked me because my brother's a pervert," Gregor snarled into Danny's ear. "Not because I'm better than him. Every wolf is whispering it, that if only Jack would stick it in a girl, our father would have picked him. Hell, if he'd even fingered a bitch, I'd be exiled instead of him."

Danny winced. He had suspected, but it wasn't the sort of thing that could be asked. Wolves didn't care who you fucked, but they'd care if you wouldn't. Packs were there to make pups. If you couldn't, or wouldn't, your rank dropped. Dog like Danny? No one cared one way or another about his cock. Someone like his ma, when the prophets said she'd not have any more wolf cubs, would have dropped to the bottom of the pack pecking order.

The Numitor? A barren Numitor wasn't even an option. If Jack couldn't, or wouldn't, knock up a pretty little she-wolf—and Danny would bet even Gregor wouldn't call one a bitch to their face—he couldn't run the pack, and Jack would never accept being at the bottom of the pack.

"So, what, you're going to hunt him down and kill him? You think that will make a difference?"

"Yes. Now, though, I have to deal with you first."

Out in the street, over the wind, a nervous voice yelled, "Over here! It was over here." Snow crunched. Then another voice. "There's blood here."

Gregor lifted his head, the dim winter light catching red in his eyes. He tightened his fingers on Danny's throat, squeezing down until his breath whistled in and out.

"Humans," Danny wheezed. "In mobs they're dangerous."

The breath on his cheek was hot, spiced with a touch of the Wild. "More dangerous than me?"

"They've wiped out wolves before."

"Not mine." The long muscles in Gregor's arm flexed, and he lifted Danny up off the ground, watching him dangle with flat eyes. Then he tossed Danny across the store. He crashed into a rack of shelves and hit the tiles. "But I have other business here. They can wait. Tell my brother I'll see him during the full moon. Tell him I have some new tricks."

Danny rolled onto his side, propping himself up on his elbow. The cold air scratched his raw throat as he coughed air back into his lungs. There were dark spots dancing in front of his eyes. He knuckled them away and dragged the fur up from under his skin. The dog scrambled to its feet and ran, not caring about getting its feet bloody. It leaped through the broken window and dashed down the street, through the small cluster of people in parkas and ski gear. They scattered, yelling and waving makeshift weapons, as it snapped and spun in circles. If they reached the shop before the wolf got outside, there would be no avoiding a fight.

When it had skin, it had faith in the humans and their clever hands. The dog didn't. The wolf would win. It might get hurt, but it would win.

A cricket bat caught it on the ribs, sending a brittle pop of pain through it, and a shovel clipped it on the head and made its ears ring. It tasted blood, flat and snotty, in its sinuses. Sneezing it out on the snow, it lunged and caught its teeth in the slippery foil of a parka. The fabric ripped, coating its tongue, with a dry mouthful of feathers.

A wildly swung cast-iron frying pan just missed crushing its skull. Before the wielder could try again, Gregor made his exit. The huge, honey-dark wolf leaped out the window, snow flying up from under its paws. It threw a snarl at the humans, the sound ripping through the air. They froze, some atavistic part of their brain shutting down their muscles, and the wolf stared them down for a long moment. Then it snorted contempt and turned its back, loping away up the street.

The dog fled too, limping and dripping blood from its nose as it ran. A few of the humans gave chase, floundering and slipping on the snow, but not hard enough to risk catching it. The lackluster pursuit ended when someone found Brock, a familiar voice screaming for someone—anyone—to come and help.

INSIDE THE apartment didn't feel much warmer than outside. Danny grabbed a towel from the bathroom and hastily scrubbed the rough cotton down his arms and legs, scraping off the blood and mud. Bruises stippled his arms and legs, a smear of purple and green down his side. He poked at the yellow spots with his fingertips, grimacing at the ache.

His ribs had healed already. When he pressed down on his skin, under the muscle and flesh, he could feel the gritty bumps of healing bone. The bruises looked a week old, at least.

It had been a long time since he healed this fast. Not since he'd left Scotland. He didn't know if it was because he'd been shifting skin more often or if it was having Jack around. Or he supposed it could be both, and he didn't have time to work it out now. He needed to make sure Jenny was okay, find out what happened to Brock.

Danny dropped his arm, wincing at the ache of muscles sliding over his ribs, and grabbed a sweater from the bed to pull on. He checked his reflection in the bathroom mirror, licking his thumb and wiping the blood off his upper lip. There, he looked human. Even if he wasn't.

It had been Jenny swinging the pan. She'd bought it at Dalton Park. Le Creuset on sale. Danny had joked at the time that she could use the bloody thing as a weapon. His nose was still leaking. He blotted the blood on his sleeve and left the bathroom.

There was no sign of Jack. Danny scrubbed the back of his neck, feeling the prickle of his hackles, and went over to check the window. Had he and Gregor found each other out in the snow? That wouldn't be good.

Danny leaned on the windowsill and stared out, looking for tracks in the snow or the glint of eyes in the shadows. It had darkened outside, the white sky of the last few days bruised like Danny's ribs. It was full of sullen, black clouds, pulling down an early twilight. They spat out gobbets of rain, splattering the glass and seeping into the snow.

"C'mon, Jack," Danny muttered, rapping his knuckles against the glass. "Move your ass, get in out of the rain."

The sudden interruption of fists battering his door jolted Danny out of his thoughts, his heart crawling up into his throat. He twisted around, hissing as his ribs protested the movement, and then caught the scent of roses and sickness on the air. Jenny.

Knuckles poking white through her skin, her face twisted up into the place where anger and fear ended up being the same thing. A grunt of effort as she tried to bring down the pan on his skull.

Danny shook his head. That wasn't fair. She'd thought he was a vicious dog; he'd been *trying* to scare them. Finding something to get angry with her about wouldn't make him feel any less guilty.

She was hammering the door with her palms when Danny pulled it open. She nearly fell into him, catching herself with both hands against his chest.

"It's Brock," she said, her eyes swimming with tears. She swallowed wetly. "He's... oh, fuck, Danny... he's hurt. He's *really* badly hurt. I don't know what to do."

"Okay," Danny said, putting his hands on her shoulders. He felt a dull wave of surprise that the man was still alive. When he'd left the shop, he'd expected Gregor to finish his kill before following him. "It's okay. We'll work something out. What happened?"

Jenny wiped her face with both hands, smearing tears back into her hair. Her fingers were covered with blood; it was on her sleeves too and down the legs of her jeans.

"I heard this scream," she said. "We all did. It was horrible. Didn't you hear it? I banged the door, but I couldn't wait for you. We had to go, and he.... God, he'd been attacked by a dog. We saw it, this big, ugly thing. Bill said it was like a lurcher or a wolfhound or something."

She sniffed and wiped her face again. "Fuck. I didn't think I'd be crying over that bastard again. But he's just so... ripped up. I can't believe a dog could do that to him. It was just a dog."

Danny didn't think knowing it had been a wolf would make her feel any better. He patted her arms in empty comfort. "We'll work out something."

She grabbed his hand and squeezed, fingers sticky and hot. "I don't want to fight with you, Danny."

"Me either. I wasn't fair." That was about as true as he could manage. "I'll get my first-aid kit."

"I think he needs more than first aid, Danny."

She was right, but first aid Danny knew he could do. Thinking about the mess of chewed blood and flesh on the floor of the co-op, he wasn't sure he could do anything else. He went into the bedroom and grabbed his jacket and the canvas bag from under the bed. Juggling them awkwardly in his arms, he stamped bare feet into his boots and hurried back out to Jenny. She didn't ask about Jack, although her eyes cut briefly over his shoulder into the flat.

Downstairs, Jenny's door was lying open, and the flat was full of strangers. Danny gave the bat propped against the wall a dirty look on the way by, feeling the hitch in his ribs as he breathed in. In the living room Brock lay on the couch, bleeding through the gray fleece someone had pressed into service as a bandage. He was pallid and sweating under the blood, and he stank. The reek of sickness on him drove Danny back a step, a retching gag in his throat. It didn't smell like a clean wound; the closest he had in his scent memory was the chemical bile curdled in a poisoned sheep's gut.

A hand settled reassuringly in the small of his back, although he thought Jenny probably thought it was the sight of gore getting to him.

"I think he's going into shock," the bald man kneeling next to him said. "Maybe we should give him some water?"

"I don't think you're meant to give someone who's been in an accident anything to drink, Bill," a young man said, shoving his hand through his hair nervously. It took Danny a second to recognize Adil, Mrs. Patel's son, without his usual quiff. He must have run out of wax. "In case they have internal injuries."

"Aren't you at medical school?" Jenny said, narrowing her eyes at him.

He gave her a frantic look. "First year! First year we don't even get to *touch* people."

Danny tossed his jacket onto the small table and swung the bag off his shoulder, dropping it to the ground by the sofa. The smell coiled in his nose, something about it making his fangs ache behind his gums. His instincts apparently felt that anything that smelled like that should be dead in a hole, dirt kicked on top of it. Instead he gingerly peeled up the edge of the bandage on Brock's thigh. Underneath, his torn jeans were glued to his legs, the coating of blood making it hard to tell what was skin and what was fabric.

"We should get him to the hospital." Bill shifted back out of Danny's way. One of the women put her arm around Jenny, trying to turn her away. Jenny shrugged it off and went into the kitchen, coming back with a handful of candles and a couple of saucers under her arm. She lit them, dripped the wax on the china, and set them out on the floor and on the bookshelf.

Danny unbuckled the canvas bag and reached in, fingers closing around the cold metal of the scissor handles. "We can't call an ambulance," he pointed out. "Bleeding like this, he'll never reach the hospital."

He snipped through the arms of the fleece and peeled the fabric, wincing in reluctant sympathy as the scabs split and tore. More blood oozed out, rank with that sour, meat taint.

"Do we have any water?"

"Mum sent some over," Adil said. He added, defending her unnecessarily, as he went to get it. "She had to stay with Mo. He's only a kid. He shouldn't see this sort of thing."

He handed Danny a sports bottle of water, the plastic seal still condoming the top of it. Danny stripped it off with his teeth, fang popping through the seal, and used it to sluice blood off Brock's leg. It was a mess. Bites usually were if the prey—victim, in this case—was alive. They didn't hold still; you had to keep adjusting your grip. The injury on Brock's thigh was worse. Danny had expected to see torn skin and excised muscle, but the mess between Brock's groin and knee was like pulled pork. He slapped layered wads of gauze on the injury and duct-taped it down.

There was half a bottle of water left. Danny passed it to Bill, then grabbed a bottle of pills from the bag. His fingers left bloody prints on the label. "Try and get a couple of these in him?"

"You a doctor?"

"Of theology," Danny said.

"Seriously? Why do you have all this stuff?" Bill asked, nervous humor in his voice as he fumbled with the pills. "Do you guys get the shivs out arguing over Corinthians or something?"

The arm was beyond any bodging that Danny could manage. It probably needed a sling or a splint, but he didn't know where to start. It flopped in a way that suggested multiple breaks, the elbow joint popped backward. He added more gauze to the puncture wounds in Brock's forearm, taping them down. Brock didn't move, but Danny could feel the vaguely sickening movement of his bones under his skin. "I grew up in Scotland—"

"Where? The Gorbals?"

"Worse. The countryside," Danny said. "We were miles away from anywhere. First aid had to hold for a while if anything happened."

He was getting better at lying without *lying*. They assumed the injured had been waiting for an ambulance; he knew they'd just been waiting to heal quicker than they were dying. Even with wolf-fast healing, a torn artery could empty you out faster than you healed up. Besides, if a bone healed crooked, it was a painful process getting it rebroken.

Danny had a lumpy collarbone that could attest to that. His ma had snapped it the second time with a pair of pliers, holding the bones straight while she lectured him on being careful and waited for them to knit.

His ma would just have put Brock out of his misery. Wiping his hands on his legs, Danny got a pack of sterile strips out of the bag. He did his best to tape Brock's face together. His lips were torn into three, the flaps hanging down to expose his teeth and pallid gums, and his nostril was split. The eye… it was a blood blister, skin puffed up and so thin Danny was scared to touch it.

"Is he all right?" Bill asked.

"No," Adil answered for Danny, voice cracking with nerves. "Look at him. Of course, he's not all right. How could you think he's all right?"

Bill's mouth tightened, and he gave Adil an irritated look, using the arm of the sofa to push himself to his feet. "I don't know, do I? I mean, he's a mess, but what are we going to do?"

"We don't know," Jenny said. "That's the problem."

Danny repacked his unused supplies back in the kit hastily, moving away from the reek of Brock's body as soon as he could. The pack of water sat on the coffee table. He ripped the plastic and grabbed a bottle. He twisted the cap off and took a drink, swilling the plastic-flat water around his mouth.

"He needs to go to hospital," he said, leaning back against the wall. His hands were shaking. He put the bottle down. "But we can't go now. It's getting dark, and it wouldn't be safe to drive in the dark."

Bill walked over to the window, shoving the curtains out of the way to look out. The moody early twilight had given way to true dusk, a heavy darkness full of the sound of running water. What had started as a drizzle had brewed into a downpour. "There's no other cars on the road. If we were careful…."

"The roads are full of wrecked cars who thought the same thing," Danny said. "There's no lights, slush on the roads, blockages. It won't help Brock any if we all end up needing medical treatment. We could try tomorrow, if anyone has a car."

"You can take mine," Jenny said. She had a Nissan Micra. It wasn't the car that Danny would have chosen to take out on the road, but no one else was offering. She went over and sat down on the arm of the sofa, touching Brock's sock-clad feet with oddly tender fingers. Looking up she caught Danny watching her and pulled a rueful face, heavy sweater sliding over her narrow shoulders. "He's an asshole, and after what he did, I wished all sorts on him. Not this."

Adil shifted, pulling his jacket close and zipping it up as far as it would go. "I can't help you here," he said. "My mum's on her own…."

"I need to get something to eat."

"I want to check on my kids."

Eventually the room emptied, and it was just Danny and Jenny, and the restlessly moaning Brock. It would be brutal if he came around all the way.

"I'll stay," Danny said. Guilt bubbled at the offer when he still didn't know what had happened to Jack. Except he didn't know how to find Jack, and Jenny needed him just now. "I just need to check upstairs, and then I'll sleep on the floor."

Jenny pulled her hair back from her face, twisting it around her fist and tying it in a knot. The ends stuck out in frayed ribbons. "You don't have to do that."

"I can't leave you alone with him."

She gave him a scornful look. "Why? To protect my virtue?" She made a wave gesture with her hand. "Ship. Sailed."

"No," he said. "But if something happens with Brock…. He's badly hurt, Jenn, and I'm not a doctor."

"You want to stay?" Jenny said. "Then come back to my bed. Move back in. Want me the way you want—" She jerked her thumb at the roof. "If you can't, don't say sorry or give me puppy eyes. Just decide whether you're my friend or my boyfriend."

He hesitated awkwardly. That was enough of an answer, he supposed. Jenny rolled her eyes at him.

"Go," she said. "It's fine. I'm fine. Go on."

"If anything happens, you *can* call me," he said.

Jenny snorted at him. "Of course I'll call. I'm showing some self-respect, Danny, not turning into an *idiot*." She stopped, folding her lips against her teeth, and added quietly. "Thank you."

He shrugged. "Of course. Anytime."

It was probably for the best. Even if Danny could have ignored the barb-hook tug of worry over Jack and Gregor, the smell would have driven him out. It was like he'd snorted a particularly disgusting essential oil up his nose, everywhere and oppressive.

He smelled Jack the minute he got upstairs: sweat, blood, and the unexplainable sap-green freshness of pine. When he got into the flat, he found Jack sprawled out, dozing skin side on the bed. In the dim light, the ink he wore looked like shadows on his skin. They poured over the hard ridges of muscle and disappeared under the waistband of his jeans.

Actually, they were Danny's jeans. Under the denim, his skin, cock, Jack would smell like Danny. The possessiveness in that thought tugged Danny's balls up to his body, hot and aching, as if a hand had cupped them. It caught him by surprise. He was usually the possessed, not the possessor. It felt oddly right, though. Maybe it was just being part of even a truncated pack after so many years.

"You coming in or not?" Jack asked, opening his eyes and squinting down the long sprawl of himself.

Chapter Fourteen

OVER THE past week, Jack had indulged a few fantasies about how Danny would finally end up back under him. Some had him pliant and submissive, neck bent in surrender. Others had him snarling, Jack's fingers digging into the nape of his neck.

None of them started with Danny throwing a balled-up jacket at his head. Jack batted it out of the air and sat up. "What?"

"I thought Gregor had found you," Danny growled, stalking across the room. "Where the hell have you—"

Jack sat up abruptly, sucking in a deep breath. He couldn't smell his brother, just Danny, blood and a lingering sourness he didn't recognize. "You saw Gregor?"

Danny paused, squinting. "Didn't you?"

"No." The admission felt like a failure on his tongue—he spat it out like it tasted bad. "When I got there, the attacker was already gone. I chased their trail through the streets and the Wild for an hour or more. I can tell you one thing, though: it wasn't my brother."

"You think that Gregor's...." Danny paused, looking for a word. "...not involved? In these murders?"

It was a human word, a human *idea*. Jack couldn't deny that it fit here, though. The bodies they'd found weren't challengers or prey, and they'd not been killed to assert dominance or from need. So, what was left but murder?

Not involved, though?

"I think that he's not *alone*," Jack said. Leaning forward, he rested his elbows on his knees and looked at Danny. He'd been *pretty* when they were younger, under the scruffy hair and defensively smart mouth. He still had the foxy bones and elegant hands, but a layer of lean muscle and a heavier cant to his jaw skewed him to handsome. "What happened?"

"He had a message for you: he'll see you at the full moon."

"That was all?"

"He called me a dog." Danny said, shrugging. "Threw his weight around a bit. He's not changed much."

"Have you told Jenny that her boyfriend's dead?"

"He's not. Not yet."

Learning that his brother was in Durham had been more confirmation than revelation. That the man was alive? Now *that* was a surprise. Jack would deny his brother plenty of virtues, but he was an efficient killer, and he had no respect for those that weren't. Gregor's adherents prided themselves on sharp teeth and quick kills.

Danny took his glasses off, leaving them on the dresser, and stripped out of his sweater, muscles stretching out long and loose under green-bruised skin on his ribs. It drew a growl out of Jack, and he pushed himself up off the bed, running his hands over Danny's side. He could feel the heat of healing flesh against his palm, Danny's natural internal temperature raised from the extra work.

"He did this?" The words were a wolf's growl forced into words by his tongue. "He touched you?"

"No," Danny said. His voice hitched through the words. His throat worked as he swallowed. "That wasn't Gregor."

"Who, then?"

"Doesn't matter."

Frustration wriggled through Jack, an irritation just under the skin. Want was easy to establish. Danny's cock was a thickening bulge under worn-soft denim, and he smelled like fucking. If he was a wolf, Jack would have rolled him over and been in him already.

This was *Danny*, though. Mouthy, snarky Danny, who'd spent too much time with humans and pretended he didn't need a pack. Jack wanted him to say it, to *admit* it.

Jack reached down and hooked his fingers into Danny's waistband, tugging the tall man in until their bodies were pressed together. There was no pretense there, Jack's hard cock pressing insistently against Danny's leg.

"She's right, your woman," he said. "You want me."

The mention of Jenny made Danny stiffen, putting a distance between them without either actually moving.

Fuck sake. Jack wasn't used to having to be charming, not with words. He was the Numitor's son, one of the strongest wolves alive. An interested look was usually enough to lift someone's tail for him.

Jack caught the back of Danny's neck and pulled him down, kissing the wariness off the other man's lush mouth. He dragged blunt teeth over the curve of his lower lip in a slow bite. That worked. Danny tilted his head into the kiss, opening his mouth to Jack's tongue. There was a hint of blood on his breath, the coppery sweetness sliding straight down to give Jack's balls a tug.

They stumbled blindly over to the bed, dropping onto the mattress in a tangle of limbs and suddenly impatient hands. It was Jack who ended up flat on his back, with Danny's long body sprawled heavily on top of him. His muscles clenched in a brief war between play and predator instincts.

"What are you doing?"

A grin slanted over Danny's face, crinkling the corners of his eyes and flashing a long dimple in one cheek. He reached down and popped Jack's fly open, sliding his hand under the waistband to cup Jack in cold fingers. It made Jack hiss, lifting his hips up off the bed.

"Guess," Danny said.

He rolled off Jack and stood up, hooking his fingers in the pockets of the jeans. He tugged, and Jack lifted his hips to let the denim scrape over his ass. His cock jutted up from between his thighs, thick and hard before anyone even touched it. Jack reached down to wrap his fingers around it loosely, swiping his thumb over the head. His mouth tilted smugly when Danny dragged in a ragged breath.

"I thought you said you didn't miss the pack, Danny Dog," he said.

"I never said that," Danny admitted. He looked like the admission wasn't something he'd meant to say, then shrugged. "Wanting isn't the same as *needing.*"

"Liar."

Danny shook his head and crouched down, sliding his hands up Jack's thighs. He pressed his thumbs against the seams of the jeans as he wrapped that clever fucking mouth around Jack's cock. Slick heat and the eager suck of his lips. Pleasure bucked through Jack, frying his nerve endings and raking hot, sweet fingers up his spine.

"Fuck," he groaned, throwing his head back.

Words. He'd never been good with fucking words.

His fingers flexed against the sheets, wringing the cotton until it tore. Danny's tongue trailed along the underside of his cock, tracing the long vein up to swirl around the head. He ran his hand up Jack's thigh and cupped his balls, squeezing just hard enough to make Jack gasp.

Jack reached down and twisted his fingers through Danny's hair. It was still damp at the scalp, cool against Jack's fingers. He pulled lightly, tugging Danny's head back until his mouth was barely wrapped around the spit-wet head.

"Remember I said I liked your mouth?" he said, voice harsh with control. "I like that you don't talk with it full."

Danny freed one hand up long enough to give him the finger emphatically. Jack laughed and shoved down again, thrusting up into Danny's mouth. He shifted his hand, cupping the smooth curve of Danny's skull just above the nape of his neck, setting the pace with the flex of hard fingers.

Hunger knotted in his stomach, cramping muscles making the long lines of ink on his stomach shift and rewrite themselves.... It had been a while since anything other than his own hand had grabbed his cock. With the wolves it had always felt that they were eyeing him midfuck, trying to work out if he was a pervert or not. With humans, there was always something a bit flat about it.

With Danny....

Jack liked him. He always had. He liked how Danny didn't have a snarky thought that didn't come out of his mouth or a horny one that didn't slide through his eyes, and he liked that thing Danny was doing with his thumb at the root of Jack's cock. He cursed himself through that one, jaw clenched and lips grimaced back from his teeth.

Little shit laughed around his cock, the sound flexing around it like another hand, and then did it again. His reaction twisted through his groin, jabbing from root to asshole. Pleasure so sharp it felt like a knife.

Danny grabbed his cock, cool against mouth-heated skin, and twisted up. Jack's hips followed it up off the bed, his hand clenching on the scruff of Danny's neck. Control hanging by a thread, he dragged Danny off his cock and up onto the bed. Danny's long body sprawled over him, damp and hot. The borrowed jeans rubbed roughly against Jack's aching cock as Danny shifted, his thigh nudging between Jack's.

When Danny kissed him, it tasted like salt-sweat and spunk, and he looked smug as he broke the kiss.

"Is that how your human girl fucks?" Jack asked, because he couldn't let anything lie, apparently. "All... cleverness?"

Surprise slapped over Danny's face, chased by anger. He shoved himself off Jack, back onto his feet, like he'd been burned. He wiped his arm over his mouth. "Fuck you, puppy prince." He turned and stalked away, bare feet and fury tight down the lean line of his back.

Jack rolled to his feet and kicked off his jeans, cock twitching wet and slick toward the flat of his stomach. He should be frustrated, aggravated. Except he'd always liked that Danny *didn't* like him all that much sometimes. It was *easy* to be liked when you were the Numitor's pup, harder to find something as honest as plain old lust.

He crossed to the door in two long strides and caught Danny before he could leave the room, shoving him flat against the wall. Danny tensed, all tight cords of muscle under Jack's fingers, and tried to throw Jack off.

"I didn't say it wasn't nice, Danny Dog," Jack said as he grabbed his wrists and slammed them against the door. He was panting, but not because of the effort. The smell of arousal was so thick in the air it was like a drug, and it was sweating the lingering human right off Danny. He grinned against Danny's neck, rubbing the roughness of stubble against the tender skin. "Didn't say I'd not want you doing it again either. It's not what you *want*, though, is it?"

Danny clenched his hands into fists, tendons shifting under Jack's fingers. He tilted his head forward so his brow rested against the wood. "So you think I want to get fucked against a wall?"

"You smell like you want fucked wherever I fucking want you," Jack said.

He felt Danny's reaction to that hitch through all those muscles, a shudder of brutal awareness. When he let go of Danny's wrist, the dog kept his fist pressed to the plaster. The Wild was a restless wind in Jack's head, wanting to break and run, howl and hunt, to chase.

That thought—Danny caught, sweaty and breathless and prone under Jack's weight—dragged an eager growl out of Jack. The thrum of the sound against the nape of his neck made Danny shudder and bite his lip. Goose bumps spread down his arms. Jack dragged his teeth across his shoulder, finding the ridges of the old scars. It wasn't easy to scar a shifter, but people had made the effort with Danny. A dotted line of scar tissue perforated his shoulder, pinching in under his collarbones. It had been old ten years ago, and Danny had always shrugged off any questions, but scraping teeth over them made him gasp.

Just like that.

"Wherever and however," Jack said smugly, licking sweat off his lips.

"Go to hell." Danny shoved backward again, shifting Jack back a few inches.

"Been there. Am there." Jack slammed him against the door again, using his body as a weight. He reached around and tugged Danny's jeans open, shoving them down his thighs. Once they were out of the way, he wrapped his fingers around the hard length of Danny's erection. Fine skin stretched and wrinkled under his grip as he moved his hand. Danny cursed raggedly and thrust against Jack's hand. "I know your mum taught you the catechism. Humans built their hell high in our world."

Danny sucked in a ragged breath and muttered, "I've tried both. Hell isn't indoor plumbing."

"Bad dog," Jack rasped, tightening his grip until Danny groaned and bucked into his hand. Muscles tightened and stretched through his long, lean body. "Time and a place to mouth off, Danny Dog."

He dragged his hand along Danny's cock, two quick, rough strokes that left Danny panting, shuddering and raggedly mute. For once. Jack sprawled against the other man's back, sweat slick between them and his cock pressing against Danny's ass.

"You don't need the humans," he said, pressing his mouth against the skin just under Danny's jaw. "You need us. You need this. Dog or not, you've got the Wild in your bones."

"I'd rather have central heating and *Top Gear*."

Jack kicked Danny's feet apart, startling a gasp out of the other man. He let go of the wrist he'd pinned to the door and grabbed Danny's jaw, wrenching his head around. "I'm going to make you howl, Danny," he promised. Threatened. "Open your mouth."

"Bite me."

"Later."

Jack shoved his fingers into Danny's mouth. The slick, wet heat and swipe of his tongue made Jack's cock twitch happily. Some human things he could get used to, he supposed. Pulling his fingers out, he kissed Danny, wet fingers in his hair to hold him still. It was all teeth and dominance—a wolf's kiss.

When Jack lifted his head there was blood on Danny's lips and no defiance at all left in his eyes. It wasn't something he'd want to last, but right now the submissive dip of Danny's eyes was sweet enough to make Jack's cock jump.

"Say you need me."

Danny's throat bobbed as he swallowed, his tongue swiping blood from his mouth. "I need this," he admitted, voice ragged and hungry. It was close enough that it should have been enough. If the moon wasn't cold in Jack's blood and the Wild still humming in his mind, it probably would have been.

He growled, letting the sound thrum through both their bodies, and reached down to push his fingers into Danny's ass. It flexed around the invasion, muscles clamping down and then relaxing. Danny's breath caught in his throat, and he jerked forward, fucking Jack's fist.

"Son of a bitch…," Danny gasped.

Jack laughed against his ear. "Too much time around humans, Danny. Your ma would wash your mouth out with pumice for that."

His patience with seduction gone, Jack slid his fingers out and let go of Danny's cock. The mewling, wanting sound of protest that escaped Danny at the sudden absence, was nearly—*nearly*—as good as him just admitting he needed Jack. He tried to shove himself off the door, muscles twisting under the skin of his back. Jack shoved him back into place against the wood.

"Stay."

Danny did. A grin tilted Jack's mouth. He was pretty sure that the minute Danny came, he'd remember to be pissed about that. He spat on his hand and pumped it along his cock, clenching his teeth against the hot ache of want that settled dully in his balls. He hooked an arm around Danny's stomach, the bony jut of hip just right for his fingers, and thrust into him.

Still tight, despite the fingers. Danny swore, and his hand clenched, knuckles pressing against the wall. All the tendons and muscles from wrist to elbow stood out against his skin, but that didn't stop him pushing back onto Jack's cock when he paused halfway in.

"Fuck me," he begged, half ordered. "God, Jack. Just fuck me. Please."

It was the "please" that did it, mewling out of Danny's mouth. Jack dug his fingers in and thrust, burying himself inside the tight, flexing grip of Danny's ass. He buried his face in Danny's shoulder, mouth moving against his skin, as he fucked.

"You're too fucking tall," he muttered after a minute.

"You're too short," Danny shot back, snarking on automatic pilot.

Frustration throbbed at the base of Jack's cock, not quite able to catch the right angle. Shifting his grip to the back of Danny's neck, scruffing him firmly, Jack dragged him off the wall and took them both down onto the ground. Danny's knees cracked off the carpet, and he braced his weight on his arms. The long muscles in his back bunched and flexed as Jack started thrusting against him.

Reaching down, Jack wrapped his fingers around Danny's cock again. The scrape of his fingers made Danny moan and drop his head, his hair hanging in a scruffy veil over his face.

"Look up," Jack ordered. He wanted to see him come.

When Danny didn't answer, Jack stretched over and grabbed a handful of hair. He used it as a handle, pulling Danny's head up and back. That pretty lower lip was caught between slightly crooked teeth, and his eyes were screwed shut, drops of sweat sliding down the side of his face.

"Please?" he hissed out through clenched teeth, pushing back into Jack's thrusts. "I want… I need…."

He stumbled over articulating exactly what he "wanted" and "needed," but that was okay. Jack already knew.

"In a minute," he promised. "You can keep up with me, can't you, Danny?"

Each thrust buried him deep in Danny, sweaty flesh sliding, and pulled the nerves in his groin that little bit tighter. It felt like a ball of hot wire, hooked into the flexing muscles of his thigh and gut. Closer and closer.

Balanced on the gray, stony ridge of orgasm, Jack slammed himself into Danny. Locked elbows gave, and Danny pitched forward, held up by Jack's dick and the fist in his hair. Jack shoved him down to the ground and came, shuddering as bruising thrusts emptied his balls into Danny's ass.

Sprawled over Danny's back, aftershocks prickling black up his spine, Jack wrung Danny's cock in his hand. Long thighs twitched, wringing another spurt of come from Jack's cock, and Danny writhed under him.

"God, yes," he panted. "Just again, just…."

Pulling back with the hand still locked in the sweaty curly hair, Jack sank his teeth into Danny's shoulder. He bore down hard enough to bruise, maybe harder than he meant to as the copper and sweet taste of blood tempted his tongue. It didn't seem to bother Danny. He came, stickiness spilling on Jack's fingers and a raw, cracking scream escaping his throat.

They both collapsed on the old carpet, breathing heavily. Jack rubbed his face into Danny's shoulder. He smelled of sex and wolf, nothing human lingering at all.

"See?" Jack said, scraping Danny's hair back from his face and pulling his head back. "I told you I'd make you howl."

Chapter Fifteen

IT FELT late when Danny woke up, the room too bright for early morning. Of course, he'd never greeted the day from the carpet before. He lifted his head and rubbed the heel of his hand over his jaw, feeling the dents from the weft of the carpet on his skin. Jack was sprawled half over his back, one arm hooked possessively around his neck. His breath was a hot, predator's pant against the skin under Danny's ear.

Danny tried to feel pissed off. Even with his improved rate of healing, his bitten shoulder itched and his hips cradled a faint dull ache. He *should* be pissed. He shouldn't feel like his body was one long, loose elastic band.

There was probably something perverse about feeling smug that it still irritated him when the words *Jack was right* popped into his head. Danny blew his hair out of his eyes and rolled over, ignoring Jack's sleepy growl of complaint. He propped himself up on his elbow and squinted at the gap in the curtains. The light that filtered in was dingy gray.

He lifted the heavy weight of Jack's arm and squirmed out from under him. At least being a dog meant he didn't get carpet burn. Glasses first, bringing the room back into focus. Then he grabbed his jeans and step-hopped into them on his way to the window.

"Shit," he breathed, staring out. It was still raining, a heavy, persistent downpour, but the temperature must have dropped overnight. Everything was frozen, glistening wet icicles dripping over the sides of the cars and down the fence.

"Fenrir's a big fan of *Frozen*, then," he muttered. "Good to know."

Jack laughed through a yawn, rolling up off the floor. "Can't see it. 'Letting Go' is kind of the opposite of his thing." He wandered over to give Danny a lazy cuff across the back of his head. "And don't blaspheme."

"You've watched *Frozen*?" Danny asked, raising his eyebrows.

"I didn't need to. We still send the cubs to school," Jack reminded him. "Even Gregor probably knows what *Frozen* is."

The mention of Jack's brother stole the brief lightness from the room. Guilt pinched vaguely at Danny for laughing when a man was dying on the floor below.

"I should go and check on Jenny," he said.

"Pining for your master's voice and a belly rub?"

The condescending lilt in Jack's voice made Danny clench his teeth. "I like her, that's all."

Jack rolled his bare shoulders in an annoyed shrug. "She's not pack."

"Yeah," Danny said dryly. "Like I said, I like her."

He turned to grab a jumper from the sideboard. Jack scruffed the nape of his neck and pulled him back, chest warm against the cold line of Danny's back.

"You liked me well enough last night." Jack said. He set his teeth to Danny's shoulder, finding the slow-healing bruises. The sense memory of the night before jolted through Danny. Rough fingers digging into his neck, dragging at his cock—bruises that took hours to fade, cock pounding pleasure through his body like a drum. He could smell the stink of lust that lifted off him. From the growl that thrummed against his spine, Jack could smell it too. "You *were* willing."

Danny twisted around and kissed Jack, mouth slanting over his at an awkward angle. It was an odd thing to worry about. Wolves didn't worry about consent that much: either you were up for it, or you shifted and chewed someone's face off.

"If I didn't want it, I'd have told you," he said, lips brushing Jack's as he spoke. "I'm not a wolf, but I'm not prey."

Jack bit his lip, a quick nip and tug.

"Then stay." He ran a hand down Danny's stomach, tracing the muscles, and cupped his cock through his jeans. "I'll let you chase me around for a while."

The rough squeeze that accompanied the offer made Danny's stupid cock jerk to half-mast. He closed his eyes and swallowed a groan. Just this once, he was tempted to bend his neck and play the submission game. Except the one reason Gregor had come hunting around here was because of Danny.

Besides, he didn't want to give Jack any false notions. Danny still wasn't a wolf, and that wasn't going to change just because he was screwing one. His ma had always tried to claim he was a wolf at heart, but he didn't think she'd even managed to fool herself.

"I promised," he said, dragging himself away from Jack. He pulled the jumper on, tugging it down over his head. "You could always come and help if you wanted."

"I know," Jack said. He stretched lazily and flopped onto the bed, hauling the duvet up over his shoulders. One arm tucked behind his head, the long muscles in his arms bunching under the skin, he shrugged. "But I won't."

"What if Gregor comes after Brock again?" Danny asked. "You could catch him off guard."

The corner of Jack's mouth curled in a sneer. "If my brother was a fool, don't you think I'd have killed him by now? Besides, if he wanted your Brock dead, he'd be dead." He sniffed the air and wrinkled his nose. "It was probably the stink that put him off. I'd not want to eat that."

JACK WAS right. The smell had gotten worse. It wasn't strong enough for *Danny* to smell upstairs, but it hit him as he stepped into Jenny's flat, the wrongness of Brock driving him back a step. After a night spent soaking in the blood and stink, the sofa was fetid with it. Even the carpet seemed to have soaked it in, releasing gasps of the stench as he stepped on it.

Jenny was sitting on the floor next to the sofa like she couldn't smell anything. She cocked her head at him, frowning.

"What's wrong?"

"Nothing." He swallowed, his throat dry and stinky. "It's just the smell."

She looked around like she might have missed something, searching for the smell in the corners. "Is it bad? I hadn't even noticed." She braced her elbow on the arm of the sofa and pushed herself up off the ground. "I've got Febreze in the kitchen."

Chemical lavender and corn molecules were not going to make a dent in this stink. Danny headed Jenny off on her way into the kitchen, putting his hands on her shoulders. She looked up at him, purple bruises under her eyes like someone had pressed their thumbs into the tender skin, and scowled.

"What?" she said.

"Have you slept at all?"

She started to nod, then changed her mind and shook her head. "I couldn't settle. Every time he moved or groaned, I thought he was… dying. Right there on my sofa. Bloody hell, Danny, we're in Durham. How can we not get someone to a *doctor*?"

"We will. Adil is going to bring around his van. Once he does, we'll get Brock to the hospital. They can patch him back together. He'll be…."

The lie caught behind his teeth, making him hesitate. Jenny folded her lips in a tight, humorless smile. "I've seen his leg, Danny. That's never going to be fine, is it?"

He sighed and put his hand on her shoulder. "Go keep an eye out for Adil. I'll watch Brock till he gets here. You need a break."

Jenny hesitated for a second, then nodded. "Thank you," she said, almost mouthing the words. She shrugged on her jacket. It wasn't heavy enough for the cold, but then nothing they had really was.

"Is it still raining?"

"It was when I came in," Danny said. He shrugged. "By now? Who knows."

It wasn't much of a joke. She laughed anyhow, a dry rattle of noise, and grabbed a hat, pulling it down over her ears. It was red. She looked like a very small, sad bear.

"It wasn't just… I did love him," Jenny said. "He was good to me. Until he wasn't."

She left without bothering to close the door behind her. Danny ran both hands through his hair and walked over to the couch, as close as he could bring himself to get. Fever had blanched Brock's face, leaving him pallid and slimy with sweat. His breathing was shallow and ragged, panting in and out of his ruined lips.

Danny had to admit, he'd expected the man to die during the night.

"Well, you did your part," Danny said, trying to talk without tasting the air. "I suppose it's our turn."

One eye fluttered open—the other still scabbed shut—and a bloodshot blue eye rolled around the room.

"Jenn? It's coming. Something's coming," he slurred. He paused and then dropped his voice to a fearful whisper. "I can feel it. I can hear it. I'm scared, Jenn."

Danny retreated a step and then made himself stop. He tried to shove the disgust and irritation away to find some compassion, or at least pity. There was nothing. Maybe he *was* more wolf than he liked to admit.

"There's nothing, Brock," he said, trying to be reassuring. "You're safe. There's no dogs here."

Brock squinted at him, angling his head to try and bring Danny into focus. "It wasn't a dog," he said. "It wasn't. I *saw* it."

"Of course it was," Danny said, making himself crouch down next to the couch. He balanced on the balls of his feet, his weight pulling the muscles in the backs of his thighs tight. "It was a big dog. Everyone saw it. They chased it off."

The correction got Brock distressed. He shook his head, mumbling about a monster, and tried to push himself up on his broken arm. A surprised whine escaped him, and he collapsed back onto the sofa, fresh blood and new stench seeping through his bandages.

"I saw him. It's coming… something's coming."

"Not for you," Danny said.

It didn't help. The fear followed Brock down into a feverish stupor, his mouth shaping illegible pleas that something not hear him. It made Danny's gums ache, his fangs pushing down. There was something oppressive about the sour smell. It put Danny's hackles up.

He pulled back and pushed himself upright, then walked over to the window to watch for Adil. It was a relief when he saw the white van sliding down the road and up onto the pavement. Danny didn't particularly want to go out into the cold, trying to get a dying man to a hospital that might or might not even be up and running. He wanted to be in this room even less.

"Not long now," he said, for the sake of hearing his own voice. Something other than the rasp and rattle of Brock's fever-full lungs. "We'll get you to hospital before the full moon, you don't have to worry about… dogs. We'll get you there."

Gregor was going to be hunting different prey that night.

FRESH BLOOD was seeping through Brock's bandages by the time they got him down the stairs and into the van. They'd tried their best, but a makeshift stretcher and icy footing had made it impossible to avoid jostling the bag of Brock-bones they were carrying. It had been a blessing in a way—the pain had knocked Brock out.

There were divots in the floor of the van to strap down boxes for deliveries. They used them to tie Brock down, lacing padded ropes across his chest and below his knees. It probably wasn't how you should transport an injured man, but it was the best they could do. Once they were done, Bill rubbed his hand over his head. Stubble was growing in in a half-moon, rasping against his palm.

"Look," he said. "I'm sorry, but this is where I leave you. My wife doesn't want me out there, not with the city still shut down."

He looked at Jenny apologetically. She glared at him. "Chickenshit," she snapped. "Go on, then."

Danny swallowed an inappropriate bubble of laughter and shrugged his helplessness when Bill turned to him. "Go home," he said. "Tell your wife we appreciate everything you could do."

Relieved at the out, Bill scrambled out the back of the truck. His trainers slid on the ice, and he grabbed the door for balance, his arm jerking as he swung from it.

"Be careful not to fall," Jenny said. "We'll not be coming back for you!"

He hauled himself up and shuffled toward the pavement, sliding his feet over the ice like he was an ungainly skater. Danny leaned out and grabbed the doors of the truck, swinging them shut with a wrench.

"I'll stay back here," Jenny said, kneeling next to Brock. "You go keep Adil company." She added, mouthing the words silently, *He's nervous.*

Danny climbed between the seats, hunching his long frame over to fit. In the driver's seat, Adil was wearing a striped wooly hat, the flaps pulled down over his ears, and a pair of heavy leather gloves.

"No heat, no music," he said, catching Danny looking at him. Chapped lips tilted in a nervous smile, his gloved fingers beating out a tattoo on the steering wheel. "We've got a quarter of a tank, and none of the garages have any petrol left."

Danny slid down into the seat, tugged the seat belt over his chest, and clicked it home.

"I don't think the police are going to be out." Adil turned the key, and the engine coughed itself back into silence. Leaning forward over the wheel, as if that would help, he tried again. It took three tries before the cold engine reluctantly turned over.

"I'm more worried about going through the window," Danny said. It wouldn't kill him. It wouldn't be pleasant either.

Adil took his hat off and scrubbed his fingers through his hair, sweat making it stand on end.

"I think I'd rather get killed than end up like him," he said, jerking his head toward the back of the van. "I wouldn't want to be injured, stuck in a car, and freezing to death—no idea if anyone is going to come and get me."

"Cheerful thought," Danny said.

Adil shrugged and pulled his hat back on. "My babba? He fought in World War II, and some of his stories are brutal. When something interrupts society, things get ugly. Look at this place? Society: Interrupted."

"It's just weather."

"I bet the mammoths said that about the Ice Age. Still fucked them up." Adil gingerly touched the accelerator and released the handbrake, coaxing the truck forward on the ice. It bumped down off the curb and spun. It wasn't a skid, just a slow pirouette like a hippo on ice. Adil swore under his breath, heartfelt and re-petitive, as he fought the wheel to get the vehicle back under control.

That was the end of conversation for the drive. Other than the occasional panic-driven curse, Adil was preoccupied with alternately telling the car to behave and informing the universe that he didn't like this.

It took over an hour to travel a few miles through the frozen-over city, melting the ice under the truck's tires and feeling the crunch of new crystals catch at the tires. Twice they gently crashed into cars left on the side of the road, scraping ice and paint off. Each time Danny and Adil had to scramble out, Jenny leaving Brock's side to wriggle in behind the wheel, and push it back into the road.

The first time they left a note; the second their hands were too cold to fumble with the pen.

"I'm worried about Brock," Jenny said, squirming between the seats as Danny and Adil got back in. She wiped the hair back from her face, shivering in layers of oversized sweaters, and then cupped her hands in front of her mouth to breathe on her fingers. Steam eddied between her fingers as she spoke. "It's freezing. There's frost on the blankets, but he's hot to touch. His fever is so high. He needs pills, treatment, something."

Adil mopped cold rain and sweat off his face with his hat. "We'll get there. It's just slow going."

The rain was coming down sideways, driven along the street like needles by a wind strong enough that Danny could feel it pushing against the van. Getting to the hospital was looking unlikely. Danny took his glasses off and polished the lens on his sleeve. He wasn't sure they could even get *back* to the flats.

Another mile, he decided. If they didn't hit cleared roads by then, he'd talk Jenny into going back. Or try. He leaned forward as Adil started inching forward again, bracing his hands on the dashboard, and squinted into the field of white. When the first hailstone hit the window with a smack, big as an egg, he jerked back.

"Shit," he said.

Another hailstone bounced off the hood of the truck, followed by a torrent of them. They hammered against the car, big enough and hard enough to dent the metal when they hit. Adil squawked and hit the brakes. The truck executed another slow spin and cracked into a bollard on Danny's side, his door deforming under the impact. The plastic cover cracked and popped in at him.

In the back Jenny yelped in dismay and Brock groaned.

"Sorry, sorry," Adil blurted, snatching his hands off the wheel and holding them up.

A hailstone, round and jagged as a white stone, caught the windscreen and punched through. Danny threw up his arm, catching the projectile on his forearm before it could hit Adil's face. Hot, cracking pain jarred up into his armpit, making his ribs ache in sympathy. The hailstone dropped into the footwell, already melting, and the windscreen shattered in on them in a thousand diamonds of safety glass.

Danny's fingers were refusing to work just yet—it was weird how numb could hurt. He twisted around, grabbing Adil's shoulder with his good hand.

"In the back," he ordered, hauling him up and shoving him through as hailstones shot into the cab and bounced. "Now."

Adil caught one on the meat of his hip, jerking at the impact. The seat belt caught over Danny's chest as he went to follow. He swore to himself as he fumbled the catch, hailstones battering against his shoulders and stomach. The seat belt finally unlatched, hissing back into its housing, and he scrambled through to join the others.

"Are you all right?" Jenny asked, voice pitched to be heard over the battering hailstones. It had gone dark, but Danny could see the rim of white shining around her wide eyes.

He leaned against the back of his seat, rubbing his hand over his chest. His lungs were cramped up, unwilling to take in enough air to answer her. So he just nodded, waving away her worry. She didn't look convinced but crawled over to check on Adil first.

Danny rubbed his chest until it didn't ache to breathe anymore. He took his glasses off to check them. The leg was crooked, the screw holding the hinge in place creaking as he twisted it back into place.

Most of the time it didn't bother him. Half the people he knew wore glasses at one point or another. It was only among wolves that nearsightedness was a novelty. Besides, the dog could see fine and had a nose that could make up for any squinting.

The wolf winter was no place for the weak; that's why the prophets didn't like dogs. That's what they said anyhow.

He put his glasses back on, fidgeting with the fit until they were more or less straight. Hailstones were still hammering down on the truck, fist-sized dents dimpling the metal. The sound was brutal, rattling around his head and bouncing off his eardrums. Some of them made it through the seats, bouncing along the floor of the van.

"Adil, you okay?" he asked.

"Yeah," Adil said after a second. He propped himself up, weight on his undented hip. "I'm okay. Bloody hell, Mum's going to kill me."

Danny snorted a laugh and tilted his head back, waiting for the assault by the weather to ease off. It lasted longer than seemed possible for a hailstorm, but eventually the hammer blows turned into taps and then faded into nothing.

"I think it's stopped," Jenny said. "We can—"

"No," Danny said. "We need to go back. There's no way we're going to get through to the hospital like this."

"The weather's let up now," she protested. "We have to *try.*"

Danny shook his head. "I'm not getting you and Adil killed trying to get Brock to a hospital. We tried our best. Now we're done."

She glared at him, the shadow of her chin tilting stubbornly. "So is this revenge because he beat you up? Or because he fucked your girlfriend? Either way, you're not—"

Danny interrupted her. "He's dying." In the confined space of the van, his voice sounded angrier than he'd meant it to. It made Jenny flinch in wounded surprise, although he couldn't tell if it was from the tone or the content. He breathed in through his nose and struggled to pull his temper back. It wasn't easy. He was cold, he hurt, and the weird stink of Brock's injuries was sweating out of him despite the cold. "Look at him, Jenny. He's torn up, he's lost a lot of blood, and his fever is cooking him from the inside out. If he were an animal, we'd put him out of his misery."

Jenny slapped the flat of her hand against the floor. "He's not some manky Scottish sheep," she said. "He needs help. We have to get him help. That's what people do. We can't just… just take him back and *wait* for him to—We can't. Adil? You'll go on?"

Under the sudden focus of Jenny's attention, Adil spluttered unhappily. He rubbed his hands together, his fingers wet and blotchy red, as he tried to wriggle around an answer. When there was no way out, he finally admitted, "I can't. The roads are terrifying, and the van's a mess. What if we get another couple of miles and this happens again? We could be stuck out here overnight. I don't want to freeze, Jenny, and I don't want my mum and my brother scared because I don't come home. I'm sorry. No."

His refusal made Jenny's face drop for a second, but she wasn't going to admit she'd lost.

"Fine," she snapped. Crawling over to Brock, she yanked at the straps holding him down, swearing snottily when the wet fabric resisted untying. "I'll get him there myself."

"Don't be an idiot," Danny said, pushing himself up onto his knees. He tried to catch Jenny's hands, getting his fingers slapped for his troubles. "What good will you freezing to death do him?"

Jenny shoved him, the heels of her hands punching into his shoulders. "At least I'm doing *something*." Her voice cracked, and she stopped to swallow hard. "We have to do something."

She went back to tugging at the knots, her shoulders hunched and mouth pressed in a hard line. Danny gave up for now. There was no point arguing about it— he wasn't going to let her go off into the snow on her own, no matter what she wanted.

They sat in tense silence for a minute, watching Jenny fight with the knots. Eventually Adil looked up, screwing his nose up as he squinted up at the battered roof. "It's stopped."

Danny pulled himself up, hunched over to stop from banging his head, and shuffled down to the back. The battering they'd gotten had warped the lock, jamming the doors shut. Danny had to put his shoulder to it to ram it open, nearly toppling out into the street when it finally popped. The wind saved him, shoving him back inside.

The idea that it might be more than coincidence snuck through his brain on chilly feet. Maybe a dog was close enough to a wolf for Fenrir and his winter? He shuddered that away as the result of spending too much time with Jack.

It might have stopped hailing, but snow had rolled in to take over. The street was a field of white, stirred into ribbons and knots by the wind. Danny could barely see his hand in front of his face, and it was cold enough he could feel his breath freezing on his lips.

"Jenny," he said, looking over at her. Snow had already blown into the van, setting in fat, white flakes on Jenny's hair and the blankets covering Brock. "We have to go back."

Her lips folded in against each other in a tight, resentful line, but she couldn't avoid nodding. "Okay." She wiped her fingers under her eyes, stretching the exhaustion-bruised skin out at the corners. "We still have to help him. He needs help, Danny. We can't just leave him like this."

"We won't," Danny said. "But it won't help him if we get killed."

Adil breathed a sigh of relief at the resolution and scrambled up back into the cab. He pulled his sleeve down over his hands and wiped the chunks of ice and

shattered glass off the driver's seat. While he was doing that, Danny hopped out the back and kicked snow
out from under the tires. Under the fluffy crunch of top
snow, he had to dig in with the heel of his boot to break
the ice. It broke a sweat under his coat, a layer of slimy
chill against his skin.

He could have sworn even that smelled of Brock's
sickness, although sweating it out left his skin less itchy
on his bones.

"You ready?" he asked.

"Yeah," Adil said. He twisted around in his seat,
arm hooked around the headrest. "You sure you're
okay pushing on your own?"

Danny slammed one of the doors shut, the warped
metal catching. "We don't have much choice. Don't
worry. If I get a hernia, I won't sue."

He set his shoulder against the door, feet braced
in the rutted snow, and threw his weight into it as Adil
turned the key. Jack could probably have lifted the
van's rear end, even with people in it, but Danny was
still strong enough to punt it out of the miring snow. Or
he would have been if the engine had caught. As it was,
the engine spluttered and died, while Danny's shove
bumped it off the curb with a final sounding crack. His
hands slid on the metal, and he went down on his knees
in the snow, the cold jolt of it jarring up to his skull.

"Shit," Adil said. "Danny, what was that?"

Since he was already on his knees, Danny lowered
himself gingerly onto his stomach. When he'd bought
the coat a year ago, the clerk in Mountain Warehouse
had claimed it was snowproof. They might have been
wrong about that.

Cold seeping damply through his skin, Danny
squinted under the van. The suspension was gone, just

snapped in half, and something was dripping from the engine. Without getting all the way under, all he could swear was that it *wasn't* oil. Brake fluid or petrol—neither made the van more drivable.

"It's dead," he said, pushing into a squat. "We're going to have to walk back."

Chapter Sixteen

AFTER ABOUT a mile, Brock came round enough to scream. He thrashed against the ropes holding him in place, blood oozing wetly from his leg and leaving a trail in the snow. The bright smears of red didn't last long before the snow covered them. A few curtains twitched as they staggered past houses with snow drifts up the windows, but no one came out to see if they could help.

Head down, trying to take the majority of Brock's weight, Danny staggered into a wind that threatened to knock him off his feet. It whistled through the narrow streets, scooping up debris and tossing it back and forth. A garden gnome bounced across the road and shattered against a gatepost, splinters of concrete flying across the road.

"It's getting worse," Adil said, shouting against a wind that was stealing the words from his lips. He stopped for a second, trying to catch his balance as the wind changed direction. His teeth were chattering so hard he could hardly get the words out. "We need to find shelter."

Jenny clung to a fence, arm hooked around the post. Her hair had whipped out of her braid and was frozen in a mat of tangles to her face. "Maybe we could find an empty house?"

"It's not much further to the flats," Danny said. He reached up and rubbed his glasses, scraping the ice off the lens with his gloved thumb. "I'd rather get there if we can. It's going to be a cold night. I'd rather not spend it snowed in at an empty house. Just a bit further."

With a sigh, Jenny started plodding forward again. She used the fences and low walls to support her against the wind.

"It's coming," Brock moaned. He'd stopped thrashing, lying still in the cocoon of blankets and coats. His swollen eyelids had finally peeled open, revealing a milky cornea floating off-center in the blood-stained white, and his eyes rolled nervously. "...feel it coming."

Still clinging to a gate with one hand, Jenny stretched out to pat Brock's shoulder reassuringly with a mittened hand. "Nothing's coming, Brock. You're safe. I promise."

Danny wasn't sure about that. He couldn't smell anything on the air but snow, but the nape of his neck was crawling with an atavistic *wrong* reaction. Something was out there.

"Just keep moving," he said.

They staggered forward. Brock shuddered and moaned, whimpering about something out there wanting him, but at least he wasn't screaming anymore. They turned to cross the road, grunting as they lifted

Brock's stretcher to fit him between the parked cars. Adil misjudged the curb and tripped, grunting as he jarred his knee. Brock listed dangerously to the side, his weight on the wet, roughly tied knots, and Jenny screamed.

Struggling to right Brock before he fell, Danny nearly missed the blur in the snow. It was a white shadow against the white background, worth noting only because it was moving against the snow. He caught sight of it and hesitated, unsure how to react, a second too long. One long, white arm lashed out, and Danny felt heat wash over him. When he looked down, blood was soaking through the torn, puffy fabric of his jacket.

"Danny?" Jenny gasped. "What happened? You're bleeding."

The wind picked up, frothing the snow into a wall of white. Danny could barely see Adil at the other end of the stretch, never mind Jenny.

"Stay where you are, Jenn," he ordered. "I'm fine."

"All right," she said nervously, then gasped hard. "Oh."

"What's wrong?" No answer. "Jenn? Jenny!"

When she finally answered her voice was shaky, but clear. "I'm okay. Something just hit me. I can't even see what it was, or you."

The pale shape leaped onto a car, the hood creaking under the impact of its paws, and Danny caught the bony jut of its jaws in profile. Then it was gone again.

"Jenn? Come toward my voice," he said. "Grab hold of my coat, okay? Then we can get moving again. We need to get in somewhere safe before the storm gets worse."

He kept talking, voice tense but carefully confident, until he felt her grab the back of his jacket. Adil had gotten back to his feet, limping on his injured leg as they crossed the road. Without the thin protection of the cars and houses, the wind pushed them into a horizontal.

Twice more the shadow came lunging out of the snow. Danny yanked Adil out of the way once, tugging back on Brock's stretcher like it was a leash, and put himself between it and Jenny the second time. Sharp teeth snapped shut on his arm, grinding down. He dropped Brock—mustering enough sympathy to wince at the man's howl of pain—and yanked his arm in. The jaws let go before he could get a good look, but he had an impression of something disturbingly *wrong*: fever-thin flesh over bone, patchy hair, eyes deep set and hateful.

At his back, Jenny tugged at his coat anxiously. "What happened?"

Blood was running down his arm, but the layers of sleeve soaked it up before it could drip. He crouched down, jerking Jenny's arm when he forgot to warn her, and grabbed Brock's stretcher again. "Something caught my arm," he said. "I'm sorry. I think I was wrong. We need to get into shelter before this gets worse."

They got over the road. Danny was neck itchingly aware of the shadow in the snow, but being almost seen seemed to have given it cause to bide its time. They found an empty house, the frosted windows bare of blinds and no "fuck off" when they banged on the door, and Danny kicked the door open.

"Misspent youth?" Adil asked as the door bounced open, ripping the lock out of the jamb.

Danny laughed, relieved to actually say something that wasn't a lie. "Youth spent in an old house with wood doors," he said. "You couldn't go to the bog without having to force a door."

They staggered in and set Brock down on the floor in his stretcher. He was sealed in with a layer of frost on the outer layers. Adil peeled his fingers off the poles, joints stiff with the cold, and sat down on a dusty chair.

"We should see if there's a bed," Jenny said, breathing into her hands and pressing her warmed palms to her face. "He can't be comfortable—Oh God, Danny, your chest."

He looked down. The front of his coat was crusted red with blood, tufts of lining sticking out gorily. "It looks worse than it is," he said, poking his fingers through the gash. His chest was too cold to hurt much, but he felt the scab of blood crack and itch. "It's just a scrape. Don't move Brock. I'm going to head on and get back to the flat. It'll be easier if I don't have to worry about Brock."

Or either of them.

HE STAYED in his skin. The dog would have had an easier time in the snow, but it was under suspicion of being a man-killer, and besides, Danny was getting tired of sneaking in naked to places. He took his glasses off and tucked them into the inside pocket of his coat. It turned the world into a blur, but the storm was bad enough it made little difference. Once the glasses were zipped in, he stripped the bloody coat off and tied it around his waist. It was cold, but he could move easier without the bulky down limiting his movements.

Telephone poles swayed and creaked along the street, the strung-taut wires singing as the wind plucked them. It was already dark and getting darker.

Danny loped along the street, long legs eating up the ground. He could feel the hunter in the snow watching him, the sense of a predator's breath on his heels, and he was wolf enough to object to being prey. It put his hackles on end, flooded his mouth with spit as his teeth ached to be fangs.

At least, though, it was hunting him and not Jenny or Adil.

It wasn't Gregor. He was the same tawny color as Jack, and solid with muscle. Not white and fever-boned. Danny had seen him hunt too. It was vicious but brutally efficient. Gregor didn't have the patience to harry.

A snarl trickled in under the storm. Danny spun to face it, and the wolf lunged past him, ice-coated jaws snapping on the way past. The sharp point of its canine caught his hand, laying it open, and then it was gone. Danny snarled after it, giving the dog's frustration voice.

He lifted his hand to his mouth, sucking at the raw meat of it. It tasted *rancid*. Danny pulled his mouth away, grimacing, and spat the taste onto the snow.

"If you aren't going to brush your teeth," Danny yelled into the wind, "at least chew a bone."

The hunter lurked out in the snow, moving restlessly with the wind. Danny wiped his bloody hand on his jeans and started running again. It wasn't too far to the flat from here. Once he got there, if Jack wanted to keep a roof over his head, he could drag his ass out and help.

There was something irritating about how reassuring the thought of Jack was.

It went for him once again, leaving a handful of cold fur in Danny's fist and taking the sleeve of his coat with it; then it faded back into the storm. After a few minutes Danny heard an animal shriek its surprised last in a nearby street. He stopped, breath panting out of him in white, wet clouds, and wiped his face on his sleeve.

It sounded like the hunter had found easier prey, but the skin along Danny's back was still crawling with nerves. He didn't trust the reprieve, but his only options were to keep going or go back. So he kept going. Halfway across the road, the hunter came lurching out of the snow.

There was something wrong about the way it moved—stiff and angular—but it was on Danny before he had time to pinpoint exactly what was bothering him. The heavy body landed on his back, claws digging into his shoulders and teeth raking at his scalp.

Danny got his arms under him, palms sinking into the snow until they hit the road, and pushed up. The hunter jumped off him, kicking up snow, and Danny grabbed its leg. The skin slid under his hand, wet and slimy, and then it kicked back into his face. A heel caught his chin, snapping his jaw shut hard enough he tasted blood, and he dropped back into the snow. His head rattled uneasily, thoughts scattered and limbs refusing to listen.

The blur of white and teeth loomed over him, eyes glittering dimly in deep-set sockets. Drool dripped hot on his face, and its breath stank of carrion and ripe acid. He swung his arm up, bracing himself for the pain, but instead of biting down, the hunter jerked its head up at the sound of an approaching howl.

It scrambled off Danny and fled, the storm closing behind it and throwing snow over its tracks.

Rolling over onto his side, Danny had managed to get up onto his knees by the time Jack came loping down the street. The wolf knocked him back down again, cold nose snorting against his neck and poking at his stomach and ribs. Kill zones.

Danny laughed, the sound catching as his ribs ached, and scrubbed his fingers over Jack's sharp ears. It made Jack grumble and shake his head, nipping Danny's fingertips with sharp teeth. The bite turned into a kiss of sorts as Jack shifted into his skin, lips against Danny's fingers.

"You smell like you rolled in shit," Jack growled. He grabbed Danny and pulled him up into a rough hug, twisting his hand in the back of Danny's shirt to shake him at the same time. "Idiot. See what your humans get you?"

Leaning into the chill length of muscle and hard flesh, Danny ignored the last bit. He hooked an arm around Jack's neck, fingers digging into his shoulder. "That wasn't Gregor."

The wide shoulders hunched under Danny's arm. "Like I said—he had supporters."

Danny leaned back, leaving a smear of blood on Jack's face.

"I didn't recognize it," Danny said, reaching up and gingerly working his fingers through his hair. The lacerations stung, but he should have lost half his scalp. The last fight he'd been in where a wolf got their jaws on his head, he'd cracked his skull and bled from his ears for a couple of days.

"You've been gone a long time."

Maybe. Wolves joined the pack sometimes, working their way up over the wall, but he couldn't imagine the Numitor letting the strange, stiff wolf be blooded in. His poking fingers bumped something tangled in his hair. He tugged on it, wincing at the pain, and came away with a snaggle of black curls and a broken, black-ened fang.

He had to fight the urge to flick the thing away from him. Wolves didn't lose teeth, not like this—in a rotting crumble. Instead, he shoved it into his pocket.

"It was strange," he said. "There was something wrong with that wolf."

Jack scrubbed his cheek over Danny's shoulder, then hauled them both to their feet. They hunched to-gether against the wind, braced against the shove of it. "There're wolves who'd say that you were strange, Danny Dog," he said. After a second, he cracked a sharp smile. "More who'd say there was something wrong with me."

It hung in the air between them, an admission and an awkward offering of intimacy. The part of Danny that had run far and fast from the wolves, and their "bite it or ignore it" approach to problems, wanted to chew on it. Except it was cold, his bones were jittering with adrenaline, and whatever problem the Numitor had with Jack fucking men, Danny didn't share it. Maybe, just this once, he could just let it go.

There was blood in Danny's ears, itching as it trickled down toward the drum. He scrubbed it roughly with the heel of his hand.

"I think you're okay," he said.

Jack laughed, a harsh bark of sound. The wind had flattened his short hair to his scalp, snow melting and freezing against his skin. "Touching," he mocked. "Your time with the humans has made you a poet."

"Changed my mind," Danny said. His voice was clipped with the cold, more irritated sounding than he was. "You're a dick. That's what's wrong with you."

He shook himself and took a deep breath, the icy air making his lungs cramp up in his chest. It helped clear the fog of fight and pain from his head though He turned around, snow crunching, and stared back the way he'd come. Other than where the fight had flattened the snow in a sludgy oval of ice and blood, his trail had been filled in. He could see shadows of pink here and there, covered over by a thin coat of fresh fall, but in a minute they'd be gone too.

"We need to go and get the others—I left them holed up in a house back there," he said. "With both of us here, that wolf—whoever it was—should steer clear."

An irritated grumble rolled through Jack's chest at Danny's dodge of Gregor's name. He didn't argue the point, though. Not *that* point, anyhow.

"They'll have to stay where you left them," he said. "At least until tomorrow."

Danny grimaced in frustration. "I'm not *leaving*," he snapped. "If you won't help, I'll get them myself. Go piss up a lamppost—"

Jack grabbed the dangling sleeve of his coat and yanked him back, tearing the fabric of his jacket more. Lumps of stained down were teased loose by the wind, blown away into the storm.

"There's no time," Jack said. "The moon is rising."

No. Danny wiped his nose on his fingers and looked up. It was still bright, the sky white with snow and frost.

"It's not that late," he said.

Jack cupped his hand around the back of Danny's neck, pulling him close enough they could taste each other's breath. His eyes, framed by frost-clumped lashes, were still wolf eyes. "It is," he said. "Selene's eye is open, and it's on us. You might insist on having human friends, but do you want to explain to them that you're not?"

Shit. Danny pulled away from Jack enough to scan the sky again. He couldn't see the moon, but now Jack had said.... The ache in his bones was from more than a reaction to a brawl. His blood was hot with the need to move, to shift, to run. Once the moon was high enough in the sky, it would be a compulsion instead of an urge.

"If we hurry, we could get them back in time?" It was a question, but he didn't need Jack to answer it. No time. Even if they got them all back to the flats—and explained naked Jack ignoring the snow—how would he explain disappearing again? "I can't just leave them."

Jack let him go, giving him an impatient shove forward. "Then leave me," he said. "Escort your pets home like a good dog. I need to find and kill my brother, not play shepherd."

He dropped back into wolfskin and turned his tail to Danny, loping away into the storm. Danny hesitated, guilt and responsibility tugging at him like wires hooked in his ribs. He was a dog, after all; loyalty was genetic. Except Jack had first claim on it, had done since he'd dragged Danny away from the fire and his girlfriend that night in the Highlands.

Jenny would be fine until morning. They were as safe in the house as they were at the flats, maybe even safer since Gregor knew the flats were Danny's territory. It was a sketchy justification, but it was all Danny had.

Hanging on to human form by his fingertips—the moon daze wanted him to turn, and sing, but it was easier to think skin side if he needed to—he ran after the smudge of Jack fur disappearing into the blizzard.

Chapter Seventeen

THE BITCH goddess was running blind tonight, the winter a veil between her and the world beneath. Jack could still feel her call in his blood, like razors and honey over his bones and a silken hand on his fur.

It felt good. Better than was safe. The bitch was a siren, calling her hounds to a mad run that would burst their hearts and crack their bones. It had been years since Jack lost himself to the moon, but every time it rose he *longed* to.

"Jack." The sound of Danny's voice rubbed down Jack's back, all softened Scottish burr and prickly temper. It made Jack shudder under the wolf's skin, the lazy wash of lust pulling the man out of him for a second. He turned a pointed nose over his shoulder and watched....

His lover? His mate? The first was too human for Jack, and he knew that the second would make Danny shy away just because it was the pack.

His. That would do. Jack watched Danny scramble over the low fence, staggering as snow and matted grasses caught at his feet. There was blood on the side of his face, flaking scabs of it. It was too cold to have much scent, but the sight of it still jarred a growl out of Jack's chest. When his da had exiled him, he'd bent his head and let the pack slip away from him without a murmur. Gregor should have been satisfied with that, not followed him down here to try and take anything else off him.

"You won. You could have slowed down," Danny grumbled. He dropped into a crouch next to Jack, one hand buried in the heavy ruff of fur around his neck. There was ice in the folds of his jumper, the wool cracking as Danny bent his arm to swipe snow out of his eyes. "It's colder tonight. Do you really think Jenny and the others will be okay?"

Jack wasn't going to try and find his skin just to talk about the fate of three humans. He shoved his shoulder against Danny's side, knocking him to his knees on the ground, and huffed his impatience with the question.

Irritation came easily this close to the hunt. Anger fed the Wild, making it prick at the edges of his senses, but the Wild wanted to listen to Selene.

No matter how many times the wolves showed their bellies to Fenrir, their curse still belonged to Selene. It was the leash around their throat, and one reason they wanted to sink their teeth in her soft belly. Dogs wore collars, not wolves.

Jack took a deep breath. It filled his lungs with the smell of Danny and snow, cool and calm things. The moon had risen, and it was time to add their own voices to the bitch's song. He threw his head back and howled, the sound melancholy with no pack to join in. The wind caught it and spooled it out, dragging the sound away from Jack.

Then Danny took a deep breath, chest swelling against Jack's ribs, and added his voice to the song. The sound was rough and thin from a human throat, all pitch and no growl, lacking the subtle harmonics of a wolf, but it was enough. Jack wasn't alone. His pack was diminished, but not gone.

And it was blood that bound the pack.

He shouldered out from under Danny's arm and growled in command, the Wild catching between his teeth. It reached down under the human skin until it found the dog's fur, catching it up to the surface. Brown eyes cracked and bled amber, his bones creaking under his skin. Danny cursed him and scrambled away from him, stripping out of his clothes with suddenly clumsy hands.

For a second he was naked, all long, pale body and scruffy curls the wind was tangling over that pretty face. He shivered under the bite of the wind, but it was from a chill, not the fact he was freezing. How had he ever managed to pretend he was human for a day, never mind five years?

Then the shift bent Danny's back and lengthened his jaw. Coarse fur thickened over spare muscle and lanky bones as he dropped to all fours in the snow. In this form, despite the long, courser's legs on him, he was a shoulder shorter than Jack's wolf.

Good. Jack flagged his tail and let a low snarl trickle out of his throat, staring at Danny until the dog pinned its ears and tucked its heel in obedient submission. Satisfied, Jack relaxed his posture and lifted his head to sniff the air.

He howled again, Danny throwing his head back to follow suit. Out in the snowy night, other voices rose in yipping chorus. Gregor. The brother he should have eaten in the womb, before twelve minutes began the fulcrum of their lives.

Later he'd sink his teeth into Gregor's throat, stealing back those twelve minutes and any other years he had left. For now, they let their voices rise into the sky together.

Let Selene hear them worship; it would make her run faster.

THE WORLD was different through the lens of the Wild. On one level the hunt played out through scrubby woodland and over fields where dirt and mud had frozen into knives. They paid the Wild lip service with rabbit blood and stringy, gamy squirrel meat, drank dank, earthy water, and ate beetles. On another they clashed like gods—with gods—amongst the massive, ancient oaks of the primeval English forest. A vast elk, antlers that spanned twelve foot from razor tip to tip, rattling the trees, fled ahead of the pack that had spawned all other packs. Jack could hear them out there, howling strange howls somewhere—somewhen—far away.

It was a world that Danny, a ragged shadow on the wolf's heels, would never see. It was a world that only wanted the wolf. There was no place for the man. Here a wolf could run forever, loping on huge silent paws through the mulch.

Until they caught the scent of prey—hormone-rich piss, grass, fear, and meat. Danny caught the scent as well, his breath huffing in with interest. He lurched forward, leaping over a tangle of fallen branches. Jack snarled his disapproval and went after him, barreling into the dog's side and sending him sprawling in the snow. The dog grunted, breath squeezed out of its lungs by the weight on it, and twisted around to snap at Jack.

All he got was a mouthful of fur, but Jack still snapped a reproof at him. Sharp white teeth clicked together just a hair in front of the black, wet nose. Danny whined an apology, laying his ears flat and licking at black wolf lips in apology.

Through the Wild, Jack could see the ghost of a wolf in Danny's shadow. It had heavy shoulders and sharper ears. Wolves didn't have words, but Jack's will hammered down the fragile tangles of pack and history that tied them together. They both saw a splash of images: shadows circling in the grass, wary deer unmoving, and raw strips of liver and lights fresh on the mud.

Still. Wait. Clever hunters.

Danny laid his ears back briefly but huffed his submission. Jack stepped back and let him scramble to his feet. They sloped to the scrub of briars that sheltered them, Danny panted eagerly, twitching with anticipation, as he saw the pod of deer grazing on the frost-wilted leaves of a blighted crop. They were muddy russet, tails flashing white and ears rotating like radar dishes.

Spit flooded Jack's mouth, dripping like froth from his lolling tongue. He shifted his weight forward, eyes fixed on the high, lean flanks. The stag twitched his head up, nostrils flaring red, and strings of ivy twisted in its antlers. Last year they had probably been fat-marbled and well-fed, destined for the dinner table. Now they were sinewy and wary, prey destined to be eaten on the hoof.

The wind shifted, and the deer lifted their heads, noses flaring red as they caught the scent of their death.

One of the younger hinds barked, a low, vibrating sound, and the pod took off as if they'd been goosed.

The flash of hooves and white haunches twitched something wired directly into Jack's bones and muscles, the urge to *chase* hitting him in the chest with enough force to make him *move*. He shoved through the brambles, losing hair to the thorns, and then Danny raced past him. Heavy muscles and long legs sent him flying over the snow, snow spraying where his paws touched down. It was more like leaping than running, like all he needed was a touch of the Wild to fly.

The deer scattered, but Danny was already among them. Hooves kicked around his ears, catching him a bruising, glancing blow on the shoulder. He snapped at all of them, sharp teeth catching on bony shanks and ripping tough hide. It wasn't enough to take any of them down, but one snapping lunge caught on a hind's leg. An incisor sliced the tough hide, carving down to bone and hooking into tendon.

The deer dropped to the ground with an almost human scream, legs flopping uselessly on the ground as it tried to crawl away. Jack ended it, putting his teeth in its throat. Blood in his mouth tasted like musky candy, potent as any human drug.

It died quickly, gurgling out its life in splurts and gasps. He held on, squeezing the breath out of it, until it finally stilled. Whatever animating force lived in prey beasts, some cud-chewing version of the Wild, vanished, and all that was left was meat. Unlocking his jaws, Jack moved to the still gurgling gut and ripped it open from anus to breast bone. Its insides spilled out in a hot, vivid tangle, melting the snow where they landed.

Jack reached down inside and dragged his skin out from under the fur. The change didn't feel natural this time, the human shape of him fitting oddly around a mind more than half-seduced into believing it was just a wolf. He dug his fingers into the deer's guts and pulled out the wet, purple-red richness of liver, tossing it to Danny.

"Fast as fuck, aren't you?" he said. The sound of his voice made Danny's ears twitch, but it wasn't enough to distract him from gulping down the liver. "The world has changed, and we're the king of the castle now. Or we will be, soon enough."

Not the castle, though. The Wild.

Jack licked the blood off his hands, iron sharp on his tongue, and stood up. The rank on his skin looked raw and fresh in the moonlight, like wet ink running down his body. The ash in it still burned sometimes, an itch too far under the skin to reach except with claws. It had seemed worth it once, but it was just patterns on his skin.

Unless he took back the meaning.

"Gregor," he yelled, voice cracking. At his feet Danny whined and looked up from his liver, ears pinned against the wind. "You said you wanted a fight. I turned up, little brother."

For a second, the only reply was the cold pant of Fenrir's breath stirring the snow. Then the heavy-shouldered, tawny wolf stepped out of shadows opposite the clearing. It shook itself, shedding clumps of frozen snow and fur. He stood in the snow, even his ink the same as Jack's. He didn't look like Jack, not to *Jack*. His hair was too long and had too much red in it, and there was a fading scar on his jaw where he'd lost the flesh a year ago. It was like the first time you saw yourself in a photograph, an undeniable similarity but from an angle that never peered out the bathroom mirror.

"I never doubted you, *little* brother," Gregor said. "You might be a sentimental pervert, but you aren't a coward."

Jack bared his teeth in a humorless grin. "We're the same from our cowlick to our balls, Gregor," he said. "Do you really like women, or do you close your eyes and think of dick just so you can do your duty and make the old man proud?"

A wolf's snarl caught at the edge of Gregor's lip, showing a sharp eyetooth to the night. "At least he *is* proud of me."

As angry as Jack had been for months, he shouldn't have cared what the old man thought. He still flinched, caught on the raw spot where their father's regard had been. So he did what he always did and evened out his pain with Gregor's. Maybe in this they weren't the same, but they would be equal.

"He's proud of your cock," he said flatly. "That doesn't mean he's proud of you, Gregor."

The jibe struck home, drawing the same flinch out of Gregor. After a second, his twin shrugged impatiently.

"Is there any point to this?" he asked. "Now?"

He was right, Jack supposed. They had bickered all these years because the old man refused to let one challenge the other, and now they didn't need his permission. Why try and hurt each other with words, when teeth cut deeper.

At Jack's side, Danny snarled nervously and shoved against Jack's leg. Under the coarse coat, his body was hot as a water bottle. Jack reached down and scruffed him, twisting his fingers in the bristling hackles.

"Danny isn't part of this," he said, narrowing his eyes at Gregor. "Whatever sick game you have been playing, if you win, you leave him be."

Through the veil of snow, Jack could have sworn Gregor looked confused for a second. Maybe it was the idea of leaving anything be. His twin had always been a scab picker and a grudge holder. Whatever the expression had been, it was quickly covered with a sneer.

"Or what?" he asked.

Jack huffed a laugh, breath misting as it left his mouth. "Or no one will ever believe that *you* beat *me* in a fight. Even if you wear my skin home for luck, they'll just think you cheated."

He wasn't *that* much better than Gregor. Over the years, he'd usually had the edge in a brawl, but when it came down to it, that wasn't even twelve minutes' worth of an edge. It didn't matter. What mattered was wolves and gossip. If Jack walked back up the Wall and announced he was the Numitor's only child, they wouldn't believe him either.

After a sullen pause, Gregor acknowledged that with a grunt.

"I'll leave him alive," he said. "I'll not leave him be. A stray dog playing house with humans will do my cause no good."

Danny snarled at him. It was a dog noise, that snarl, all throttled rage and threat. Slaver bubbled between teeth and off his lips, clotting and freezing in the snow. Wolves growled and postured, but by the time you were that angry, you were already fighting. Jack cuffed Danny around the ear with the back of his hand.

"For once, Danny Dog," he said flatly. "Shut that mouth and know your place."

The dog gave him a sidelong look and tucked its tail. As submission displays went, it was halfhearted. There were times when Jack thought the man was easier to deal with than the dog.

Gregor huffed impatiently, stepping through the cloud of his own breath. "Enough. I didn't run all this way to watch you make a fool of yourself over a dog, little brother. I came to kill you. Now let's get it over with. I want to be back north for the cub's first shift."

Humans talked about their feelings. Wolves just had them. Still, the need for *something* caught in Jack's throat as he stepped away from the big dog. He didn't know what it was, though, just a caught bone of need in his throat, so he thumped the dog roughly.

"Stop collecting humans," he said as he walked away. "They'll get you killed."

There should have been chains to limit their range of movement, binding them to the challenge as Fenrir was—had been—bound, and a priest to speak the words. Neither of them needed the ritual to wind themselves up to murder, not one they'd been planning since they opened their eyes, but there should be something said.

"It would have been an easier life if we didn't hate each other," Jack said.

Gregor shrugged. "But we do."

They shifted at the same time, going for each other in a snarling knot of hair, teeth, and claws. Snow rose up in a powder-dry cloud as they rolled in it, settling in their ruffs and on their backs like grizzle. It was bitter enough the fur crunched between their teeth, but it did nothing to cool their blood. Gregor's fang punctured Jack's nose—painful and bloody, but not fatal—and Jack caught the tip of Gregor's ear between his teeth and took it away. Blood stained the snow in dark puddles and splatters; chunks of fur and skin mulched into the snow.

There was a smug sliver of moonlight caught between the trees—a goddess come to watch.

A snap of powerful jaws caught a leg and bore down, the bone-snap sound echoing over the snow. For a second, closer to his brother than he'd been since they were in the womb, Jack wasn't sure whose teeth and whose leg. The hot splash of pain that poured through exposed marrow cleared that up. He yelped in pain, the weakness startled out of him, and lashed out in vicious panic. His teeth scraped down the side of Gregor's face, gouging his cheek down to the bone and blinding his sharp green eye.

The flood of fluids that filled Jack's mouth tasted like copper, salt, and the wet, slippery flatness of vitreous fluids. He spat it out, lips wrinkling back from the taste.

Both injured, they broke apart and circled each other, Jack hobbling on three legs, awkward in the stained, rucked-up snow, and Gregor twisting his head to keep his unruined eye on Jack. Outside the makeshift ring of the challenge, he could see Danny pacing back and forth. The lanky dog was whining and unsettled.

It was Danny who saw it first, pricked ears flattening hard to his narrow skull. He barked, a jarring, alien sound in the Wild. Jack trusted him enough to take his attention off Gregor for a second and look to see what had upset his dog.

The narrow ribbon of moonlight that he'd seen at the start of the fight was moving, lurching from tree to tree. It was... wrong. Jack let his jaw drop, panting in hot, worried gasps as he tried to taste what it was on the air. Even Gregor, stiff and bristling with suspicion, got into position to watch both Jack and the trees.

From a distance, through the snow, the thin ribbon of pallor had seemed like moonlight. It wasn't. As it got closer, Jack made out the blotchy discoloration that marred it and the tattered, blackened edges that ripped in the wind.

Wrong.

It was a man who hobbled out of the trees on crooked legs, shaggy and ruined. Grizzled hair hung in filth-matted elflocks to wasted shoulders, and a flayed woman hung from his shoulder. An empty arm flapped, and the torn remnants of her mouth lipped at the man's ear like it was telling him something.

Jack had been right—it was a goddess come to watch them fight—he'd just been wrong about *which* goddess. Hel had come early to Winter. A high, strangled noise whined out of his mouth, rattling around the bones of his skull, and was picked up by his twin.

In the depths of the trees, the shadows moved. Hel hadn't come alone.

Chapter Eighteen

JENNY KNELT on a dusty rug in front of the hearth, the corners of the blanket wrapped around her hand as she fed damp logs into the fire. It spluttered and spat, cinders scorching the knees of Jenny's jeans. Smoke belched out in huge, ashy clouds, filling the narrow lounge. Jenny could feel it settling on her hands, like dust, as she drew out the business of rearranging the coals with a poker.

She was so cold that the warmth hurt, turning her skin red and blotchy with radiator burn. It still took an effort of will and a hard jab from her conscience to make her shuffle aside enough to share the heat with the others. Part of her wanted to keep it to herself, just suck it all up and curl up in a corner while she waited for Danny to come back. Like some sort of needy ex-girlfriend lizard person. She snorted out a half laugh at that, rubbing a dusty hand over her face.

"What?" Adil said, shuffling closer to the fire. He held his hands out, and pulled them back as the heat bit at cold-white fingers. Grimacing, he shook his hands and stuck them under his arms for a second before the lure of the fire got too much, and he tried again. "What's so funny?"

"Nothing," Jenny said, shaking her head. Behind them, on a bed of sofa cushions and pillows they'd managed to roll him onto, Brock mumbled and gasped in his sleep. Whatever little bubble of self-loathing humor had briefly distracted Jenny dried up and blew away. "Nothing at all."

She hunched over her knees, not wanting to look at Brock and feeling guilty for not wanting to look at Brock. Not that long ago she'd loved looking at him, the heavy slabs of muscle on his back, the scarred knuckles that he popped when watching TV, even his badly done and sort of regretted tattoos. He was the boy her parents—who'd gotten over their disappointment she was dating a white boy with Danny too quickly to satisfy her desire to rebel—would *never* have approved of.

"I love him," she'd told people, because admitting she'd broken up with Danny because she wanted a hard fuck with a bad boy was out of the question. It wasn't the sort of thing a good girl like her did. Now... she didn't know if someone she'd *loved* was dying badly while she sat and did nothing, or if someone was dying badly because she'd kept him around so she could pretend. She didn't know which was worse.

Adil shuffled closer to the fire, coughing as he breathed in the smoke. "My awa always said we didn't know what a winter was. She was born in Auli, up in the mountains, and when she was a girl—" He broke off to cough, cupping his hands over his mouth. "I used to mouth off that she should have thought herself lucky, that I *wished* we had good skiing in the Lake District. I was a spoiled brat."

Reaching over, Jenny gave his shoulder a gentle shove. "Come on, it's not like you wished this on us," she said, waving a hand at the window. "You wanted a white Christmas and a hill to sled on. Not food drops and dog attacks."

"No," he said, smiling wanly. "Not that."

They sat quietly for a while, listening to the fire pop and the feverish mumbles from Brock. He got louder and louder, his muttering about someone coming sounding almost gleeful now. Eventually Jenny made herself get up and go check on him, hating herself for not being able to do it sooner. She crouched next to him and stroked his hair, the cropped red bristle feeling dry and stiff under her hand. His skin was so hot he wasn't even sweating, and the stains on his bandages weren't red anymore; the cotton was clotted with yellow and brown. It smelled sickly and sweet, reminding her nauseatingly of overripe apples full of wasps.

"Here," she said, trying not to show her disgust as she put water to his lips. "Try and drink something, Brock."

Before the water had just trickled over his cracked lips, through the makeshift stitches. This time he fastened onto the bottle like a baby to a nipple, scabs splitting as he sucked the water down frantically. When Jenny tried to pull it back, surprised at the sudden energy and wondering if that much water was good for him, he grabbed at her with his unslinged arm and dug hard fingers into her wrist.

"Can you hear them?" he asked. His voice was raspy, the words slurring through swollen lips, but he sounded almost... normal. That unwound as he kept going, madness unraveling in his words. "They're waiting for me. I'm late, but I didn't *know.* Did you know, Jenn? Did you? Did he tell you to keep it a secret so he didn't have to share? He *should* have shared."

She pulled her hand free and scrambled backward over the floor, away from him. He rolled his head to the side, glaring at her with a bloodshot eye. It was stupid, he was too sick to sit up, but for a second she was scared of him.

Then he seized. His body arched up off the bed, muscles wrenching bones as if he was trying to fold himself in half. A terrible, rattling noise gargled out of his tight throat, like he was trying to scream but there was nowhere for the sound to get out. His fingers clawed at the pillows, at the bandages holding his ruined arm down.

"His fever must have gone up," Adil said, scrambling to his feet. "He's going into convulsions. Jenny, help me hold him down."

Jenny hesitated. She'd had epilepsy since she was six—she knew that you weren't supposed to hold someone down or put anything in their mouth. She also knew that those were rules for people whose only problem was a seizure, not like Brock, who was so broken already. It just felt *wrong* to get any closer to him, some atavistic rejection prickling the hair on the back of her neck.

She shook it off, not understanding it after everything she'd done to nurse Brock so far, and threw herself over his legs to hold them down. Fresh blood oozed from under his bandages, darkening the existing stains on them. It felt like his muscles were twisting under his skin as he bucked.

She wondered briefly if this was what it was like when she had a seizure? Then Brock went limp, his breathing huffing in and out of his chest like a dog.

Jenny pushed herself off his shins, sitting down heavily on her ass. It was still cold, but she'd broken a sweat under her coat. Adil pulled his gloves off with his teeth and pressed the back of his hand against Brock's forehead, then peeled his lid back to check his pupil. He frowned, chewing on his lower lip.

"Is he okay?" Jenny asked.

"...no. But then he wasn't before." He stopped and shrugged, face pinched and gray hued. "He's still alive. Under the circumstances, that's doing okay."

Tears burned the back of Jenny's eyes suddenly, a terrible mix of fear and frustration hitting her. She was cold and scared, and Danny had *left* her to deal with this. It probably wasn't fair to be angry with him— Brock was nothing to him—but she was. All these years, he'd *always* been there for her. It wasn't fair to get someone used to that and then just abandon them because they fucked up.

"Good," she said, scrubbing her face with her sleeve. Adil pretended not to notice, keeping his hands busy rebinding Brock's dressings. When the tears didn't stop coming, Jenny scrambled to her feet. "I just... I'm going to see if I can find some clean sheets, or a towel or something. We can change his bandages."

She scrambled to her feet and ducked out of the room, then headed upstairs. She ducked into the icy bathroom, sat down on the toilet, and had a quiet, hard cry. It left her face raw and her hands shaking, but at least the tears didn't feel like a salted stone in her throat anymore.

It reminded her that she'd not taken her meds. She sniffed and fished in her pocket for the strip of pills. They were old, the foil cracked and peeling on the back. She'd run out of the trial meds yesterday.

"Danny's kind of a badass, huh?" Adil called up the stairs, his voice brittle with forced cheer. "I mean, who'd have thought it of a guy who wears cardigans?"

"I certainly never did," Jenny admitted to the blue-tiled walls.

"What?"

"Nothing." she called back. Standing up on the toilet, she pushed the bathroom window open to look out. It was dim outside, the snow covering the garden until only a few branches of a hazel tree stuck up out of the white blanket. There was no sign of anyone moving around out there. "I'm okay, Adil. I just needed a minute. I—"

He screamed, a shocked yelp turning into a tumbling litany of profanity. Jenny fell off the toilet, cracking her shoulder against the bath. The pain blinded her for a second, stealing her breath, and then she scrambled up off the floor. Downstairs there was a thud, and Adil went quiet.

"Adil?" She bolted out the door and took the stairs two at time, boots thudding off the sea-grass carpet. "What's wrong? Are you...?

She swung around the doorframe into the main room and stopped, confused, as her brain tried to catch up. The makeshift bed they'd made for Brock was torn up, pillows and cushions ripped up and stuffing kicked over the floor like snow. Adil was lying crumpled against the hearth, the side of his jacket starting to pucker and wither from the heat.

There was no sign of Brock.

Jenny licked her lips, breath tight and fast, and then hurried over to grab Adil and drag him away from the hearth. There were singe marks on his coat, and when she touched the back of his head her fingers came away bloody. What the hell had happened?

Something smashed in the kitchen. Jenny laid Adil down carefully, whispering apologies, and crawled over to peek through the door.

It was an IKEA kitchen, all glossy red surfaces and magnetic strips. There was a Belfast sink and a built-in microwave, a butcher block island in the middle of the space. Brock was hunched over it, leaning on it, as he shoveled broken chunks of half-frozen meat into his mouth. It must have been cold enough to keep the freezer icy even without power, because Jenny could hear the grinding noise of his teeth on the wood-tough steak.

"Brock?" she said, her voice wobbling with uncertainty.

He jerked his head up and around, staring at her. Jenny gasped, shoving her hand against her mouth like her knuckles could hold the sound back. Brock's face looked like a plastic surgery botch job. His torn lips were swollen and split in the middle, all the way up to a nose that had flattened and spread like a boxer's. Even his skin looked coarse and inflamed, like he'd had a bad peel.

"Something's wrong," she said, using the door to pull herself to her feet. "Brock, you're not well. You need to come back and lie down."

She took a step into the room, her boots scuffing over the tiled floor, with her hands out and petting the air soothingly. Brock hunched over his pile of meat, something wrong with the high arch of his back, and snarled at her like an animal. Drool dripped from his ruined mouth, thick strings of it that hung.

Excuses—*explanations*—ran through Jenny's brain like a ticker tape of options: lockjaw, delirium, or even Ebola. Her gut didn't care; it just wanted out. She took a deep breath, nearly gagging at the stink of sickness and sour sweat, and tried his name again.

"Brock. Please, you need to listen to me. This isn't right. You're not well."

He hauled the fevered weight of his body up onto the island, the chunks of meat and broken plastic containers digging into his knees. Clubbed, bloody fingers clutched the edge of the counter, the tough plastic splitting, and he was still making that unsettling, inhuman snarling noise.

There was nothing in his face that recognized her.

Jenny took back the step she'd taken into the kitchen, moving carefully as if he was an animal that she couldn't risk spooking. She kept the tight, nervous smile on her face and took another step, weight settling back onto her heel.

The heavy slope of Brock's shoulders moved under his skin, and he screamed, mouth gaping open until she could see the frozen meat caught in his jagged, broken teeth. Shocked into screaming back at him, Jenny threw herself back out of the room. She landed hard on the carpet and kicked the door shut, bracing her back against the sofa. Brock hit the door hard enough that she felt it up into her knees, making them ache.

"Oh God, oh God," Jenny chanted. Her heart was thundering against her chest, and she couldn't get a breath around it. After a minute, Brock stopped. Jenny stayed where she was until her legs started to cramp. Then she gingerly rolled to her feet, trying to be as quiet as possible. She could still hear him on the other side of the door, breathing in those wet, growling wheezes.

She grabbed a chair and quietly as she could, wedged it under the door handle. Then she crept over to Adil, trying to shake him awake and get him back on his feet. His eyelashes fluttered, bleary brown eyes trying to focus on her. She plastered her hand over his mouth to shush him.

"Something is wrong with Brock," she whispered. "We have to get out."

Her lips were stiff and numb from shock, and her brain was full of ideas that made no sense. It was the full moon. She'd seen it, briefly, when she looked out the window. It was the full moon, and Brock had been attacked by… something. Except that was crazy, even without going as far as putting a name to it. She got Adil up into a sitting position, then dragged him back toward the door.

Then Brock hit the door again. The chair splintered, and the door smashed open, the handle burying itself in the plaster wall. Brock shambled through the door, and maybe Jenny's crazy ideas weren't that crazy.

She screamed, and then he crossed the room in a limping run and backhanded her into silence.

Chapter Nineteen

WOLVES WEREN'T religious in the way humans were. They didn't respect their holy men; they reviled them. Prophets held a higher rank than dogs in the pack—barely—but even the most iconoclastic wolf, even Gregor, would rather associate with a dog. Maybe even an actual all-the-time dog.

So the dog didn't understand why Jack and Gregor were ear-flat, tail-tucked cringing in front of the ragged old prophet in shabby hides. The prophet should have been fur side, the moon so fat and ripe overhead, but strong enough wolves could find their skin. It barked, an uncertain stutter of noise, and turned the noise into a snarl when the prophet looked at it.

Job. Pack whispers had it that he'd been the Numitor's brother/son/rival before he lost his fangs and the Wild to the old king's edict. It had been he who'd laid the charges of barrenness against the dog's mother when she whelped a wolfhound instead of a wolf.

"Run away, dog," Job said, the edges of his words lisping as they slid through the gaps where his incisors should have sat. "Go cower by the fire. We're the Kings of the Wild now. I'm King of the Wild now."

He absently stroked his coat as he spoke, running declawed fingers through the matted hair. His mouth twisted in a hard smile. In the back of the dog's brain, a thought of Danny's tried to push its way past the distraction of Selene's siren song. Something about dry, coarse hair and a fang that cracked and stank.

The prophet shrugged the coat on, sliding his arms clumsily into too tight sleeves. Heavy thread pulled at the shoulders, tearing at the hide. Not hide, skin. The dog couldn't smell tannin or piss, nothing that would have cured or tanned the garment. Just skin, blood and….

"I'm the new Numitor," the prophet said, reaching over his shoulder. He pulled the head up, the wolf skin's head flopping over his face. Limp ears sagged over bloody, empty eye holes, blood and pus scabbed in tear ducts and snout.

No. Not just a wolf skin, a skinned wolf. Job, the prophet, had skinned one of their people and was wearing him like a badly kept waxed jacket. Or another skin, the dead wolf's skin remembering the Wild and pulling the prophet's flesh with it. He sprouted knots piebald, hybrid hair, his skull a knobble of ill-fitting bone pieces and his jaw bristling with too many fangs to fit in a mouth. It was a horror, but it gave the prophet back his fangs and his claws.

The prophet raised his arm, mutilated hands turned into clawed mauls, and beckoned monsters out of the trees: two things that loped on their knuckles, curved, white claws bending back to gouge their arms, and chewed the air with fangs that didn't fit into their twisted mouths. Gregor and Jack snarled as one, moving like mirror images as they forgot their differences in the face of this challenge, and attacked.

Big as the twin wolves were, the monster things were bigger. They were clumsy, though, and awkward in odd ways—like their joints were trying to move in ways their muscles had no memory of. Gregor darted under a slap from a maul-like paw and ripped through the ragged remains of Minion pajamas into the thing's stomach. At the same time, Jack grabbed the dangling scarf tied around the throat of one monster—its pale, hairy flesh growing over it like a grown-into collar—and shook the onetime Magpies supporter until there was the popping snap of dislocated vertebra. Jack lost a cut of flesh along his side, raw meat and muscle steaming as the cold air got inside his fur, but the monster thing pitched forward. Its face plowed a rut in the snow, and it lay there twitching. It wasn't dead, but it would take time healing, and in the meanwhile Jack joined Gregor in harrying the first thing.

Not a wolf, not a dog, and not a human—not anymore, at least. It was impossible, or it was a nightmare from the old stories. The ones that wolves too old to hunt told children before they went to sleep.

Danny would have had too many questions. He'd have been confused. He'd want to understand what had happened, what was going to happen next. It was simpler for the dog. The things were wrong, the prophet was wrong, and they needed to be killed.

It wasn't a fighting dog, though. To the small and furry, it was death on legs, but the only scars it had to boast of were from the fights it *lost*. Instinct, and the hot-wire tension of the pack's anger, sent him darting in to snap at heels and the raw, spinal lumps that might have been tails.

Their blood in its mouth was too thick and too rich, salty enough to make it gag and with a strange, acrid undertaste that was almost more of a smell. A slap from a thick arm, heavy muscles wrapped around bones that looked too thin for them, sent it flying; a kick ripped its chest open, thick nails slicing through hair and muscle, and bowled the dog tail over ears across the snow. It struggled back to its feet, each breath cramping pain through it as it waited to heal, and lurched back into the fight.

Its paws sank into the snow, cracking the frozen crusts of blood, and it stumbled. One of the wolves spun out of the fight and snarled at him, sharp, white teeth snapping at the air fiercely. It was so bloody and shredded—half an ear dripping blood down its neck and one lip torn back to show gum—that the dog didn't know if it was Jack or Gregor. Either way, the message was clear.

It wasn't a dog's fight.

The dog dropped back, tasting iron on his tongue as he panted through the pain of his mending breastbone. The two wolves were giving a good account of themselves, their eyes flashing green with the Wild and their wounds healing almost as fast as they were inflicted. That *almost* would damn them, though, and the monster Jack had put down was starting to move again.

The long muscles in the dog's haunches bunched and twitched with the urge to run, but he resisted. What good was it going to do against monsters like these? All he'd ever been good at was running away.

He hesitated, dropping his chin and staring at the fight. Bracing itself, the dog waited for a space to open up between the writhing bodies and snapping white teeth.

The piebald prophet, coat a knot of red and black, grabbed one of the wolves and shook him like a rag. The heavy, tawny body smacked into a tree and dropped limp to the ground, the wolf taking a second to scramble to its feet. Blood dripped from his nose in bright red blobs.

The dog was in motion almost before it registered the opening, long, lean body streaking across the snow. It darted under one of the monster's upraised arms and lunged for the prophet, sinking his teeth into his ass until they grated on bones. The monster screamed in surprise and swung around, lifting the dog off its feet. It hung on as long as it could, but the meat slid from its moorings, and it went flying. The dog's shoulder hit the ground with a thump, shocking the breath out of it, and the prophet turned. Under heavy sockets, its eyes glittered with specks of bile-bright yellow.

"Dog," it said, somehow managing to work contempt into the guttural noise. It barked out a rough, chewed-on laugh. "Pack of... perverts and *dogs*."

The mouthful of wet, slick meat that felt wrong in the dog's throat. It spat it out and growled, even though it sounded thin and unsure. Behind the monster the injured wolf had staggered back into the fight, leaking blood from his ears. He was wobbling like a drunk.

The dog took a deep breath and darted forward to bite the monster's nose. Bone crunched, blood and snot filling its mouth with copper and thick salt. The monster shrieked and reared up onto its feet, hauling the dog up with it by the grip of his teeth. Let go or bite down. The dog chose to bite down, teeth scraping through bone, and shook itself like a terrier with a rat, whipping its long, gray body back and forth viciously. The prophet howled, nearly deafening the dog, and backhanded it with one big, heavy arm. The dog went flying. Midair it occurred to it that if it hit a tree, this plan wasn't going to work so well. It twisted, trying to think like a cat and work out the intersection between ground and feet. That didn't work. It hit a fallen stump and then a rock, finally landing hard on the ground. There was blood under its muzzle, but there didn't seem any point in working out which generalized ache it was coming from.

Up. Its paws twitched, pain shocking up long legs, but that was about it. Blood bubbled under its black nose with every heaving pant. It hurt too much to move.

"Dog," the monster roared. Except its voice sounded different—clearer—and the dog's mouth was full of old skin and loose hair. "*Dead* dog."

The dog dragged itself to its feet, the wolf skin hanging like a torn shirt from its teeth. Where it had ripped off the prophet, his skin was raw and dripping with no sign of healing. Even better, he'd lost the shape he'd taken from the dead shifter, and he was mutilated again. His jaw hung empty of fangs, and his ruined legs folded and tightened under him without the brace of stolen legs.

The prophet staggered back, lurching and naked. He rammed the stumps of his fingers toward the dog.

"Get him!" he screamed. "Kill him and bring me back my skin!"

Gregor—the dog thought it was the wilder wolf— was on the ground, ribs crushed under the callused heel of a monster. Jack was still fighting, but he was a wolf of blood and raw skin for now. The monster pinning Gregor hesitated, one hand clenched around Gregor's head.

"Get him!" the prophet yelled. He fled into the woods, the shadows wrapping around him. "Now! Go, you mindless fucks. Get my skin!"

The two monsters—werewolves, the old stories called them while laughing at the idea—turned to look at the dog. Teeth still clenched in the skin, it turned and took off into the forest at a dead run, ignoring the branches whipping its head and ears. The huff of its own breathing filled its ears, but it didn't need to hear it to know the monsters were on its tail. It could feel the heat of them, see the impact of their weight muscling through the trees.

They were slow. Slower than the dog, anyhow. Those meat-hook claws hobbled them, making them fight the ground for every step. Hopefully.

The dog ran and didn't look back.

After a minute, it felt the Wild rush up around him. It smelled of ancient trees and tasted of ice-melt water. It prickled in the back of its nose, sharpened its attention. It didn't do anything for the aches and pains—the grate and rub of a tearing tendon in its knee, the yelp of broken ribs every time he sucked in a breath like he was drowning—but the path smoothed under his paws, and the gaps through knots of brambles were just big enough he didn't have to slow down.

It wasn't much help, but it would take what it could get. Pain jabbed the end of its tail—jolted its spine all the way to its skull—and lost its grip when the dog jolted forward. It *needed* what it could get.

Short an inch of tail and tattered skin flapping from its jaws, the dog burst out of the trees and onto a narrow road. The surprise of the harsh winter had cracked the tarmac from its moorings, leaving it scattered over the frost-coated road like clippings. It slid under its toes, chunks of loose tar poking up into the tender skin between his pads.

The Wild faded, his gratitude for this broken remnant of civilization splitting his connection with it. Without it, the dog felt its gait alter, trying to limp. No time. It pushed aching legs to keep going, just until they reached the water.

The monsters roared behind him. It sounded almost like words, but between the pain stinking up the air and the clutter of saw teeth in raw gums, they never quite made their way out. The dog looked back over its shoulder as the first shoved out of the trees and rolled down onto the road, brambles wrapped around it like garlands. Except the bloody scrapes and punctures were already healing themselves up. "…fukka… a'tard. Kill ou."

It was too close, and the dog was flagging on legs leaden with fatigue poisons. It dragged one last burst of speed out and made it to the end of the road, staggering around the corner like a drunk. The bridge was gone. A charred Tesco truck hung over the gap, melted wheels just caught on the broken road. The corpse of the driver was still wedged in the cab, frozen and pallid inside an ice cube of sealed metal.

Exhausted now, the dog scrambled up onto the parapet. The damaged stone shifted under his weight, crumbling bits of stone dropping into the river below. The water was frozen, a rime of translucent ice over the slow pour of it. The dog hesitated, taking another glance back.

The monster was up on its feet again, walking along the road like it had all the time in the world. There was an expression on its malformed jaw that might have been a smirk. It knew there was nowhere left to run. While the dog watched, the second monster came lurching out of the forest.

There was nowhere else to go. The dog gathered itself and jumped. It almost reached the other side, paws scrambling at snow-covered stone, but not quite. It dropped like a rock, landing *on* the river with a crack that knocked the air out of him. The ice held for a second and then cracked, dumping the dog into the icy current. It splashed its way back up, sneezing water and sucking in a coughing breath. The river pummeled it, slapping it backward and down until it rolled under the ice. A stray rock caught the dog in the back of the head, hard enough to sprinkle stars in its eyes and fill aching lungs with stale water. The skin was gone, leaving a grease of rot on the dog's tongue.

Through the glaze of the ice, it saw the monsters scrambling awkwardly down to the bank of the river.

HE WOKE up draped over a fallen tree, the bark scaling his bare stomach. His arms were hanging in the ice-prickle water, fingers water-withered and numb enough to be a worry. A rough hand grabbed his hair and pulled his head back. Green eyes in a hard, pretty face looked down at him.

"The dog's still with us, then," Gregor said.

Danny sneezed a gross, muddy mixture of blood and river out his nose. He could feel the pressure of what was left in his sinuses.

"Get away from him," Jack said flatly, shouldering his brother out of the way.

He grabbed Danny under the arms and hauled him up onto the bank, kicking the snow away to bare a square of hard, black ground to lay him on. Danny sprawled there for a second, staring up into a blurry sky, then rolled onto his side and puked up the river.

He couldn't have been out that long—his bones still hurt, and his spine throbbed with phantom tail pain. And while he couldn't *see* the sky that well, he could still feel the moon strung up there over the clouds.

"How?" he asked, voice raspy with puking, as he poked at his face with fingers he shouldn't have had.

Danny wasn't the Numitor's pup. Even if he'd been a wolf, he'd be the late-life get of a Glasgow she-wolf with a nasty streak and a willingness to go for the underbelly. His mum didn't ride the Wild—it rode her.

Jack squeezed Danny's shoulder, then shrugged and pushed himself to his feet in one fluid flex of muscle. Last time Danny had seen the pack leader, he'd been shredded and bloody. Now he was all tawny skin and moonlit tattoos, not even a scar left. He held his hand out to Danny.

"Either you pleased the Wild," he said, as Danny took his hand and got yanked to his feet, "or Selene gave you the wink for a good show. Don't look a gift horse in the mouth. Dogs aren't good at grabbing lifelines."

Danny would have put his money on the Wild. Whatever—he wasn't stupid, he had the word for the thing in his head, but he didn't want to spit it out—the monster was, the Wild didn't like it much. He staggered, the muscles in his thighs informing him the Wild didn't like him enough to patch him up like Jack, and leaned against the wolf's hard shoulder.

"I have to go," he said. "I need to get back to Jenny."

He felt the growl under his arm before it escaped Jack's throat. It should have been warning enough, but he didn't react in time. Jack shoved him up against a tree, hand around his throat and thumb braced under his chin. Chunks of frozen snow dropped like winter-born fruit, splattering on the ground.

"There are monsters roaming the forest, affronts to the fucking Wild, and one wearing a dead wolf's skin like a parka," he growled, pushing Danny's head back until it pressed against the bark of the tree. "And all you can think of is your humans? You might be a dog, but you don't have to be a pet."

Danny punched him. His mum would have rolled her eyes, a blind, windmill of a roundhouse that caught the point of Jack's chin. No technique. No skill. It was surprise that made Jack stumble back more than the impact, earning a rasping laugh from Gregor.

Taking a step back, Jack rubbed his jaw. The controlled anger in the way he breathed in, shoulders squaring, was more frightening than the hand on Danny's throat had been.

"You had a good reason for that?" Jack asked.

Resentment tasted like bile and river water. Danny swallowed it for later and jabbed a finger at Jack.

"Do you know *what* that prophet was?" he asked instead. "*Did* you know what he is?"

For a second, Jack's face stayed stonily unmoved by the question. Then he dropped his chin and grimaced, glancing at Gregor.

"When I was exiled, Job offered to make me a legend, or a monster," he said. "I turned him down."

"Same offer; same response," Gregor said. He squatted in the snow, hands laid casually over his knees and cock hanging between lean, scarred thighs. Sharp green eyes watched Jack warily, whatever tender ceasefire this was not nearly deep enough to be trusted. "I told him I didn't need his help to do my killing. As my brother would have found out, if we hadn't been interrupted."

Jack curled his lip back, showing blunt teeth that should have been fangs. "Don't worry, Gregor, we'll finish that soon enough."

Pushing himself off the tree, Danny stepped forward. "We've all heard legends about wolves who could balance the Wild to hold a half form. When we were good as kids, Mam would howl us them at night. My sister used to try so hard to do it at moon hunt that she looked cross-eyed. Those others...."

Gregor shrugged and reached down, idly jabbing three holes in the snow with his finger. "Some wolves have no pride. Or maybe they're dogs. They stank of cities."

The stained white-and-black scarf flashed into Danny's mind, folds of hide bulging around the pus-stiff knots of it. No shifter would turn wearing something like that. It was the sort of thing you did once as a cub and had to be chewed out of it by caretakers. They hadn't moved right either. Even the prophet, squeezed into his stolen skin, had moved with the confidence of someone whose *idea* of their flesh was... shifting. The two monsters had lurched and struggled on new bones and unhappy muscles.

"I think there was a good reason for that," Danny said to Gregor. The wolf gave him a sour, squinting look, annoyed at having a dog talking to him. "They were...."

He lost the guts to spit the word out at the last minute. So Jack said it for him. "Werewolves," he said. "Humans who've stolen our curse."

The idea of it made Gregor growl, shoulders hunching as his rage dragged the wolf up out of him.

"Stories to frighten children," he said. "And dogs. The curse is *our* bloodright, not some cock-rot disease that you can *catch*."

"Fenrir's a story to frighten children too," Danny said. "*We're* stories to frighten children, and the prophet *stank* the same way Brock did. Does. You both saw him; you both smelled it."

Doubt settled the wolf back down under Gregor's skin—most of the way. He looked over at Jack.

"Da would never allow it," he said. "The Wild is *ours*."

"I never thought Da would exile me because of where I stick my dick," Jack said. "The wolf winter is coming, and maybe he doesn't think *either* of us is ready for it?"

It wasn't an idea that Gregor wanted to hear. He snarled, handsome face wrinkling ugly with emotion, and stalked away from the conversation. What he didn't do, though, was deny it.

"What if Brock's like them?" Danny said. "I have to go back. I won't let Jenny get hurt because of me. Not again."

Jack grabbed Danny by the scruff and dragged him in close, yanking him down until he had to crane his neck to look up at Jack. The wolf pressed a hard, hot kiss on Danny's mouth, biting his lips until they both tasted blood. There was probably a wire loose somewhere that explained why that claiming cruelty made Danny so hard it ached.

"We'll go back to the city. Not for your pets, but because we need to know if this is true," Jack said, breaking the kiss. He licked red off his lips and shoved Danny away from him impatiently. "And that wasn't a good reason to hit me. We'll talk about that later."

He walked away, him and his brother shifting at the same time, and Danny watched them go. He could taste Jack's kiss and his blood in his mouth.

Later. Fine, he could deal with later as long as Jenny was okay. And if he couldn't, if she wasn't... he could always run.

Ask the monster, ask his mum, ask anyone—he was good at running away.

HE STAYED human. The Wild had been generous to him tonight, but assuming it would let him shift on a whim seemed like pushing his luck. So did a pack of wolves running up to a farm where there had just been a serious animal attack. Or whatever you'd call the prophet now. So he stole a pair of ragged jeans and an old Durham University sweater from a house they passed, the cloth damp against wet skin.

He was feeling the cold less than he had been. Something to do with shifting more? Or maybe this dog was more wolf than he'd thought.

The two wolves loped through the woods, slipping silently between the trees and around fallen logs. Both of them looked a bit more ragged than they had at the start of the night. It wasn't slowing either of them down.

Keeping up with them was tiring on two legs, but there wasn't much farther to go. Now that he'd been skin side longer, Danny was starting to doubt himself. Gregor was right. The legends he'd been worrying about were the stuff of nightmares, not real life.

Said the shape-shifting dog, running through a forest with wolves who were sometimes men.

Chapter Twenty

THE REEK of something *wrong* hung in the street. It was strong enough that Danny could taste it on his tongue before he even set foot on the tarmac. There was no quantifying or categorizing it, no "like." It was just wrong. Gregor stopped so abruptly he nearly tripped over himself, sneezing and shaking his head until his ears flapped. Jack snapped at his tail and nearly lost his ear tip to a retaliatory nip. The twins shoved at each other, banging shoulders, and then Jack shrugged back into his skin. He stayed low, crouched down in the snow, so no one in the snowed-in houses could catch a glimpse of him.

"It didn't smell like this before," Jack said.

Danny leaned over and braced his hands on his knees, trying not to wheeze like an out-of-condition academic. His legs ached from the run, and he had a stitch in his side that felt more like a stab. A human couldn't have made the run at all, but for a dog he was in disgraceful shape. He caught his breath and shoved his wet hair back from his face. The sweaty curls were cold to the touch, the ends stiff as they started to freeze.

"It did," he corrected Jack. "It's just much worse now. I thought it was some sort of infection."

After a second Jack shoved Danny's shoulder. "Get me some clothes," he ordered. "We'll go and see what is happening. If it is—"

Someone screamed in one of the houses. It was the sound of someone in pain, a noise that came clawing out of their chest like it or not. Danny took off at a run, ignoring the ache in his ribs and the sound of Jack angrily barking his name.

The snow had buried his earlier tracks, disguised the scent marks he'd usually use to find the building. It still didn't take him long to find it. He'd broken the lock to get in; whatever had come *out* had just broken the door. Shattered plastic and metal lay on the pavement, bits of glass sparkling. They were covered with a light skin of snow, but barely. Whatever had happened, it hadn't happened long ago.

Danny jumped over the debris, nearly falling into the puddle of blood in the hall. His heart clenched with dread, but it was clotted with the sour taint of the prophet's bite. *Not Jenny's. Fenrir's fangs, don't be Jenny's.*

He faltered for a second at that thought—if Brock bit her, would she end up tainted too? Then someone called his name.

"Danny? Is that you?"

He wasn't squeamish. You didn't grow up eating raw squirrel and get to be squeamish. The thought of stepping through that stinking blood revolted him, though. He took a long step over it and into the living room. Adil lay on the floor, his face gray and sunken-looking. The shadows under his unfocused, dark eyes looked like purple paint. There was a bruise spreading across his temple, black under his skin, and his left leg was twisted so it pointed the wrong way.

"I'm sorry," he said, stuttering over the words. "I tried to help. I tried to stop him, stop it, but.... Danny, you didn't see him. He attacked me, and his *face*, Danny. You should have seen his face. It was...."

There were rules. Humans weren't meant to know about the wolves that lived in their cities and used their public transport. The ones who found out were silenced. Maybe it was a different world now. Danny wasn't willing to take the risk.

He grabbed Adil's chin and squeezed until the young man's eyes focused on him. More or less focused on him. "You were knocked out. You were woozy. You didn't see anything clearly. You understand?"

"No," Adil said, shaking his head. "What do you mean? Why would I—"

Danny covered his mouth and glanced over his shoulder. It might be too late already. Wolves had sharp hearing.

"Adil, what did you see?" he prompted.

He lifted his hand enough for Adil to mutter "nothing" against his palm.

"Good." He dragged him up off the floor and into a chair. "Scream if you want."

Adil looked confused. "What?"

Danny pressed his hand against Adil's sternum, fingers sinking into the down of the jacket, and grabbed his ankle with the other hand. He didn't know enough to do this, not on a human, but leaving the leg the way it was would do more harm. Tightening his fingers, he pulled and twisted. Adil didn't scream. The pain shocked him too much for that. His mouth just gaped open, a thin whine escaping him, as the joint ground back into place in the meat of swollen skin and torn muscle.

He screamed when it was done, finding his voice on a torn shriek.

"Sorry," Danny said. "It's going to hurt, but if you're careful, it should be okay. What happened to Jenny?"

Adil couldn't get the words out for a second, too busy panting. He finally sniffed back snot, wiping his sleeve over his face. "He took her. I thought he was going to kill us. Fuck sake, Danny. He was—"

Danny's fingers twitched on Adil's knee, and the boy gasped out a curse and writhed in pain. It hadn't been on purpose. He'd not meant to hurt the kid, but it worked. Whatever Adil had been about to say, he kept to himself.

Snow creaked outside, and Jack stepped into the hall. He had found a pair of jeans from somewhere, but that was all. He stayed out of the angle of Adil's peripheral vision. The smell of Jack's anger—like green wood burning—cut through the smell of the taint.

"Danny." Even in human form, the way Jack said his name sounded like a growl. "What happened?"

He gave Adil a quick, warning look and let him go, turning to look at Jack. With the amount of anger and adrenaline floating around, he made sure to keep his eyes low. "It took Jenny. I don't know why... or where."

Jack crouched and dipped his fingers into the puddle of blood—the crust breaking around his fingers—and sniffed at the liquid. His nose wrinkled. "You were right," he admitted. "It was Brock, but he's gone now. And we have other fish to fry."

He left, walking through the blood and getting it all over his feet. It was the prophet he was interested in, and the monsters. Not Jenny. Danny pushed himself to his feet, then hesitated. He glanced guiltily at Adil. "I'm sorry. I have to go with him. Will you be…?"

Sweat soaked Adil's face, staining his collar. He nodded. "You have to go, and I didn't see anything," he said.

"I'm—"

Adil shook his head. "Just go get Jenny, okay? And, whatever I didn't see? What I saw was scary, okay? Be careful."

Danny went to grab one of the blankets from the floor, but Adil shoved it away. The reek of infection and monster sweat was strong enough to curdle in even a human's nose.

"Go," he repeated. "I'm fine. I'll be fine. I won't say anything. Just get her back."

"I will," Danny promised.

He got up and hurried back outside, looking for Jack and Gregor. They were already leaving. Danny cursed and ran after them, grabbing Jack's elbow as he caught up.

"We need to go after Brock," he said.

Jack shook his head, grimly determined. "Job's the problem. Kill the monsters first, he can just make more. That's what he's been doing, the dead people were just… accidents. Not a message. He just couldn't control himself when he was able to bite again. We need to kill him, and then we'll look for your human friend. The old bastard has broken nearly every law we have. He'll destroy everything we are if we let him go on."

"No, you're wrong," Danny said, stepping in front of him. "Don't you remember the stories your ma used to—"

"Our ma died," Jack said flatly. "And the old man had more important things to do than fill our head with fairy tales."

"Maybe it is more a fairy tale, but so is what is happening here," Danny pointed out. He talked quickly. "It was a story my grandfather told my mum, even that wasn't firsthand. An old priest had told him that was what happened to the Coaldown pack."

"I've never heard of them," Jack said impatiently. It was Gregor who interrupted with a growl, pressing his shoulder against Jack and staring at Danny with intent green eyes. Jack rolled his eyes but gestured impatiently for Danny to get on with it. "Tell us your fairy tale, then."

Danny rubbed wet palms down his legs. "They didn't call them werewolves, but... there was a priest, and they were monsters. Ma said they'd gone cannibal, but they'd not known at first. It had been a harsh winter, and the priest had fed them their own dead to try and keep the pack alive. They turned into monsters, lost to the Wild, and the Numitor had to put them down. Only the priest got away, or tried to. The thing was his wolves were loyal as dogs. Even when he wanted them to leave him running, they'd follow on his heels. That's how your da found him, in the end. My mum, although she said her dad swore it was true, never really believed in it. She said it was just a scary story." He twisted his mouth into a tight smile. "Even scarier if it's true, though, if it was something like what Job has done to himself."

He waited. Jack didn't look convinced, rubbing his thumb dubiously over his lower lip, but he hadn't dismissed Danny out of hand. In the end, it was Gregor who tipped the balance in Danny's favor. He shoved a cold nose in Jack's colder hand, green eyes meeting and a silent something passing between the twins.

"Could it have been Coulsden?" Jack asked. "Not Coaldown?"

"Maybe?" Danny said, shrugging. "It was an old story. She never spelled the place names out for us. Why?"

"Job's a Coulsden wolf," Jack said slowly. "Pack's long gone, like so many of 'em now, but the line's still inked in his skin. If the story's true...."

"Maybe that is how he knew to make monsters?" Danny finished for him. He hesitated, not wanting to undermine his own argument but unable to let it alone either. "There was no mention of humans in mum's story, not as anything but victims."

A small, cold smile curved Jack's mouth. "There wouldn't be, would there? Stories about sharing the curse with humans? Da would go to his grave with that story unhowled. Even if he gave Job his blessing for this, it's not something to add to the catechism. Like the dogs, like half the things no one else remembers now—he'll commit his sins and wait for time to wear the memory down."

The truth of that gave Danny pause for a second. He was the one who loved history, books—*records*. Yet it had never occurred to him before how much of the Numitor's biography was whispers and hints. There were *myths* Danny studied with more archaeological provenance than their pack leader.

"If I am right," Danny said, dragging the focus back to where he needed it, "then Brock will lead us straight to Job, from the monster to the monster-maker."

"And if you're wrong, you still get your girlfriend back," Jack said.

Gregor laughed a wolf's laugh at that, letting his tongue loll like a dripping ribbon out of his mouth. The mockery got him a kick in the side from Jack, but it didn't faze him. He shook himself, heavy fur shifting, and gave Jack another of those looks.

It was strange. There was no sudden fraternal bond, no sibling affection in their mannerisms. They held their ears like they hated each other still. Yet they seemed more like brothers than ever before. It was the ease that they hated each other with, so familiar that it didn't distract them from the hunt.

"You were right about Job giving the humans fur and fangs," Jack acknowledged after a second and a shrug. "Maybe you're right about this. We'll follow Brock and your mouthy friend."

THEY RAN out of that street and through others. Whatever Brock had become, he apparently didn't see any reason to be discreet about what he was doing. The tracks of his lumbering, knuckle-swing run led down a street and through a fence, shards of wood rolling over the snow as the wind poked at them.

A flash of lightning stitched across the sky, ripping through the low, heavy clouds and lighting up the streets. Danny was still blinking the dazzle out of his eyes when something big, heavy, and dark lunged out of an alley. It hit him in the ribs and knocked him flat on the ground, breath grunting out of him.

Teeth raked at his throat and claws punched through denim to dig into the heavy muscles of his thighs. For a second it didn't hurt; all he could feel was hot blood on cold skin, then the pain hit. Danny sucked in a scream, clenching his jaw, and got his arm up into his attacker's throat.

It snarled and dug its teeth into his collarbone, a snarl vibrating through Danny's bones. He heard a crack, pain splintering down his spine, and this time the scream escaped him. Squirming on his back in the mud, he shoved until the thing made a choked, gargled noise. It hung on.

Lightning flashed again.

The dirty straggle of wet ginger hair—and the noose of a football scarf—identified it as one of Job's monsters. If it wasn't for those identifiers, Danny wouldn't have guessed the thing used to be human once. Maybe the werewolves of human legends spent most of their life skin side and tame, but it was hard to imagine that this ruin of a thing could mend itself. Its face, close enough to Danny's that he could hardly breathe for the stink, hung like a cheap rubber mask on a skull that was all broken bones and putty. Torn lips peeled back from protruding gums, blood and his own flesh caught in ragged predator teeth that stuck out between cracked incisors. All of which were currently buried in Danny's flesh.

It was the shift without the wolf, a body breaking apart with no template for putting itself back together.

Danny grabbed the monster's face with his free hand and dug his thumb into the soft, wet bulge of its eye. The swollen marble of it popped, wet gobbets of infection and jelly dripping onto Danny's jaw and throat. He gagged and choked back bile as he gouged his thumb deeper, nail scraping against grit and sinew.

The thing screamed and wrenched its head back, swinging its arm in an awkwardly jointed roundhouse punch. Danny jerked his head to the side in time, the bone-padded knuckles cracking against the side of his skull instead of crushing his face. The impact rattled through his brain. On top of him the monster made a thick satisfied sound, the noise dying on its tongue as its head suddenly collapsed in on itself with a wet, cracking sound.

The twisted mass of bone and flesh went limp, the horrors the shift had inflicted sliding back into the more commonplace horror of torn flesh and infection. As the dewlap withered back into a human neck and chin, Danny could see the broken knobs of bone and sunken planes where it had been crushed. Gobs of brain leaked out of its eye. It would have finished off a wolf, and it seemed to have done so for the monster.

Jack dragged the corpse off Danny and crouched down, grimacing as he looked over the damage. The throat, Danny thought with odd clarity, had to be a mess. He was having trouble breathing through it.

"Hold still," Jack said, shoving him back down against the snow when he tried to get up. "Still, dog-boy."

"Fuck. Off," Danny hissed between clenched teeth. Then Gregor padded into view, head low and ears set a dangerous angle, and closed his jaws around Danny's throat. The pin prickle of sharp teeth pinched the wound shut, scraping raw nerves against the cracks in the bone. He sucked in a hard breath, feeling Gregor's teeth tear his skin as his throat moved. "What're you doing?"

The answer buckled his body as the Wild reached through his blood and drew the shift out of his bones. It was slow, hair poking itchily through his skin and reshaping muscle sliding along bones. Then Gregor let go, and Jack grabbed Danny's jaw. He shoved the change back down, making Danny wheeze and splutter. It didn't hurt, it just felt… strange, like that jerk-awake moment that ends a dream about falling.

Jack let go of his throat and sat back, wiping his hand on his thigh.

"That," he said.

Getting his elbows under him, Danny sat up. When he rubbed his throat, the skin was whole, and there was only the memory of an ache in his collarbone. He poked at it gingerly, looking for cracks. It just felt bruised. On his own, it would have healed. Eventually. If someone with a grudge or a shovel hadn't found him.

GREGOR WAS watching him with intent eyes, furred shoulders hunched against the whipping snow. He looked like he was waiting for something.

"Thanks," Danny said, trying not to sound as resentful of that as he felt.

It wasn't easy for a wolf to sneer. Gregor managed it, turning his back on Danny with clear contempt. He scrambled up awkwardly, not looking for help and not being offered it. Wiping his nose on the back of his hand, he looked down at the monster. The dead man lay in a spreading puddle of blood and snowmelt. In the sporadic flashes of lightning, he didn't look peaceful. Just horrible and dead. Danny tried to feel the right sort of things, the feelings that a professor of theology would feel looking at a brutalized corpse. All he felt was a sort of repulsed pity—it didn't seem like enough.

He braced his foot against the dead man's ribs, feeling them crackle and give, and shoved him out of the way. The black-and-white scarf trailed over the snow, although between blood and other liquids, the white had gone more yellow and green. "I was right about Brock going after Job. We must be getting close."

"Maybe," Jack said.

When Danny glared at him, he shrugged broad, bare shoulders. It was cold enough to brush pallor over his skin, making the black ink livid, but he didn't bother to register it otherwise. "It could have followed us from the river. If not, we're walking into a trap. What else would a wolf prophet want with your ex?"

That dug a chill into Danny's gut that had nothing to do with the weather.

Chapter Twenty-One

FEAR TASTED like sour vomit and salt.

Jenny huddled on the ground in the corner of the gutted kitchen, as far away from Brock as she could get. Chunks of ripped masonry pressed against her hip as she shifted, cradling the side of her face in one hand. The cheekbone wasn't broken—probably, she wasn't a nurse but poking at it didn't make her scream—but it throbbed with dull heat. Her nose, on the other hand, was broken. It had popped when Brock hit her, a star-burst of snotty pain, and last time she'd touched it, she'd nearly passed out.

She didn't know why she was here.

She didn't know what Brock was anymore.

But she knew her nose was broken, and her cheek-bone (probably) wasn't.

There was no reason for that to be a comfort, but somehow it managed to be. Maybe it was just *knowing* something, when every other solid fact she'd had about the world had turned to putty. Whatever Brock was, he wasn't natural. Even if she accepted the furthest, *SyFy*, *Piranhaconda* definition of what science was, she couldn't make Brock fit. The only thing that came close to fitting, dredged up from the memory of a sleepover spent watching banned horror films at her best friend's when they were twelve, was "werewolf."

Just thinking it made her stomach lurch, as if acknowledging this one anomaly meant she couldn't depend on the world to keep spinning neatly on its axis. That wasn't the worst part, though. The worst part was that Brock didn't seem to realize *what* had happened to him. He knew something had happened, but it hadn't registered that he was… grotesque.

"Brock," Jenny said, trying to sound… normal. She didn't. Her voice wobbled with fear and tears, her throat closing up when he shuffled around to look at her. "I just want to go home. Let me go home, okay?"

He growled, a rumbling sound in his chest, and shook his head. Drool splattered the old, dusty concrete floor as he loped over to her.

"Not yet," he said. The words were slurred, twisted by his malformed jaw, but he already sounded clearer than he had. He was getting used to his new body. "You gotta meet 'im first. He'll make 'ou like me."

Something that she thought was meant to be a smile twisted his mouth. He stroked her hair carefully with a callused, bone-clawed hand, yanking knots of it out despite his obvious attempt at being gentle.

"I'm sorry," Jenny choked out and swung her fist. The chunk of masonry she'd grabbed—one side still painted kitchen-grease magnolia—caught Brock on the temple. Overworked bone cracked, one swollen eye bulging in its socket, and with a howl Brock slung her across the room. Jenny hit the floor with a yelp, her ribs creaking and her face throbbing with fresh pain. She rolled with it, scrambling onto her feet and bolting for the door.

The rough planks that covered the floor dug into her bare feet as she ran, leaving bloody smudges behind her. She hit the door, a soft *oof* escaping her, and staggered into the hall. There was no front door, just torn wood and a rusting metal grille. Jenny fled toward it, the sound of Brock screaming at her like a hand shoving her back.

The snow hit her like a wet towel as she ran outside. She'd already been cold. Now she was abruptly frozen. Her ears and nose burned, her chapped lips stinging as she breathed in. Wharton Park. She recognized the place suddenly. The old park-keeper's cottage. She knew where she was and how to get home from here.

"Bitch!" Brock slur-snarled, and something hit Jenny hard on the back. She was thrown forward, sliding over the wet grass and mud. Her shoulder was hot and numb, refusing to cooperate as she tried to push herself up. She rolled over onto her back, cracking her elbow on the bit of bloody masonry Brock had tagged her with.

The snow came down on top of her. If it had been rain, it would have felt like drowning, but letting the drifting snowflakes cover her seemed almost peaceful. Better than whatever Brock had planned for her, once "he" got here.

A dark, misshapen shadow fell over her, and Brock grabbed a handful of her hair, dragging her up until they were nose to snout. He moved his ravaged mouth carefully to make sure the words came out right.

"Now look what you made me do."

He cocked his arm back. Jenny squeezed her eyes shut and sniffed in a hard breath through her nose. A terrible, stupid sort of pity filled her stomach. Brock's dad had beat his mum like a drum, and he'd sworn he'd never be like that. He'd hurt Jenny, the things he said and the things he did, but he'd never hit her. Not until—

"Enough!" a hard voice cut through the storm.

The hand in Jenny's hair let go. She dropped back into the snow, tears freezing as they hit the snow.

"You'll have to forgive him," a rough voice said. The accent, all burrs and warmth, sounded like Jack. Or like Danny when he'd had a few too many. It was older, though, and there was something brittle in it, like he was barely not screaming. "My dogs are loyal, but not well-trained. Not yet."

Not looking wasn't going to help. Jenny wiped her nose on her sleeve and looked up. The man was tall and spare, with a ragged beard and pale, strange eyes on either side of a badly broken nose. He was wearing ragged old clothes and smelled old and... earthy. If she'd seen him on the street, she'd have crossed the road. Apparently she'd have been right to. Something shuffled behind him, a strangled growl creaking out of it.

Dogs, he'd said, she realized. Plural. It was another *thing* like Brock.

The man picked her up, ignoring her attempts to struggle, and carried her back into the house. He set her down next to a rusted radiator, lashing her ankle to it with a loose cable. She cringed back from him, pressing her back against the radiator until the edges dug in through her ragged coat.

"Please, just let me go," she said. When she swallowed, her mouth tasted like walnuts. "I don't know anything. I just want to go home."

He gave her a flat look. "Has no one ever told? You can't go home again, girl. Keep squealing, though. You're my Judas goat, and I need you bleating."

He chuckled to himself like it was the best joke in the world. Once it stopped amusing him, he stripped down to his skin. It wasn't…. Jenny looked away—she felt her cheeks flush hot and her palms go sweaty with that old fear—it didn't seem sexual. As far as he was concerned, they were sexless as side tables. He kicked his jeans off and stretched, all heavy muscle and Scot-pale skin. Under his clothes, he was wearing a shabby vest or… skin. It was the wet skin of some animal, soaked and smearing pink slime over his hair-matted chest.

Her nose and ears were still prickling. It wasn't from the cold. The doctors had said that if she stopped taking the experimental meds, it could intensify the episodes. She swallowed and tried to push it away—like that was possible.

The man seemed to be having his own seizure, grunting and jerking. When his bones started to break, Jenny tried not to look. It was like a horror movie, though. She couldn't help but peek through her fingers.

A blood-red stain crawled over his skin as blood blisters popped on his follicles, his jaw visibly wrestling itself out of alignment with the pop and tear of tendons. He panted through his nose, nostrils flaring and the whites of his eyes bleeding, as his spine bulged and rippled under his skin. The bloody, bony tip of it pushed through his skin, curling between his legs as flesh and fur congealed around it.

Maybe it was going to happen anyhow. Maybe it was fear that pushed Jenny over the edge. For her it was usually just a pause, an absent minute or so before she came back to herself in a body that was all bruises and aches. This time she saw… something.

Overlaid, overcracked, damp-scaled concrete walls, raw stone stretched up toward the winter sky. She could taste snow and pine on the air. It tasted *fresher* somehow, cleaner. Brock, leaning in to sniff at her with his split nose, was a bone-armored, red-eyed hound. The Scot was…. Jenny whimpered and tried not to look, but her body not being her own was still the same. He was a wolf, twice as big as the mastiff her best friend used to own, but rot crawled over half of his body. Mangy hide hung loose from wasted muscle, bone showing through rotted holes. Maggots squirmed in its eye socket, and the reek of it made her gag and choke.

The wolf lunged at Brock, tearing a chunk out of his throat, and then turned to look at Jenny. First with a wicked amber eye, then with the rotted hole on the other side.

"You see us," the wolf said, leering at her. "That's interesting."

It had been years since Jenny believed in anything but science and the Internet, the only prayers the empty ones she mouthed in her parent's line of sight to keep them placated. When she'd been little it had been different, and suddenly she was there again. The old prayer soaked up from where it had hidden in her mind, bringing with it the memory of her grandmother's age-soft hand and the warm childish faith that it meant everything.

It couldn't really help, but somehow it did anyhow. The absence washed over. When she came to, she was lying in a puddle of her own tepid sick, and the hip on her tethered leg felt like someone had tried to twist it off.

She sat up slowly, wiping puke off her face, and leaned over slowly, working at the cord with both hands. Her fingernails broke down to the quick, blood welling, but she kept going. She didn't know if anyone was even looking for her. The only one who might be was Danny, and could she trust him?

Brock had said Danny knew.

Chapter Twenty-Two

LIGHTNING CRACKED down from the sky, a thunderstorm caught up in the snow. It caught in the branches of a tree, cracking it in half with a sizzle and a snap. Char sizzled down the trunk, and the snow melted in fractal scars, steam rising from the roots of the tree. The smell of burned air and cooked sap hung in the air. It was almost strong enough to drown the stink of the monsters. The next bolt smacked into the upraised claw of an excavator, scarring the yellow paint with black ash.

The Wharton Park regeneration. Danny had signed petitions supporting it a year ago. He supposed it wasn't going to be finished anytime soon. All the dug-up grass had been buried under snowdrifts, hard frost sealing the tracks to the ground. If nothing else, it gave the wolves cover as they reached the end of the trail.

Danny crouched between a roll of cold-cracked tarmac, squinting toward the narrow, weathered house in the middle of the field of snow. The ghost of the monster's stink hung in the air, but the storm was smoothing it assiduously away.

The thunder rumbled overhead, a belated underscore to the lightning.

Danny shifted, wincing as his joints protested. His bones ached, and his shift-abused muscles were twitching with erratic pops of hot pain. It was shift-fever, something that only adolescents who spent too much time playing with their skins got. After tonight he was going to be sick as a... dog... for a week.

He grunted to himself and tucked his chin, wiping cold sweat on his shoulder. That was assuming he wasn't *dead* as a dog after tonight, of course.

Jack dropped down next to him in the dirt, breathing hard and controlled. He slung one arm casually over Danny's shoulder, leaning into Danny's side as he talked. It would have been annoying if it hadn't felt so good.

"Gregor is circling around. There's no sign of any more of Job's wolves, just the two."

"That was enough before," Danny pointed out. He ran his thumb up along Jack's side, tracing the muscle-padded ripple of ribs. "They nearly killed you."

The fist under his jaw lifted, making Danny tip his chin back to show throat. "We were already injured," Jack said, a growl just laid over his words. It wasn't real anger, just a rebuke. "And they caught us by surprise. Now we know what they are, it'll go differently."

"If you say so," Danny said. He grabbed Jack's wrist, tugging his knuckles from under the point of Danny's chin, and went back to staring down at the house. In a sick sort of way, he wanted to see one of the monsters again.

They weren't wild, or *of* the Wild. They weren't tame. They were just wrong—and the train wreck of that was compelling. Even as it turned his stomach.

"Do you really think that the Numitor, that your da, could have put his seal on this?" he asked.

"Maybe," Jack admitted after a second. "I don't think he wanted Job giving our curse to humans, but…. What's a monster or a hero to a wolf? They say my da could do a half shift too, back when he was young and balls to the Wild." He paused, jaw working as he clenched his teeth. "I can't do it, and Gregor only wants to run in his wolfskin. If Da thought that Job could give one of us the power to kill the other, to settle the question of who should rule the old way? Maybe."

ON THE other side of the clearing, in the lea of the cottage, Gregor's huge, tawny frame appeared for a second through the trees. He glanced their way, finding them unerringly. Then he was gone again.

A second later Job loped out of the cottage, wearing his dead wolf's skin over his own. Mangy patchwork fur was soaked to his body, picking out the strained tendons and trembling sinews struggling to balance that mass of bone and muscle.

Somehow, though, Danny thought the hide's dip in the river had… lessened it. He squinted, trying to bring the wolf into focus, and saw bald patches on his shoulders and hips, raw and weeping like lick granulomas, and it seemed to slide on his bones more. Two monsters, one of them Brock, squeezed out the door behind him, snapping at each other as they jostled for preference, and squatted like knots of muscle and bone at Job's side.

Job looked around, searching the snow-filled predawn.

"Cowards and weasels hide," he yelled. Pausing, he worked his tongue around the inside of his mouth, then spat out a chunk of broken tooth. "Should we make the dog's bitch scream? Will you come out then?"

Jack pressed down on Danny's shoulder, growling a command to "shh" in his ear. It was only then that Danny felt the growl vibrating in his throat. He bit the inside of his cheek until he tasted blood and swallowed hard, gulping the anger back down into his chest.

"While we deal with Job, go get your woman," Jack said into his ear. "Get her out of here. Understood?"

It made sense. Jenny would just be in the way, and Danny wasn't much more use in a knock-down fight. Making sense didn't make it any easier to swallow. His loyalty *should* be to Jenny. Even if he never loved her the way she—the way they'd both—wanted, he did love her. Except, the thought of leaving Jack to fight with only Gregor to have his back....

It had always been too fucking easy to love Jack, and too damn hard to stop.

Still he needed to get Jenny out of here. It was his fault she was involved in this, and whoever he loved, he owed it to her to keep her safe.

"Okay," he said, voice stiff.

Jack stared at him for a second. Once he was sure Danny was under control, he stood up and stepped out into the open. Lightning cracked again overhead, forking through the snow in a brilliant flash.

"The Numitor will kill you for this," Jack said, stalking toward the broken fence. Job stood, one hand on Brock's head like he was a favored pet, and waited.

"I might be exiled over the Wall, but I'm still his son. And he named Gregor his heir."

A smile on a wolf's face was a horrible thing. "Gregor disobeyed his da when he chased you down here. He sent me down here to make a wolf out of one of ye, and if that don't work? He'll wash his hands of cubs, and the Numitor will lead us into the wolf winter," Job said. "He's right too. Except *he* thinks that will be him."

"And you think it'll be you?" Jack asked, contempt in his voice. "*You're* going to challenge my da?"

There was something sly in the slide of Job's eyes, the wet lap of his tongue at his chops. It gave Danny a familiar sinking feeling in his gut, the same one he'd had when he turned up at university thinking he knew everything and found out he was wrong. The realization the world was keeping *secrets*.

"Why not a prophet?" Job asked, still sly. He reached down and petted Brock's wet, bloody head. "You damn us to this, *sentence* us to it, and then spit on us for our service. Now our prophecies are proven right, the gods are coming, and why should we be your whipping boys anymore? Let the wolf winter rage, and under our—my—leadership, the gods will see we can still serve. The wolves might spit on us, but the gods will see our loyalty!"

Jack spat in the snow. "Never met a prophet that didn't mouth off against dogs. Now we know why: you envy their collars."

Rage twisted Job's gray lips back from his dual row of teeth. He clenched his fist in the hump of loose skin on the back of Brock's neck and threw him toward Jack. Brock staggered, then caught himself and raced over the snow. Drool flew from his outthrust jaw, splattering the snow with dirty commas of spit.

Jack met the charge, shifting into a wolf between one step and the next. He bit Brock's face, ripping a chunk of flesh from eye socket to jaw and spitting it out like he tasted foul. Brock howled, broken teeth visible through his torn face, and swung his arm in a brutal, hammering blow. It caught Jack on the shoulder, and he went flying nose over tail. He landed in the mud, skidded and jumped back to his feet. His lips wrinkled back in a snarl as he shook his head, trying to shed the dizziness.

Danny lurched halfway to his feet and then froze, his debt to Jenny locking his joints.

Maybe Brock remembered the first fight with Jack, in the car park of the flat. He roared a challenge and skidded through the snow toward the dazed wolf. He moved like a gorilla, only putting his weight on the heel of his hand instead of absent knuckles.

Job roared with laughter. "Beat by a monkey with claws," he gnawed out the words. "Won't have to kill the old man; he'll die o' shame."

Before he could finish gloating, Gregor came flying out of the trees and hit Brock in the shoulder. He was a big man, a bigger wolf, and he staggered him. Snapping teeth tore his ear, scraped the bone on his front leg. Brock slipped in the mud, landing awkwardly on his hip, and Jack darted in to worry at his face.

Mood quickly curdling, Job kicked the other monster and sent it—her once, maybe—lumbering out into the fight.

Chapter Twenty-Three

JACK SPUN and sank his teeth into the monster's leg. The huge muscles in his jaw clenched down until he felt bone grit and crack against his fangs. Sour flesh and sourer blood flooded his mouth. He resisted the urge to spit the taint out—the Wild world of ancient trees and clean air fading as what the man wanted took precedence over the wolf's instincts—and shook violently. He felt the distinctive snap of it in his jaw.

The thing screamed like it was still human and reared up onto her back legs. She swung him up off the ground, still dangling like an idiot, and slapped him into a tree. His own blood in his mouth still tasted clean. He felt his ribs bow inward until they snapped; then the Wild breathed into him until he was so full of it his ribs popped back into shape. Like he was a deflated balloon instead of a living thing. By the time he hit the ground, he could fight again.

Gregor darted in and bit the fatty curve of Brock's mostly human ass. He'd always been a dirty fighter, Jack's little brother. Sharp fangs tore off a chunk of hard flesh, retching at the stink of it, and the thing whirled on him. Quicker than the bulk of him would suggest, Gregor dodged backward. The snaps and snarls of him, teeth clicking shut just shy of its nose, kept the thing after him.

The fight was a tangle of pulled fur, blood, and fangs. Gregor and Jack had the advantage of a lifetime of animosity, the familiarity of knowing how each other fought and the weaknesses they'd catalogued. The monsters were slower, clumsier. They kept getting into their own way, fouling their partner's strikes.

Except that didn't stop them, didn't even slow them down. Either they didn't feel the pain, or it was nothing compared to the agony of broken bones and reshaped flesh.

It wouldn't be *enough*, not with the Wild's favor on Jack. He *could* kill him. The only question was if he could do it in time. The monsters hardened with every bite, every blow, their bodies looking for the right shape.

If Danny had been here to give them numbers....

Jack let the thought wash over and out of him. "If" was empty thought; the wolves knew there was no point to it. He cut around one of the monsters, blue-and-yellow cotton knotted between her heavy muscles, and tore the hamstrings out, savaging the back of her knee like it was his first kill. Shredding like that took longer to heal, and without someone to pull the tendons together, it wouldn't be clean. It would collapse under the monster's weight.

"Get down!" Danny yelled, his voice cracking and the smell of his fear pungent. "Now!"

Without thinking about it, Jack did as he was told.

There was a crack, and the monster's head jerked to the side. It looked like nothing, but blood and brains were sprayed over Brock's face. Chunks of it caught in his ears, the bits that got in his mouth making him hack and scramble backward. The monster in yellow and blue swayed in place for a second and then toppled over, flopping onto its side with a boneless finality. Most of the front of her face was gone, peeled off as its head exploded.

Danny stood behind it, looking nearly as surprised as Jack felt. His eyes were wide, oddly soft when they weren't peering through glass, and he held a bright yellow nail gun plastered in peeling safety stickers in shaking hands. Vapor was coiling around the edges of it.

Gregor shrugged off his surprise and went after Brock.

Before following him, Jack cocked his head questioningly. Danny bared his teeth in a quick, shaken smile. "I'm good. Go."

Once they could tag team Brock, it didn't take long to take it down. Gregor jumped on his back, clawing at his ribs and gnawing his way down to the spine, while Jack harried him hard enough to stop him scraping his brother off.

Brock. He'd met him briefly. He'd not cared then, or now, but monsters needed a name in a tale. If their father was behind this, Jack would be damned to Selene's wake if he was going to let it go.

Finally Gregor got his fangs in Brock's spine and something cracked. The monster dropped, eyes glazing over and sides heaving with the desperation of air going nowhere. Gregor pried his jaws free and slid off the thing, ears flat and nose wrinkled with dislike at the taste. He shook himself, shedding frost and blood, and then shared a wolf grin with Jack.

They might hate each other, but they'd just fought monsters and won. It was a thing of legend.

"Jack!"

It was Danny, his voice sharp and anxious, who broke the rare moment of fraternal affection. Jack turned hard, gaze snapping first to Danny and then to what Danny was staring at. Job limped out of the house, dragging Jenny with him. His hand was wrapped around her throat, claws drawing blood from her collarbones.

Jenny struggled, clawing at Job's fingers. "Danny! Danny, what's going on?"

"Let her go," Danny said, shifting his weight forward. His hands worked around the gun he was still hanging on to. "If you hurt her, I'll go north myself and tell everyone you failed. Just another prophet, howling his shite to the wind."

That hit close to the raw spot in whatever passed for Job's soul. It made him flinch, claws digging deeper into Jenny's shoulder. She cried out and then bit the noise back, teeth digging in her lower lip until it went pale.

Jack dragged back his human form. It took more effort than usual, his bones burning as the Wild reluctantly ceded its hold on him. "Cowards and weasels hide, remember?" he said, throwing Job's words back at him. "What do you call someone who hides behind a human woman?"

Yanking Jenny in front of him, Job hooked his arm around her throat. He pressed a furred paw-hand against her temple, pushing her head over his forearm hard. "Should I just break her neck, then?" he asked. A coarse laugh scraped through his jagged teeth. "It's not as if you have any use for her, pup prince."

Gregor went for him, two hundred pounds of muscle and bone latching onto Job's crooked arm. Thrown off-balance by the flailing wolf attached to his arm, Job staggered backward. He let go of Jenny, kicking her back into the house, and swung his arm to slam Gregor against the brick side of the house.

"Shoot him!" Jack yelled. When Danny hesitated, he roared, "Now, dammit! Shoot him!"

The gun fired. Jack wasn't sure if Danny had obeyed him or just flinched. Job staggered back, blood spurting from his shoulder. A second shot caught him in the barrel chest. He staggered, blood dripping down his body, and snarled in pain. The stolen skin he was wearing was ripping, leaving him raw and wet underneath, as Gregor thrashed and raked at him with frost-sharpened claws.

Roaring in pain, Job grabbed Gregor by the back of the neck and wrenched. Gregor hung on, stripping Job's arm down to the bone in long, oozing rents. The stolen skin caught in his incisors, peeling fur and finger-ends off in a slimy, maggot-dripping mess. Grabbing Gregor's back leg, Job swung the wolf against the side of the building until Gregor went limp.

The sharp jolt of fear and grief as Job dropped his brother to the ground surprised Jack. If anything, he'd expected to feel relieved, not concerned.

"Don't stop now!" Jack snarled, turning to look at Danny. "Shoot the fucker."

"I can't," Danny said, shaking the gun like it was a misbehaving remote. "It's been in a shed in the cold for a month. Fuck sake, Jack, I was lucky it worked *once*. It's dead now."

Of course it was. The Wild loved its wolves, but it loved chaos more. Jack threw his head back, letting the rain sluice over his face, and laughed. He could taste the water on his tongue, the sting of ozone masking the chemical flatness of it.

"Run now, Danny," he said. "Get the girl and run."

"Fuck off."

The denial was flat, steady at his shoulder. Jack opened his eyes, swiping his sleeve over his face. Job had kicked the fence down and was lumbering toward them, blood pumping sluggishly from the hole in his chest. It was already healing, layering more muscle over it like a pressure bandage.

"No," Jack said. Then his voice rose to a shout, almost a scream over the noise of the storm. "Fuck him. Fuck you, Job! You whining, pathetic *asshole*. We sentenced you to be a prophet? Your *sins* made you a prophet, and now you're a monster. You could have had my da's ear during the wolf winter, and now you've got nothing."

A horrible, blank rage washed through Job's twisted face, and he threw himself into a lunging run across the snow. For a second the world Jack saw was tinted green, shadows of great trees stretching up into the sky, and a pack sang in the dark. It wasn't the worst moment to have before you died. Jack reached out to the Wild and breathed it in, filling himself with it until he felt the "Jack" of him starting to wash away.

Lightning flashed, blinding them all. Someone screamed, and the smell of scorched meat and burning hair washed over both of them.

When they could see again, Job still stood on the path where he had been. The monster was gone, leaving only the man. For some reason it seemed like he was going to say something. They stared at each other for a second, then Job's cooked-pale eyes rolled back into his head and his knees went out from under him.

A hand brushed down his back, from his shoulders to the small of his back. Danny pressed against his shoulder, and he was Jack again. Mostly. It felt different in his head, or his heart, like he'd given something over to the Wild, and it hadn't returned it.

"Is he dead?" Danny asked.

"I fucking hope so," Jack muttered. He started toward his brother and nearly fell over, exhaustion hitting him like a mallet. It had been a long night. He'd ridden far into the Wild, and now he had to pay the price.

Danny slouched down so Jack could sling an arm over his shoulder, and they stumbled down to where Gregor lay. Jack gritted his teeth and lowered himself into the mud, creaky as an old man. He reached out to grip the thick, furred shoulder. Under Jack's fingers, the fur slid away, and Gregor slipped back into human skin.

If Gregor had enough of the Wild left to survive that, he'd live. It would take a while to mend—the Wild was fading with the light—but he would. And maybe one day Jack would regret not finishing it now, but…. There'd never been any love lost between him and Gregor; there probably never would be. Their da loved him, though, and he deserved better than knowing his son died in the mud because of something he'd set in motion.

"You'll survive," Jack said, slapping the back of Gregor's head.

His brother groaned and rolled over, hugging his splintered ribcage together with his arm. "Ask me later if that's a good thing. Get me up."

Between them Danny and Jack hauled Gregor to his feet, bruises spreading under his skin like spilled ink. They staggered over to the dead man. Dead and cooked, from the smell of him. Leaving Danny to hang on to Gregor, Jack kicked the body over. The lightning had burned Gregor's lips black and left nothing but chalky marbles under his eyes. Livid burns cut through the rank ink on his pale, heavy body. The scars looked like one of the ancient trees of the Wild, scorched into his chest and thighs. Jack stared down at him and tried to feel something. All he had was a sort of weary dread, because this wasn't over.

"Fuck. If my da ever asks, tell him I said something worthy of an Edda?"

Gregor laughed at him, wincing as it jarred his guts. Taking one last look at the dead man, Jack left him and went over to take his brother's weight off Danny. "You should go," he said. When Danny blinked at him, Jack nodded toward the house. "Your friend's still inside."

Danny hesitated, glancing around at the dead monsters, the dead prophet. "What about them?"

"That's my job." Jack shrugged. "You need to know she's okay. And I know where your loyalties lie now."

Chapter Twenty-Four

JACK'S WORDS replayed on a loop in Danny's mind as he headed toward the house. After Job had dropped her, Jenny had crawled back into the house. It would be easier to work out what he'd meant if Danny knew himself. There was blood and brains on the ground, and he still wasn't sure. Not sure.

Wrong thing to think about. He could still feel the punch of the gun in his elbow and shoulder, that dull thump of the monster's head exploding. The satisfaction at making the kill flooded his mouth with spit before he could remind himself it was—had been—a person, not dinner.

His stomach turned sickly at the memory, his heart cramping as if his breastbone had shrunk. It was hard to breathe. He stopped at the front door, leaning against the wall, and closed his eyes. Just for a second, so he could focus on the rain soaking him and not anything else.

Wolves didn't have panic attacks. Wolves didn't get the shakes after killing someone.

It was a shame he was just a dog. He'd not mind being braver. Instead he just had to make do with being responsible. And right now, that meant finding Jenny.

"Jenny?" he called. He tried again, louder this time. "Jenny? It's me. It's safe now."

After a second, a tight voice answered from the back of the house. "Here."

He huffed a sigh in relief and hurried toward her, finding her curled up in the closet under the stairs. There was blood in her hair, on her jacket. Her hands were bruised, the nails torn down to the scabbed quicks.

"You have no idea how glad I am to see you," Danny said, his grin feeling weird on his face.

Jenny reminded him why. "Your face is covered in blood, Danny."

"Oh." He wiped his arm over his face. It probably hadn't helped much. Jenny was still staring him as if he was a monster. "Sorry. I.... There was a fight. I... anyhow, I'm fine. Let's get you out of here."

He crouched down next to her, reaching for her. She flinched away from him, tucking her foot under her calf. "Don't touch me. What are you?"

It was the question he'd always known to expect. It still hurt more than he'd thought. "This isn't the time, Jenny."

He tried to pull her out from under the stairs. She hit him, fist catching his cheek, and then shoved him, punching him back with her fists. It wasn't effective, but Danny let it work. He dropped back onto the ground, hipbones taking the impact, and folded his arms over his knees.

"What are you?" she repeated. "Are you like them? Like Job and Brock?"

"I'm not a monster, Jenny. I'm just Danny. Come on, you don't want to stay here. Please, we can talk later."

He waited, hands dangling over his knees, while she studied him with narrowed eyes. After a long moment, she took a deep breath and crawled out from the dusty alcove. Danny went to help her out, but she shied away from him. He had to let her struggle back to her feet on her own. She wiped one hand over her neck, smearing blood.

"I want to go home," she said stiffly, not quite looking at Danny.

"It's a long way," he said. "I could carry—"

"No." She shook her head, matted hair swinging over her shoulders in elflocks. Refusing his arm, even, she limped over to the door. It was still snowing outside, but the dim light was a little less dim. The garden was empty, the dead gone. Danny didn't know where and didn't want to know. Not yet.

"It's over, Jenny," he said. "You'll be okay. Just try and forget about it."

She sighed and rested her head on his shoulder. Her breath was hot against his throat, and he could smell how scared of him she was. "Are you human?" she asked.

He hesitated, which he supposed was answer enough for her purposes. "Yeah," he said at last. "Just something else too."

IT TOOK a mile before she let him pick her up and take her the rest of the way home. Then he went to get Adil. Both of them had questions he couldn't answer.

Except he thought he probably could have. Like Jack had told him, the world was different now, and the Numitor had other, better, reasons to kill Danny if he wanted.

He didn't, though.

"You had a seizure and a fever when I found you," he told Jenny instead. "Maybe you were hallucinating. After everything you went through with Brock, it's not surprising."

He lied, and they both knew it. Jenny chose to accept it anyhow. Just one more crack in the foundation of their friendship. Without her....

All Danny's posturing about how this was his home, and it took so little to take it away.

There was no sign of Jack. Danny supposed he couldn't complain about that. It was what he had wanted, wasn't it? To be left alone. Well, finally everyone was doing just that.

And he was over the fucking moon—so what if that was just another lie.

So he wore his old glasses, squinting through a four-year-old prescription, and kept his packed bag kicked under the bed. He thought about going home too, for the first time in years. Not that he imagined some teary reunion, but his mum had done her best for him. It had been brusque and sometimes cruel, but it had been all she had, and she'd given it to him.

It would be a long walk, and cold, but he should let her know about what the prophets had planned.

A COLD hand over his mouth woke him up. He sucked in a shocked breath through the hard fingers and tried to struggle free, flailing about violently until his brain caught up with his nose. Pine, blood, and old high places.

He stopped fighting, his long body relaxing into the mattress. After a pause to make sure he wasn't just faking it, Jack moved his hand.

"Where have you been?" Danny asked, rolling over and squinting at the shadowy blur perched on the edge of the bed. He immediately grimaced at himself, because that didn't sound needy at all. "I mean, what happened after I left?"

"I was waiting for you," Jack said. He picked up the candle from the bedside table and held it in both hands. The flickering twist of a lit flame was visible in his eyes a second before the wick sizzled and caught. Now he was just a blur. Jack picked up something from the table and slid them onto Danny's nose, bringing the room into focus. "You're late, Danny Dog."

Danny sat up, hitching the quilt up over his shoulders. He adjusted his glasses, shoving them up onto the bridge of his nose.

"I hate that," he said.

"Yeah? I like it," Jack said. He tilted his head, candlelight glazing his eyes. "So, are you back to playing human, Danny Dog?"

No. He supposed he wasn't. He'd spent the past week lying and keeping his distance, too sick with shift-fever to work at remembering how to fake it. Adil and Jenny didn't have anything to accuse him of. They'd not seen *him* do anything. It didn't matter—they knew he had secrets. They knew that whatever he was, he wasn't one of them.

"I'm not playing wolf either," Danny said.

Jack rolled his eyes and shoved Danny down on the bed, straddling his hips. He dug his hands into Danny's hair, holding him still.

"Good," he said. "I like you, my dog-loyal, dogged dog."

Danny showed his teeth. "Fuck off, wolf boy."

Jack laughed and kissed him, slanting his mouth roughly over Danny's. He dug his thumbs into the side of Danny's jaw until he opened his mouth, claiming his mouth with his tongue. With a frustrated sigh, lost in Jack's mouth, Danny ran his hands down the heavy muscles of Jack's back. He lingered on Jack's ass, digging his fingers into the taut curve of muscle and then around to tug at the fly of his jeans.

"I'd rather fuck you," Jack said, pushing himself off Danny long enough to shove his jeans down and kick them off. He threw the quilt off Danny, grinning at finding out he was wearing nothing underneath. A callused hand stroked up his thigh, muscles twitching under the touch, to cup Danny's balls. "You're my dog, remember?"

Danny arched up into Jack's hand, digging his fingers into the sheets until they ripped. His breath was ragged against his teeth. "That's kind of offensive."

"Yeah?" Jack snorted. "Your cock doesn't think so." He wrapped his hand around it, dragging tight fingers from base to tip. Then he sprawled out on top of Danny, his erection pushing damply against Danny's thigh. "Neither does mine."

There were probably a lot of things Danny should have said. A vague, hormone-dazed "um" was all he got out.

Shifting position Jack shackled their cocks together with one hand, using the other to shove Danny back into the mattress when he tried to sit up. "I've been thinking. The humans should know you don't need fucked." He thrust, his cock sliding hard and slick against Danny's, Jack's fingers rough on both. "Don't want them thinking you need fixed or something."

Danny had squeezed his eyes shut, breath hooked in his throat as hot pleasure clenched the muscles in his thighs and gut. He squinted one eye open long enough to punch Jack in the shoulder.

"Not. Funny."

A smirk tugged at Jack's mouth as he leaned down to kiss Danny, catching his lower lip between his teeth. "What? Did you get picked up by the dogcatcher?"

Trying to buck him off just ground Danny's cock against the hard line of Jack's stomach. Sensation dragged at him like spiced honey, slick and hot under his skin. He cursed raggedly, throwing his head back into the pillows as he struggled for control. Jack occupied himself by biting his way down his neck to his collarbone, all teeth and hot, wet, sucking mouth.

He didn't move his hips or his hands until Danny stopped swearing; then he rolled his hips and twisted his hands. And… fuck. Danny came over his fingers, his spent seed smearing fingers and stomachs in a messy clot. His throat hurt a bit as the euphoria slid away, and he was pretty sure everyone in the building had heard that.

"Humans ain't the only ones that can be clever," Jack drawled, brogue thick enough to taste. He rolled Danny over and shoved his thighs together. He slid his cock into the wet valley of skin and taut muscle, a short growl escaping him as Danny clenched his thighs together.

One hand scruffed the back of his neck as Jack rubbed against him, the hard length of him grinding against Danny from asshole to balls. Danny cursed raggedly as nerves twitched and fired in his already spent cock, and he pushed back into each thrust.

Jack was silent when he came, just hot, ragged breathing and the weight of him flopping on Danny's back as warm come soaked into the bed. They sprawled there, catching their breaths and cooling down. Jack didn't move once he had, just growled lazily when Danny tried to elbow him.

"I don't give a fuck if you're a dog," Jack said, shifting to tuck his knee between Danny's legs and stretch his arm over the bed. Fresh black ink scored the skin, up in welts from the aconite used. "I ain't pretending you're suddenly going to sprout a pointier nose and your ears will stop flopping over."

"They don't *flop*," Danny grumbled, trying to find his annoyance when all his body cared about was sleeping.

Jack licked his ear, scraping his teeth over the curve of cartilage. "They do a bit, at the top. It's kinda cute. Stop running away from jabs that ain't coming, Danny."

"...okay."

A sharp chin tucked into his shoulder, and Jack craned his head around to squint at him. "Okay? That it?"

Danny shrugged the best he could with a wolf lying on him. "What else do you want?"

After a second, Jack blinked and went back to using Danny as a pillow. "We need to go back over the Wall. Da...."

"I know. I'm packed," Danny said. He ran his fingers through Jack's hair, feeling the contented huff of reaction along the line of their bodies. "Will your brother be keeping us company?"

Jack snorted and shrugged. "Probably," he said. "He took off once he could stand on his own, but if he's not heading back to warn our da, he'll probably tag along to try and kill me."

The old, hard enmity was back in his voice. Apparently it took more than abominations and an apostate prophet to reconcile the Numitor's sons. Danny sighed and dropped his head against the pillows, staring up at the ceiling, where he was probably never going to get around to filling that crack in the plaster now.

"I guess I can't deny the wolf winter's here anymore," he said.

"Here?" Jack said, not bothering to move. "Danny, it's barely started."

Sequel to *Dog Days*
A Wolf Winter Novel

When the winter arrives, the Wolves will come down over the walls and eat little boys in their beds.

Doctor Nicholas Blake might still be afraid of the dark, but the monsters his grandmother tormented him with as a child aren't real.

Or so he thinks… until the sea freezes, the country grinds to a halt under the snow, and he finds a half-dead man bleeding out while a dead woman watches. Now his nightmares impinge on his waking life, and the only one who knows what's going on is his unexpected patient.

For Gregor, it's simple. The treacherous prophets mutilated him and stole his brother Jack, and he's going to kill them for it. Without his wolf, it might be difficult, but he'll be damned if anyone else gets to kill Jack—even if he has to enlist the help of his distractingly attractive, but very human, doctor.

Except maybe the prophets want something worse than death, and maybe Nick is less human than Gregor believes. As the dead gather and the old stories come true, the two men will need each other if they're going to rescue Jack and stop the prophets' plan to loose something more terrible than the wolf winter.

Chapter One

"I'M A pathologist," Nick had protested as the hospital administrator shoved a clipboard and hi-vis vest at him. "What good am I going to be to a relief effort?"

No one had listened. It was all hands on deck as the SNP proved they could manage their own disasters without any help from England. Except they couldn't, and it was small comfort that, by all accounts, neither could anywhere else in the UK. The winter had swept across the country with brutal, climatic efficiency, and all their glorious civilization ground to a frozen halt.

Helicopters were grounded, train tracks frozen over, and most importantly, the off-licenses were either sold out or looted.

Nick only had one bottle of whiskey left, and that would not be enough.

Faced with the prospect of an unstocked liquor cabinet—otherwise known as a filing cabinet—Nick added an extra shot to his tepid coffee. He took a drink and grimaced as the bitter burn hit the back of his throat. At this point he could probably just drop the pretense and admit it was just whiskey in a coffee mug.

Nick took another drink, apparently determined to chase that empty bottle, and closed his eyes for a second. Last night's hangover poked at his eyelids with raspy fingers, and the little bit of professional pride that wasn't numb with the cold hissed reproachfully at him.

"Fuck you," he told it. His voice echoed back to him dully as it bounced off the walls. "This is your fault anyhow."

He sighed and opened his eyes. The world had gone to hell, and Nick was apparently going to face it sober, but there was still work to do. He turned and cast a grim eye over his makeshift base of operations.

It was billed as an *Entertainment Center* on the sign outside.

Even at its best, Nick couldn't imagine it had been that entertaining. It was a corrugated iron box with a flat plastic roof in the middle of a run-down trailer park, probably sweaty hot in the summer and definitely Baltic in the winter. There was a heavy cover that turned the small pool into a stage and a poster still taped to the front door. The paper was yellowed and the tape brittle. It advertised a tribute act to the pop band Bucks Fizz (Buck the Frizz) as a headline event in the 1980s. From the layer of dust in the pool, it had been drained since that concert, but the smell of chlorine still lingered in the air.

Not even the real Bucks Fizz could liven up the atmosphere now. Frost crusted the dips in the metal, the paintwork was fractured and peeling where the ice crystals had pushed through, and corpses wrapped in tarps and plastic sheets were laid out along the edge of the pool. It looked like a particularly macabre holiday brochure photo.

Nick was the only doctor in Ayr who still had a full practice list.

He fished his voice recorder out of his pocket and turned it on... probably. The cold had cracked the casing, and the LED had given up the glowing ghost a week earlier. It didn't look like it was working, and there was no way to tell if it was or not until he stumbled over to the Trauma Base to use the only computer hooked up to the generator.

Until then—Nick tapped his thumb on Record—he just had to take it on faith.

"This is Doctor Nicholas Blake," he said. His accent slurred down-market as he talked. Exhaustion and, to be fair, booze had eroded a natural talent for mimicry and one year of elocution lessons. His vowels had gone all Glasgie. He thought about caring and decided he didn't. "I am continuing to process the dead recovered from Ayr."

It was stark, said out loud like that.

Nick tucked the recorder into his breast pocket, where hopefully it would still pick up his voice. He looked at the body laid out on the flimsy Formica table he'd dragged over from the kitchens to serve as a makeshift slab—not ideal under normal circumstances, but these were hardly normal circumstances, even for Scotland.

He remembered scoffing over weak tea with his colleagues in Edinburgh as the snow piled up outside. They'd made fun of the soft Southerners who thought a bit of snow was the end of the world and joked about missing *I'm a Celebrity* this year. The Scots were used to bad weather, cold winters, wet springs, and the legend of summer. When winter came early, it was just something to grumble about and stock up on whiskey.

Even as the helicopter took off from the hospital roof and Nick perched on a box of antibiotics and saline and peered with that familiar queasy fascination at the retreating earth, he'd thought it was all under control. It would be a few hard months, and once it was over, farmers would apply for compensation for their dead sheep, the *Guardian* would write op-eds about global warming, and the odds would be significantly better for a white Christmas next year.

He'd been wrong. They all had. It probably didn't make any difference to the dead, though.

"Deceased is a teenage female," Nick recited for the record. He picked up his digital camera and breathed on the lens to melt the glaze of frost. The first photo was of the girl's pale face, bruises discoloring her temples and the hollows around her eyes. Even in death the cold pinched her lips and left them chapped and dark. The clips still in her hair, rhinestone butterflies against wet-dark curls, were quietly macabre. Nick lifted her arm. The flesh was stiff and chilled under his gloved fingers. "Identifying mark of a rose tattoo on inner forearm. Initials *I-C* are included. No ID was found with the remains."

He snapped a picture of that, the ink dull under dead skin, and set the girl's arm back down on the table. Two more pictures, to chronicle the mole on her hip and the scar on the back of her ankle, and he set the camera aside.

"Cause of death is presumed to be hypothermia."

Nick put the envelope containing the girl's personal effects on her chest and sealed the body bag. He scrawled a number in Sharpie on the plastic, and job done. The girl would join the rest of the logged remains in the deep end of the small pool and then be transferred to the shallow, temporary grave site in the waste ground outside the trailer park.

And that was it. Nick's job was done. On to the next corpse. Sometimes the body would present with injuries inconsistent with the cold as a cause of death, but even then, all he did was chronicle the injuries the same way he did scars and tattoos. It wasn't a job that really required twelve years of medical school and nearly a decade of experience. A janitor with a checklist to work off could have done the same job.

Not that Nick had anything else to do. He was only meant to be there for three days—an in-and-out mercy mission to drop off medical supplies and evacuate the critically ill and vulnerable to a world-class hospital with an emergency generator and prepared staff. That was four weeks ago.

The medical supplies had been used up. Contact with the world-class hospital had begun with platitudes about finding a way to get them out and ended with silence. The critically ill were mostly under Nick's care now.

So Nick logged the dead, tried not to think about how much he missed picking them apart, and waited for his whiskey to run out. Once it did—he picked up the mug and took a gulp that warmed him up just enough to make him realize he was freezing—he'd see what came next.

The cold was brutal, and the equipment they'd been given wasn't sufficient for the conditions. Nick was nearly forty, nearly fit, and he drank too much even before the snowpocalypse. His fingers had lost sensation. He needed booze to control the scratchy cough that woke him up at night, and he'd skipped meals because his stomach ached as though it couldn't digest what he shoved in there. It might have been years since Nick treated a live body, but if he put his mind to it, he could probably diagnose himself.

But once he did, there was only one real resolution on the table and he wasn't ready to lie down in the pool with the rest of the corpses—not yet. There were still a few shots of whiskey left and plenty of remains to chronicle.

Nick shifted the girl's corpse. The next in line was a contorted, naked man with bloody hands and feet.

"Presumed cause of death is hypothermia," Nick said tiredly. "Injuries are consistent with 'terminal burrowing,' and with the state the remains were—"

Someone hammered on the door. It made the whole building rattle as it vibrated out along the metal walls. Up in the corners of the roof, ice cracked and dropped onto the corpses. Nick jumped in reaction and nearly knocked the dead man off the table.

"Fuck," Nick spat out. His heart skipped a beat and then another before it finally, sluggishly started again. It felt as though it were wedged in the base of his throat, like a chicken bone. He swallowed hard and rubbed his knuckles against his chest to shift the ache. "Shit."

He yanked the dead man back onto the center of the table and folded the tarp over him, as though he might still care if someone saw his frostbitten genitals.

Whoever was outside had stopped banging on the door. Apparently it wasn't as urgent as they had thought. Nick grumbled under his breath. Before they decided to give up, they'd woken every dog in the area and set them to howling. Nick stripped the gloves off as he stalked to the door. He yanked it open, and the blast of cold that blew in shocked the irritation out of him. It had gotten dark while he was working under the glare of portable generator-powered lights, and the storm had picked up again. There was no fresh snow to add to the grubby drifts piled up against the nicotine-beige caravans, but a wind armed with ice had blown in off the sea.

The dogs filled the night with frantic, aggressive noise that bounced off the metal sides of the trailers. It made it difficult to place anything.

"Hello?" Nick asked sharply. The cold worked under the heavy cuffs of his jumper and dug down into his bones. It dried out his nose as he inhaled. "Nelson? This isn't funny, you idiot."

He grabbed his coat from beside the door and shrugged it on as he stepped outside. The snow came up to his ankles, a bitter trickle down into his boots, and the wind flapped the long tails of his coat behind him. It splayed his shadow over the snow like grubby wings.

"Nelson?"

He took a step forward and looked around for the idiot paramedic. Back in Edinburgh, Nelson had been a "two sugars in a sugarless tea" joker. The last weeks stuck in a shoddy trailer site on the edge of a shrinking, snowbound town had edged the practical joker into an almost manic need to coax a laugh from someone. It wasn't working.

Nick held his coat closed over his chest with one hand and ventured another precarious step outside. He squinted against the wind and wiped his nose on his sleeve.

"Hello?" he said.

Something familiar and bitter teased at his nose. He had a good sense of smell. He'd always been the "do you smell that?" guy. But he couldn't quite place that smell. The cold dulled everything. He took another step. His feet were already soaked.

"I'm not in the mood." Nick scowled into the dark. "Jim? What is it? Does Jepson want to see me?"

Someone groaned in the dark. The sound was low and wet and suggestive. Nick would have blushed if he weren't so cold. He licked his lips and felt the sting of spit in open cracks.

"Go to hell."

Nick turned and stumbled through the snow, back toward the still-open door. His shoulders were hunched and tense, the muscles knotted into a tight ache. He shouldn't have slept with Nelson. It would have been a bad idea even if they weren't stuck there until the weather eased off.

If. A paranoid voice creaked a correction in the back of his brain. If it eased off. It was his gran's voice, old Scottish pessimism to the point of preaching the apocalypse and a clip around the ear if you left your shoes on the table or your hat on the bed, or the other way around, just to be safe.

She was born around here, he remembered—up north a few miles—a "proper Highlander" as she always said.

Nick reached the threshold and kicked the clumped snow off his boots. "Go ahead and freeze, then," he tossed sourly back over his shoulder.

But something made him hesitate in the doorway—maybe the smell, still naggingly familiar, or the second groan that clawed its way over the wind. That time it sounded… thick instead of wet. Across the trailer park, he saw lights flicker down at Jepson's trailer. The trauma leader was still up and at work. Her silhouette paused in front of the grubby net curtains, and someone joined her there.

Maybe not at work. Nick started to turn away, but then he stopped and looked again. Heavy jackets and layers made everyone the same shape, more or less, but the second figure was shorter than Jepson. So unless the surgeon had decided to kiss a girl and see if she liked it, that meant it was Nelson.

Blood.

The scent finally worked its way far enough up his nose that he could pick the copper and salt stink of it out from the sharp ozone smell of the snow and the distant salty reek of the sea.

Nick lurched back out into the snow. "Copeland! Harris!" he yelled for his neighbors. The wind caught his voice and stretched the words out thin and tinny from his lips. "Someone's hurt out here. Help!"

The door on one of the shabby vans creaked open, and Copeland looked out. Her hair was matted down on one side, and her broken arm was strapped carefully across her chest. She used her teeth to pull her heavy padded jacket over her shoulder as she gingerly came down the metal-grille steps.

"Who is it?" she asked, eyes wide and afraid.

"Don't know," Nick said. "I thought it was Nelson playing silly buggers, but...."

He jerked his head toward Jepson's caravan. Copeland looked in that direction, and, even though there was no one visible at the window anymore, she blushed.

"Maybe they're just... I mean, Doctor Jepson is married."

He snorted.

Copeland pulled a flashlight out of her pocket with her good hand and thumbed it on. The narrow beam of bright light flicked back and forth over the snow for a second and then stopped abruptly on a patch of dark, half-melted snow in front of one of the unused caravans. "Doctor Blake. There. Oh my God, they're bleeding."

Nick shifted direction and lumbered toward the stain. The snow was up to his shins as he veered off the trodden-down path and into the heavy, iced-over drifts. He caught his foot on something—a pot, an old bit of fence—and pitched forward onto his knees.

Other lights were going on across the park. He heard doors open and some voices demanding to know what was going on and others yelling at the dogs to shut up.

The beam of the flashlight flittered away and played randomly over the side of the caravan as Copeland hammered on the side of Harris's van.

"Wake up. Come on, man, we need help," she yelled.

Nick scrambled back to his feet and batted the ice off his knees with both hands. The wind caught his coat and viciously flapped it back and forth. Despite the cold, he had broken out in a slimy sweat under his arms and an itch at the back of his neck. The blood trail went from blotch to drip to smear before it disappeared under the trailer, dragged under the cracked brown latticework that covered the base. Old horror-movie instincts made him hesitate at the hole, where the smell of blood was so strong that it was impossible to mistake for anything else.

"Hey, are you okay?" Nick asked. Stupid question, but he felt like he had to break the silence. "Do you need any help? I'm a doctor. If you're hurt."

A rough rattle of air, almost lost under the wind, was his only answer. Nick took a deep breath, tasted the whiskey still on his tongue, and crawled into the gap. Snow soaked through his jeans, the chill of it jabbed into his knees like needles, and he had to fumble blindly in front of him to avoid the metal bars and pipes.

"...go...."

Nick squinted into the dark. He could just about make out a figure curled up against the trailer's tire, half-naked with a dark blanket hitched up over their hip. Something about the voice was.... Did he know them? It wasn't someone from the Relief Team, though. Maybe it was just the accent. Everyone up here burred their words like his gran had when she got merry.

"It's alright." Nick grimaced as he caught his shoulder against a sharp strut. "We can help. You're going to be okay."

Behind him he heard Copeland and Harris arguing as they got closer, her voice quick and panicky over his sleep-blurred questions. Nick was almost close enough to the man to touch his white sleeve when Harris demanded, "Who the hell is it, then?" and turned his torch under the trailer.

It wasn't a blanket. Blood coated the man's leg and stomach in a thick, almost syrupy film over raw skin. His chest was dappled with it too—arterial dark splatters that dripped onto the frosty ground in slow, persistent splats.

Nick didn't know him. The torch picked out the sharp lines in his lean, angular face and bounced back oddly from green eyes that looked too bright for the amount of blood. He was beautiful. It was an odd thing to notice in all that gore, but Nick couldn't help it.

"I don't need your help," he rasped out, his lips curled back from the words. "I don't need anyone's help."

"Of course you don't," Nick said. "You look like you're thriving under here."

His brain scrambled to pull up the half-forgotten, heavily depleted list of supplies stored in the old toilet block.

"Harris! Get in here and help me. You're the emergency medicine expert."

"I told you. I can die… on my own."

The man lifted his head off his arm, and Nick realized that the awkward lines of his folded body had created a sort of tourniquet that was now released. The steady drip of blood turned into a gush that steamed as the cold air hit it. Some ingrained habit from med school, back before they all agreed he was better with the dead, made Nick lurch forward and clap his hand against the man's throat. With his body pressed against the man's shoulder, he was close enough that it felt like an embrace—but somehow more intimate, with the bubble of the man's life caught in Nick's hand. The wound was wide and ragged, the edges bulging around his fingers as he tried to pinch them together.

"Who is it?" Harris persisted in the background. "What are they doing out here?"

Copeland's voice cracked. "Does it matter? We have to help him."

"What if it's a trick? What if those idiots come back to try and steal drugs we don't have?"

It felt alien. He was used to cold blood, still and settled under the skin. Not this hot gush, eager to escape and soak the ground. The man struggled against Nick's attempts to help him, his bloody hands slick and slippery as he pushed at Nick's arm and face. Blood smeared up over Nick's eye and into his hair. Through the glaze of red, he saw, for a second, a woman hanging off the man's shoulders by one wasted arm. Her fingers, so sharp and hard they looked like shrink-wrapped bone, plucked at the edges of the wound to try and open it.

Nick gasped and tasted rot and wine in the back of his throat. As though she could feel his attention on her, the woman looked up. Dirty, elflocked hair swayed back from her face, and Nick saw the sharp blade of an eroded nose and a glimpse of a dry yellow eye.

His bladder clenched and nearly spilled a night's worth of whiskey down his leg. He didn't want to see any more. Nick squeezed his hand tighter, resisted the pick-pick of dry fingers, and ducked his chin to wipe the blood off his face with his shoulder.

When he looked up, the woman was gone. He shuddered in relief, and the injured man stared at him as though he could tell what Nick had just seen.

"Tell him."

"Who? I don't know who that is. You'll have to tell him yourself," Nick said, the taste of metal and copper slipping onto his tongue. He glanced over his shoulder and yelled at the dithering Harris. "Just get in here and *help* me. He's bleeding."

"Tell the Old Man," the man said. The sharp clarity had faded from his eyes, leaving them dull and angry. He sagged against Nick, a heavy weight of muscle and bone and despair. "Tell him... I died first, if nothin' else."

"You're not dying. I got you," Nick insisted. He could feel the blood push against his fingers and run down his arms. The warmth of it was almost pleasant, even if it was in danger of making him a liar…. "Besides, I don't even know your name."

"Gregor." The man's head fell forward, and his chin braced against Nick's hand. "Tell him his favorite son died, but I went first."

TA MOORE genuinely believed that she was a Cabbage Patch Kid when she was a small child. This was the start of a lifelong attachment to the weird and fantastic. These days she lives in a market town on the Northern Irish coast and her friends have a rule that she can only send them three weird and disturbing links a month (although she still holds that a DIY penis bifurcation guide is interesting, not disturbing). She believes that adding 'in space!' to anything makes it at least 40% cooler, will try to pet pretty much any animal she meets (this includes snakes, excludes bugs), and once lied to her friend that she had climbed all the way up to Tintagel Castle in Cornwall, when actually she'd only gotten to the beach, realized it was really high, and chickened out.

She aspires to being a cynical misanthrope, but is unfortunately held back by a sunny disposition and an inability to be mean to strangers. If TA Moore is mean to you, that means you're friends now.

Website: www.nevertobetold.co.uk

Facebook: www.facebook.com/TA.Moores

Twitter: @tammy_moore

BONE
TO PICK

TA MOORE

Digging Up Bones: Book One

Cloister Witte is a man with a dark past and a cute dog. He's happy to talk about the dog all day, but after growing up in the shadow of a missing brother, a dead-beat dad, and a criminal stepfather, he'd rather leave the past back in Montana. These days he's a K-9 officer in the San Diego County Sheriff's Department and pays a tithe to his ghosts by doing what no one was able to do for his brother—find the missing and bring them home.

He's good at solving difficult mysteries. The dog is even better.

This time the missing person is a ten-year-old boy who walked into the woods in the middle of the night and didn't come back. With the antagonistic help of distractingly handsome FBI agent Javi Merlo, it quick-ly becomes clear that Drew Hartley didn't run away. He was taken, and the evidence implies he's not the kidnapper's first victim. As the search intensifies, old grudges and tragedies are pulled into the light of day. But with each clue they uncover, it looks less and less likely that Drew will be found alive.

www.dreamspinnerpress.com

SKIN AND BONE

TA MOORE

Digging Up Bones: Book Two

Cloister Witte and his K-9 partner, Bourneville, find the lost and bring them home.

But the job doesn't always end there.

Janet Morrow, a young trans woman, lies in a coma after wandering away from her car during a storm. But just because Cloister found the young tourist doesn't mean she's home. What brought her to Plenty, California… and who didn't want her to leave?

With the help of Special Agent Javi Merlo, who continues to deny his growing feelings for the rough-edged deputy, Cloister unearths a ten-year-old conspiracy of silence that taps into Plenty's history of corruption.

Janet Morrow's old secrets aren't the only ones coming to light. Javi has tried to put his past behind him, but some people seem determined to pull his skeletons out of the closet. His dark history with a senior agent in Phoenix complicates not just the investigation but his relationship with Cloister.

And since when has he cared about that?

www.dreamspinnerpress.com

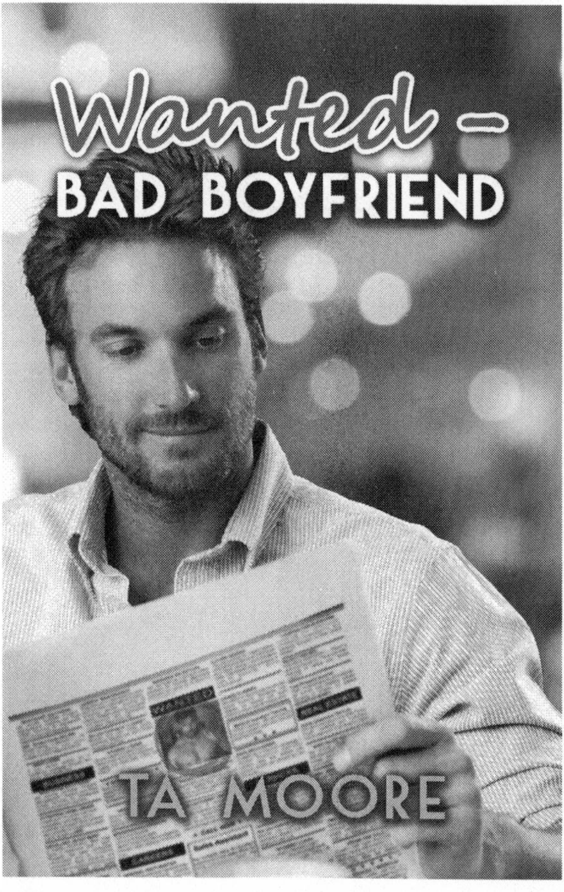
Wanted –
BAD BOYFRIEND
TA MOORE

Island Classifieds: Book One

His mother. His best friend. The barmaid at the local pub. Everyone is determined to find Nathan Moffatt a boyfriend. It's the last thing Nathan wants. After spending every day making sure his clients experience nothing but romantic magic, the Granshire Hotel's wedding organizer just wants to go home, binge-watch crime dramas, and eat pizza in his underwear.

Unfortunately, no one believes him, and he's stuck with lectures about dying alone. Then inspiration strikes. He needs the people in his life to want him to stay single as much as he does. He needs a bad boyfriend.

There's only one man for the job.

Flynn Delaney is used to people on the island of Ceremony thinking the worst of him. But he isn't sure he wants the dubious honor of worst boyfriend on the entire island. On the other hand, if he plays along, he gets to hang out with the gorgeous Nathan and piss off the owners of the Granshire Hotel. It's a win-win.

There's only one problem—Flynn's actually quite a good boyfriend, and now Nathan's wondering if getting off the sofa occasionally is really the worst thing in the world.

TA MOORE

EVERY OTHER WEEKEND

Divorce lawyer Clayton Reynolds is a happy cynic who believes in hard work and one-night stands. He also believes that being an excellent lawyer means he never has to go home to the miserable trailer park where he grew up and that volunteering at a women's shelter will buy off the conscience that occasionally plagues him. So when Nadine Graham comes in with a broken arm and a son she desperately wants to protect, Clayton can't turn down their plea for help.

Taking the case means appealing to investigator "Just Call Me Kelly" for help. That wouldn't be so bad if Kelly weren't a hopeless romantic… and the hottest man Clayton's ever met.

Kelly has always had a crush on the unobtainable Clayton Reynolds. He agrees to help, even though he has enough on his plate with the motherless baby his widowed brother left him to care for.

As Nadine's case turns dangerous and the two seemingly opposite men are forced to work together, they discover they have a great deal in common—but solving the case and saving Nadine's life might cost Kelly everything.

www.dreamspinnerpress.com